Book 1 in the Amber Ridge Series

unafraid

NYSSA KATHRYN

An NW Partners Book
Cover by Deranged Doctor Design
Developmentally and Copy Edited by Kelli Collins
Line Edited by Jessica Snyder
Proofread by Amanda Cuff and Jen Katemi
Cover Photography by Andrey Bahia at Wander Book Club

❀ Created with Vellum

A new town. A fresh start. An old enemy.

Aspen Davies had three reasons to move to the small town of Amber Ridge: to get away from her overbearing mother; to escape the clutches of her psychotic ex; and Jesse Hayes. Okay, maybe Jesse isn't a reason to relocate her entire life. After all, he's just a friend. A housemate. And someone she absolutely is *not* going to date. At least…that's what she keeps telling herself.

Discharged from the military, Jesse Hayes is back in his hometown of Amber Ridge. Only, he's not alone, as he expected. His new housemate is right down the hall, and every day with Aspen is a new form of torture. She just got out of a relationship, and she's not looking to get into a new one. He knows that. Doesn't make wanting her any easier. He needs to keep his distance, for both their sakes.

But when Aspen's past follows her to her new home, keeping his distance is no longer an option. Jesse needs to keep Aspen safe and in his sights. Because the enemy is proving formidable—and clearly playing for keeps.

ACKNOWLEDGMENTS

Thank you to my amazing team who helps me tear my stories apart and put them back together—Kelli, Jessica, Amanda and Jen —they're always so much better after you've touched them.

Thank you to my ARC team and readers. You enable and inspire me to write the next book.

And to my family—Will, Sophia and Alexia—I love you more than you know, and it is only with your support, that I am able to work a job that I love.

CHAPTER 1

*H*e'd bought flowers. Expensive flowers. A freaking bouquet of them.

Who were they for? A friend? A date? When had he gone on a date?

Aspen Davies tapped her indigo-painted nails against the marble kitchen island as she stared at the receipt like it would somehow answer her questions.

Maybe he'd bought them for a sick aunt?

No. These were pink roses. A man didn't buy pink roses for a sick aunt. Lilies? Sure. Tulips? Absolutely. But *not* pink roses. Pink roses were romantic. They were an I-like-you-let's-date flower. An I'm-attracted-to-you flower.

Was he dating someone? Was he *attracted* to someone? Who? Nancy from the grocery store? She hadn't been able to take her eyes off him when they'd gone in for rice last Thursday night. Or maybe it was Lorelei from the library. She was cute. Sweet. Had a girl-next-door vibe that guys usually loved.

Did *Jesse* love that?

Argh. Why did she care? Jesse was a roommate. Heck, he was her landlord, if you considered the fact that he owned the house and she was just renting a room.

She didn't care. There was absolutely no caring happening here. None.

So why was she standing in the kitchen, stressing about some flowers on a receipt like she was crazy?

Her phone rang, Callie's name flashing on the screen.

"I'm losing my mind without you," Aspen said to her best friend, not even bothering with a hello. "Two entire months and poof, my mind is gone."

"I miss you too."

"No, you don't understand. I'm *really* losing it."

"Your whole mind or just a little bit of it?"

"You don't believe me? This morning, I left the conditioner in my hair and didn't realize until I was out of the shower and pulling on jeans. I put my shirt on backward. Now I'm obsessing about something that should absolutely *not* be taking up space in my head."

"First of all, every time I've left conditioner in too long, it's just made my hair softer. I'm sure your blond locks are glowing. Second, if the shirt is a plain color with no logos or words, no one will notice. And what are you obsessing about?"

She nibbled the inside of her cheek, gaze returning to the receipt. "He sent someone flowers."

God, it sounded as silly out loud as it did in her head. He was nothing but a friend to her…she shouldn't care.

"He, as in—"

"Jesse. You know, the former Ghost Ops soldier who offered me a room in his house. The man who's a million feet tall, with gorgeous tattoos down his arms and brown hair that's far softer than it has any right to be."

"How do you know how soft his hair is?"

"You can tell by looking at it."

"I can't."

"Can we stick to the matter at hand, please? I'm going crazy without you."

"That is not the matter at hand. The matter is why you care if Jesse sent someone flowers. You keep telling me you're just friends."

"We *are* just friends, and I don't care. I just... If he's dating someone, I should know."

"And why is that?"

"Because we live together and that's etiquette. He's bound to bring said date home, and I would like a little heads-up."

"Flowers don't mean he's dating someone. He could—"

"Pink roses."

"Oh."

Oh, exactly.

"So ask him."

Was she out of her mind? "I can't ask him! He'll know that I snooped on his receipt, and he'll think I'm jealous."

"*Are* you jealous?"

Yes. "No."

Callie chuckled. She obviously wasn't taking this seriously. "Okay, how did you find the receipt?"

"It was sitting on the kitchen island this morning." Mocking me.

"Interesting."

"What's interesting?"

"Well, it's just a very obvious place to leave it. Maybe he *wanted* you to see?"

"Why would he want me to see that he bought someone flowers?"

"Maybe he wanted you to be jealous."

She snorted. The sound was so unladylike that it was lucky only Callie heard. Not that she would care if a certain six-foot-four hunk of gorgeous heard. "He didn't. We're friends."

"You keep saying that."

3

"We are. We've gotten into this really good routine where he cooks and tells me I'm welcome to his food. Sometimes I throw his laundry in with mine. We even make each other coffee when the other's up."

That all screamed friends...right? Exactly how she wanted it...how she *needed* it.

There was a small pause before Callie's voice softened. "Would it be so bad if—"

"No." Aspen shook her head. "I mean, no, I can't date him if that's what you were about to suggest. I can't date anyone. I need a break from...that."

"That" being men. Or trusting men on a romantic level. After Dylan, she wasn't sure she'd ever trust another man again.

His name made a shudder course down her spine. Once upon a time, she'd thought *he* was a good guy. Sweet. Charming. But it just showed, you never really knew a person unless they wanted you to know them. Unless they *chose* to show you all their sides.

It was a lesson she'd learned the hard way.

She forced her nails out of her palm and her breathing to even out.

"Aspen."

Oh no, Callie was using her soft, hard-talk-for-her-best-friend voice.

"You've moved away from Dylan now. He's your past, and the next guy you date will be nothing like him."

It wasn't just about the other guy though. It was about her. About her readiness to jump into another relationship. About her new inability to trust her own judgment. About how far she'd deviated from the person she'd been before Dylan.

She sucked in a sharp breath. "I know you believe that. You're with your soul mate."

"But that wasn't an easy journey."

No. It hadn't been for either of them. But they'd gotten to

where they needed to be, and Aspen was so incredibly happy for her friend.

She shook her head. "Enough about me. Tell me about Lock." She needed a change of subject. "Are you two still doing well?"

Callie and Lock had a complicated past. One that most people wouldn't have been able to work their way through. They had, and now her best friend was happier than Aspen had ever seen her.

Callie sighed, like she knew Aspen was changing the subject on purpose but also knew how stubborn she was. "We're great. He's great. Still super protective. Still so gorgeous I can barely take my eyes off him."

"Good. And how's our little bun in the oven?"

"Getting bigger every day."

And Aspen was missing it. Sometimes she hated that she'd left Misty Peak. But she hadn't had a choice. She'd *needed* to get out. Between her ex and her overwhelming mother, she'd been on the verge of a quarter-life crisis.

"I'm—"

"Don't say you're sorry," Callie interrupted. "We've talked about this. You needed to leave, and Jesse offered you a way out. Taking it was absolutely the right decision. Other than the flowers fiasco, how are you doing out there?"

"Still fielding daily calls and texts from my unhinged mother, but I'm not having to deal with her shit in person or run into Dylan on the street, so my days have a bit less stress in them."

"I hate that she can't be the mother you deserve."

"Me too." Although, after a lifetime of the same hot-and-cold treatment, she was used to it.

"And how's your book coming?"

Aspen cringed. A big don't-ask-me kind of cringe. "I wrote a thousand words yesterday. Then I deleted *four* thousand, so I'm going backward now."

"Why did you delete four thousand?"

Aspen dropped her head into her hand. A bit dramatic maybe, but this called for drama. This was her income they were talking about. The way she earned a living and, you know, paid for things. She was a self-published romance author, and if words didn't get written, books were not released and money was not made.

"Because the words were wrong," Aspen finally said. "But I can't seem to put *any* words to the page that sound right at the moment."

"Are you sure they were wrong? Maybe you're just being overly critical."

"No, trust me, they were terrible. My hero sounded like an ass, and there was no chemistry between the two main characters. None. Zip." And the chemistry was kind of important in a romance novel.

"Hm."

Aspen lifted her head. "What does that mean?"

"Just that, maybe—"

The front door opened, and Aspen shot up straight, shoving the receipt behind the fruit bowl.

Jesse.

And holy fucking shit. He was shirtless. Tiny beads of sweat were making his skin glisten like he was a freaking sports model, and those muscles...holy hell, those muscles. They were glorious.

"I have to go," Aspen said quickly, not hearing a word her best friend said after Mr. Tall, Dark and Handsome walked in. "Jesse's back from his run."

"Say hi for me."

"Uh-huh." Aspen hung up.

As Jesse toed off his shoes, his gaze swung to her. The grin that spread across his face was huge and *it was beautiful.*

"Hey." His deep, rumbly voice slid through her belly like lava.

She cleared her throat. "Hey. Good run?"

Good work. She wanted to give herself a big pat on the back for how unaffected she sounded.

He crossed the living room and walked into the kitchen, the muscles in his stomach contracting as he moved. "Yeah. I used to love running with my team. It's harder since I got out and don't have them pushing me. I've lost a bit of my fitness. I might get Becket to start running with me."

Lost a bit of his fitness? What had he been like before? The Terminator? Right now, he looked and moved like a gladiator. But then, so did his brother Becket, who was a former Navy SEAL. It must be a special operations thing. The men were just built different.

He nodded toward her phone before grabbing a bottle of water from the fridge. "Was that Callie?"

"Yep, she called to check in."

One side of Jesse's mouth lifted, showing the sexiest dimple she'd ever seen. "You tell her how terrible it is to live with me?"

"I absolutely told her about our mess situation."

The mess situation being *her* leaving messes and Jesse getting on her back about it. She wasn't a messy person. In fact, she'd always considered herself quite tidy. Sure, she left the occasional coffee cup on the table. The odd pile of clothes in the bathroom. Jesse was just a bit of a clean freak.

"I trust she and Lock are on my side," Jesse said.

"Do you know anything about how female friendships work? No matter how wrong I am, that woman will defend me until her last breath."

"So you admit you're wrong."

"Never."

He chuckled, and the sound was beautiful.

Stop it, Aspen. Every inch of him may be unbelievably gorgeous, but you're not dating for a very, very long time. Years...maybe centuries!

He walked around her to the sink, and his arm grazed hers. The gesture almost made her shudder...almost.

He did that a lot. Little grazes here and there. Small touches. Torture. It was all torture.

"What are you doing today?" he asked.

"Well, I was supposed to write three thousand words yesterday, but I ended up writing minus three thousand, so today I need to write six just to catch up to where I'm supposed to be." Did she think that would happen? No. But she could dream.

"How do you write minus three thousand words?"

"You don't want to know. But I'm trying a new writing location. It's called The Tea House, and I'm hoping it inspires me." So far, she hadn't felt like writing in any of the places she'd tried around town. The diner. Public parks. The library. They all sucked for inspiration.

He frowned. "We have a tea house in Amber Ridge?"

"I thought this was your hometown?"

"It is. I'm just not much of a tea drinker. My mom might know about it. You don't want to write at the diner?"

"No. That's where I wrote my minus three thousand words yesterday. Plus, their coffee sucks."

"All the coffee in Amber Ridge sucks."

She wouldn't have believed that if she hadn't experienced it firsthand. How not a single business in an entire town could make a good cup of coffee, she had no idea. "Maybe this tea house has good coffee." Did tea houses sell coffee?

He gave her a keep-dreaming smile. "Do you want a ride?"

More one-on-one time with Jesse? Heck no. She'd sold her car before leaving Tennessee for Montana and was getting everywhere on foot. Luckily, the town was small, and Jesse lived close to everything.

"I'm okay to walk." She straightened. "Hey, I forgot. It's your first day as sheriff, right?"

He'd become a deputy when he'd returned home from the military and had quickly proven his worth in the department.

8

Now the sheriff had fallen ill, which meant while he was out of the office, Jesse was his replacement.

Jesse dipped his head. "It is. Wish me luck. I think I'm gonna need it."

She scoffed. "You don't need luck. One look at you and the whole office will fall into line, especially the women."

Her eyes widened, lips snapping shut.

Shit. Had she really just said that out loud?

One side of Jesse's mouth lifted, and he stepped closer, his sandalwood scent all she could smell. "Did you just pay me a compliment, Davies?"

"No."

"Really? Because it sounded like a compliment. It might have even sounded like you were implying I was good-looking."

"No siree. Unfortunately for you, I do not find you good-looking. Not even a little bit. You look like a friend. A roommate. A landlord." Jesus Christ, what words were coming out of her mouth? Someone get some tape and stick her lips together.

Jesse's smile widened. "Don't worry, I won't tell anyone." Then he lowered his head so that his mouth was beside her ear. "And just so you know, I think you're cute, too."

Then he walked away like he hadn't just made her belly do the biggest somersault it had ever done in its life.

CHAPTER 2

*J*esse pulled into the parking lot outside the sheriff's station, still smiling at the memory of Aspen's eyes as they'd flared. At the small separation of her lips as he'd whispered into her ear.

God, she was cute. Hell, cute didn't even do her justice.

He undid his seat belt and climbed out.

It wasn't all sunshine and roses though. Living with her was getting harder every day. Her scent was everywhere. *She* was everywhere. Some days he wondered what the hell he'd been thinking by asking her to live with him.

But he knew exactly what he'd been thinking. That he didn't want to leave Misty Peak, because she was there. That the couple months they'd spent getting to know each other weren't enough. And that he'd wanted her away from that jerk of an ex of hers.

He shook his head. He needed to get Aspen out of his mind and focus on his job. It was his first day as sheriff, a position in which he hadn't expected to find himself. A position that was important. The sheriff of Amber Ridge needed to take sudden leave because of his health, and the likelihood of him returning was slim.

The town was counting on him to do a good job, and he couldn't do that if his mind was on Aspen all day.

Bea, the young receptionist, smiled up at him from behind the front desk as he stepped inside. "Good morning, *Sheriff*."

"Jesse is still fine, Bea."

"Hey, hey! It's the big boss man!"

Jesse looked up to see Luke, one of the deputies, heading down the hall toward him, two mugs in hand. They'd gone to high school together, but since getting back, Jesse had found it hard to connect with his old friend.

"You don't need to call me boss man," Jesse finally said.

"Of course I do. You're my new boss and it has a good ring to it." Luke nudged open the door beside him. "Your new office awaits."

Jesse stepped in. The space was big, with a desk at the end in front of a window and storage cabinets to either side. "Tell me again why I want this job?"

"Because you wanna be in charge of locking up the bad guys and cleaning up this town."

Jesse scoffed. "Amber Ridge is the size of a shoe, and the only real crimes are the coffee and Burt's terrible pizzas."

Terrible was underselling it. They were somehow both burnt and soggy, often with a fishy aftertaste. It was an art Burt had perfected over the years.

Jesse dropped behind his new desk. "And doesn't everyone hate the sheriff?"

"They hated Rowan because he was a grumpy old ass. *You* are young and vibrant and loveable."

"I don't think any of those things apply to me."

"Of course they do. Maybe not today though. Today you're looking a little worse for wear. Trouble at home with your *roommate?*"

Shit. He did *not* want to talk about Aspen. "No trouble. In fact, she seems completely unaffected by me."

Luke cringed. "That must hurt the ego."

"My ego's fine." The other parts of him? Not so much.

"Why did you ask her to live with you again? Because you like torturing yourself?"

He could have laughed because wasn't that the same question he'd been asking himself all morning? Hell, all month. "She needed to get out of Misty Peak, and I had a room."

"Oh, yes, because of the ex and the unstable mother. And maybe you were hoping that if she stayed with you—"

"No. I wasn't hoping anything. She just got out of a bad relationship. She's not in a place to date." She'd said that more than once, and he needed to respect it, dammit.

Luke's nose wrinkled. "You poor son of a bitch. You know what you need?"

"A drink?"

"Let's agree you need a few things, but first, coffee."

Jesse took the outstretched drink. What the fuck? "The mug has breasts."

"You're welcome. And the second thing you need is a date."

"No." Hell no. He couldn't date when Aspen was all he could think about.

"Yes. And I know just the right woman. I met her in yoga."

"You do yoga?"

"Hell yes, I do yoga. Have you *seen* the women there?"

"I thought you were dating Margot?" Margot was a deputy here at the station, and honestly, Jesse didn't know if they were dating or friends.

Luke lifted a shoulder. "You should know that no woman can tie me down."

Jesus Christ. This was why he'd found it hard to reconnect with Luke since coming back. While Jesse had grown and matured, he wasn't so sure Luke had.

"Come on." Luke leaned forward. "One date. The two of you might hit it off over a slice of pizza."

"I'm not dating a woman from your yoga class. And even if I was, I wouldn't be doing it with Burt's Pizza."

"Chinese then."

"I need to check my emails." He turned toward his computer.

"Fine, but I'm picking this conversation back up at lunch."

"Close the door on your way out."

Luke laughed as he stepped into the hall.

Jesse's computer was just booting up when a text came through from his brother.

Becket: We still on for drinks at CJ's Saturday night?

CJ's was one of three bars in town. It was the most popular because there was pool, often a band, and it was right in the center of town.

Jesse: Depends, is Clara buying?

Becket: Which sister are you talking about? It can't be ours.

Jesse: Sorry, I forgot. I've been away for too long.

Becket: Damn straight you have. So are you coming?

Jesse: I'll see you there.

He dropped his phone and turned back to his computer.

The best part of being back home was all the family time he'd missed out on while in the military. His brother had retired as a Navy SEAL a few years ago and was the town's fire chief.

His sister was now an acupuncturist but had once been a lawyer. One year into her first job, she'd been diagnosed with Hodgkin lymphoma.

Every muscle in his body tightened at the memory. It was a tough time for everyone. He and Becket had wanted to come home and look after her, but both she and their mother had refused to let them. Five years had passed since treatment, and there were no longer any signs of cancer in her body, but she still suffered from chronic fatigue. And that meant at times he and Becket were more protective than Clara liked.

Then there was his mother. She was a powerhouse of a

woman, raising three kids on her own since their father had died when they were young.

Jesse's family was the main reason he wouldn't consider living anywhere else.

He logged into his inbox to see it full of emails. Damn, looked like a day of admin.

He spent the morning with his butt plastered to his seat. Some emails were easy questions he had to answer; others were fires to put out.

At first, he'd been surprised to be promoted to lieutenant over Luke, since Luke had been at the station much longer. But then Luke had told him he didn't want the position. And since spending more time with him, Jesse could see why. He probably didn't want the responsibility.

Whereas Jesse liked the challenge. Hell, he needed it. And right now, he also needed the distraction from Aspen.

CHAPTER 3

*W*hat in the ever-living hell *was* that?

It wasn't coffee. It couldn't be. More like warmed-up dirt water. Heck, it was worse than dirt water.

Maybe she hadn't tasted enough. It surely couldn't be that bad?

Aspen took another sip.

Worse…so much worse.

"Everything okay, dear?"

She choked on the hot liquid before looking up at the older woman with an English accent standing beside the booth. Hot liquid sloshed over the sides of the mug, barely missing her fingers. "Is this the latte with almond milk?"

"Yes. Is something wrong with it?"

It wasn't a mistake. The older woman had intentionally made it to taste like this.

It was terrible.

But how on earth could she express that to this kind elderly woman who seemed to have no business in her little café? And really, this was probably her own fault for ordering coffee in a tea house.

She set the mug onto the table. "You know what? I was just looking at your tea list. I'm not much of a tea drinker, but they have me intrigued."

Excitement lit the older woman's eyes. "Oh, all the teas here are marvelous. They're loose leaf and mostly organic. Unfortunately, when I opened this store a few years ago, I found there aren't many tea drinkers around. I'm not sure if it's a Montana thing or a—"

"It's an American thing. Not big tea drinkers. But I'd love to try some." Kind of. It had to be better than the coffee.

"What kind would you like?"

"What do you recommend?"

"Earl Grey is a favorite of mine."

"Earl Grey sounds wonderful."

If it was terrible, she'd ask about sweet tea. It didn't seem to be on the menu, but maybe… "I'm Aspen, by the way."

"Mrs. Gerald. I'll go get your tea."

When Mrs. Gerald walked away, Aspen cast her gaze around the empty store. There wasn't another soul in sight. Was it always like this? The place was big, with stairs to a mezzanine level upstairs. It wasn't styled in an overly tea-house kind of way. In fact, it looked kind of like a normal coffee shop.

She eyed baked goods in the display case. Now *they* looked good. Pies, scones…even the mini chocolate cakes.

She looked back at the screen of her laptop and tapped her nails against the wooden tabletop. She was procrastinating. Procrastinating when she should be working. But the blank page was a great example of the fact that not a lot of work was happening.

She wanted to blame the quiet tea house because she tended to like noise and movement around her when she worked. But that wasn't fair. Lately, it didn't seem to matter where she was, there were no ideas to be typed. None. Squat. Her head was empty. Completely and utterly empty.

Okay, Aspen, if there was any time to be inspired, it'd be now.

She put her fingers on the keyboard, trying not to let the blank page intimidate her.

She wrote a sentence. Then deleted it. She wrote another sentence...and deleted it again.

Dammit, Aspen, come on. This is your job.

Maybe she needed to read the previous chapter she'd written...that sometimes helped.

She scrolled up and started reading.

Five sentences in and she hated it. Not just a little bit. Huge, gigantic belly punches of hate. Her hero sounded like a pompous prick, and her heroine did nothing but complain. They weren't likeable characters, not even a little bit. *She* didn't even like them, and she'd *written* them.

Her finger hovered over the delete key, but she hesitated. What if she wrote negative words again? And what if every day she deleted a bit more until she had nothing? No book. No new release. But was no book better than a bad book?

If she couldn't write anymore, she'd have to get another job. But she wasn't good at anything else.

Maybe if she just stared at a blank page long enough, the words would come to her.

Ha. She'd tried that yesterday...didn't work.

"Here you go." Mrs. Gerald set a pot of tea onto the table with a teacup, saucer, and a little pot of milk beside it. "Let me know what you think."

"Thank you."

Instead of walking away, the old woman watched.

Oh, she wanted her to try it right now. That was a bit of pressure.

She poured some tea into the cup and added a dash of milk before taking a sip. She flinched when the burning liquid touched the tip of her tongue. Holy crack on a cracker, it was hot.

"Not good?" Mrs. Gerald asked.

"Oh no, it is good." Not really true. Well, not for her. She was a coffee person. But no part of her wanted to break this little old lady's heart. "Just hot."

Her smile returned. "I'm so pleased you like it. Sing out if you need anything else."

Aspen smiled at the woman, but the smile immediately dropped when she looked back to her page. Still empty. No magical writing fairies wrote the chapter in the few seconds she'd been turned away.

All right, time to type. She was *not* going to accept another no-word day. She was going to get words down, dammit.

She pulled out her AirPods, pushed them into her ears, and played her favorite instrumental playlist. It was her go-to when she had to get writing done.

She scrolled back and deleted her last five sentences then rewrote them, forcing more words out.

It was an hour and one thousand rewritten words later when she sat back and decided to read what she had.

It was crap. A full thousand words of crap that no one would want to read.

She wanted to drop her forehead to the table and ask whatever higher power was watching her—why? Why was writing something good suddenly impossible?

Her phone rang. When she saw her mother's name flashing on the screen, she cringed. If there was anyone who could make a bad day worse, it was her mentally unstable mother. She was pretty sure her mom had undiagnosed borderline personality disorder...and maybe bipolar disorder.

She answered the call, knowing if she didn't, her mother might spiral. "Hi, Mom."

"When are you coming home?"

Well, hello to you too. I missed you as well. Thank you so much for checking in.

All words that would likely *not* enter the conversation.

"I told you, I'm not sure."

"You've deserted me. Did you think of me at all during this move? Or Dylan?"

Her fingers tightened around her phone, her stomach doing a nauseous roll at his name. Aspen hadn't told her why they'd separated—she hadn't told anyone. But her mother *certainly* knew Aspen wanted nothing to do with him.

"Dylan and I broke up."

"I know. But if you'd stayed, he might have taken you back."

Taken her back? "I left him, Mom."

"I know. You said that."

Said that? Did her mother not believe her?

She sighed. "I need to go, Mom. I'm working."

"Wait. I need your address so I can send you some of your things."

"What things?"

"A ring you left here. A T-shirt. A—"

"Keep them."

"I don't want them. What the hell am I supposed to do with things that aren't mine?"

She scrubbed her face. Her mother had always hated clutter. She had the most clutter-free house Aspen had ever seen. "Then throw them out."

"No. I don't want to be blamed later if you decide you actually want them."

"I won't change my mind."

Her mother huffed. "Honestly, Aspen, I don't know why you're so difficult. Do you know what I sacrificed to have you and raise you? A lot. And now you're forcing me to keep clutter that isn't mine."

She massaged her temple. She'd heard similar spiels before. Heck, she could just about recite it word for word.

The funny thing was, this was her mother being *nice*. When

she wasn't nice, Aspen often needed to block her number for a few days just to get a break from the threats and curses.

She looked back at her laptop. Everything was annoying today…and it had all started with those damn flowers.

"Fine," Aspen finally cut in. "I'll text you my address now."

"Good."

Then her mother hung up. She just freaking hung up. No "goodbye." No "have a good day." Nothing.

Un-freaking-believable.

CHAPTER 4

*A*spen watched through the window as Dylan's gray Toyota Tacoma reversed out of the driveway. Fear pitted her belly. A fear that ran so deep it made her feel physically sick. Every part of her wanted to just go. Leave her things in his house and get out. But she had to be smart. She had to get everything she owned out of his house so she never had to come back. She had to be done with him for good.

His truck disappeared down the street, but still, she didn't move right away. She had to be sure he was gone. Because if he caught her leaving with all her things...

A shudder rolled through her body. No. He wouldn't catch her.

Two entire minutes ticked by, and in those minutes, the silence beat into her. Almost absently, she ran her fingers over the place on her arm he'd just grabbed. She cringed at the dull ache. It would bruise. It had bruised last time.

Now, *Aspen whispered to herself.* You have to move now.

Straightening her spine, she forced her feet to cross the living room into the bedroom. They'd been dating less than a year. She didn't have a lot in the house. Little bits and pieces here and there. Spare deodorant. A couple pieces of clothing. She needed all of it. She needed Dylan to have *no reason to come to her. No possessions to return. No messages to pass along.*

She grabbed a couple of T-shirts and some leggings from a drawer. The drawer Dylan had emptied for her. She could still remember the smile that had stretched her face when he'd shown her. She'd been excited that he'd made room for her in his house.

That was before any of this had started.

Stupid. So stupid. He'd been so good at hiding the ugly parts of himself. The angry parts. The downright scary. But she still should have seen the warning signs. The loss of temper. The raised voice.

She threw the clothes into a bag before checking the laundry basket, then under the bed. When she was sure everything was clear, she moved into the bathroom. Her deodorant sat on the counter. Moisturizer and some concealer in the drawers.

There shouldn't be so much here. There shouldn't be anything here. She should have left long ago.

Weak. She felt so weak and stupid and pathetic for staying. She'd always prided herself on her strength, but maybe she'd never been as strong as she'd thought.

Sudden tears pressed to her eyes, and she scrunched them shut. She didn't want to cry. *He didn't deserve her tears.*

She grabbed everything that was hers from the bathroom and dropped it into the bag on the bed.

Next, she moved into the living room and set her bag on the couch. A charger and a couple of things in the kitchen...then she'd be gone.

Her fingers shook as she pulled the charger from the wall. In the kitchen, she grabbed her mug and a Thermos.

There. That was everything. In a few hours, Dylan would return to his house and there'd be no sign that she'd been here apart from the note. She reached into her back pocket and pulled out a piece of paper. The edges were scuffed and the page crinkled from spending too long hidden away.

She'd written it days ago. But only now, after their disastrous morning, did she have the strength to leave it. The morning when he'd grabbed her arm for telling him she wasn't staying over that night. Yelled at her like she was nothing. Like she was a possession of his.

She set the note onto the kitchen island.

She wished today had been the first time he'd hurt her. God, she wished that so badly. It wasn't. And she hated herself for that.

She stepped back into the living room and had just put the mug into her bag when the click of the front door unlocking sounded.

Her heart crashed into her ribs, gaze flying to the street... Dylan's gray Toyota Tacoma. It sat in the driveway.

He was home.

He stepped into the living room. His gaze moved from her to the bag on the sofa, then back to her. There was no anger on his face. No shock or frustration. In fact, his face was eerily clear of emotion.

And for some reason, that was even more terrifying than the anger.

"I thought something was off with you. It's why I came back." He stepped closer, his voice sharp, cutting into her skin like a razor. "You're leaving."

It wasn't a question. But she answered as if it was. "We're over, Dylan. I can't be with you anymore."

Still, there was nothing on his face. And it made the fear in Aspen's belly triple.

He inched forward. "I don't want us to be over."

Some of the fear shifted into something else. Something darker. Something easier to feel.

Anger.

"It doesn't matter what you want. I'm done walking on eggshells around you. I'm done making excuses for you. I'm leaving. And if you don't like it, you should have thought about that before you—"

He was across the room in a second. His fingers wrapped around her upper arms in a grip so tight that she cried out in pain.

"You're not leaving me."

She shoved at his chest. "Let go of me. Now!"

"I'm not losing you."

"You don't have a choice. I don't love you—"

His arm swung and he backhanded her. She screamed as she fell back, hitting the coffee table so hard that the glass shattered beneath her.

* * *

JESSE'S EYES SHOT OPEN. Something had woken him. What?

He sat up silently...listening. Waiting for whatever had woken him to sound again.

A soft cry sliced through the air.

Aspen.

He shot out of bed and reached behind his bedside table to pull the Glock from his hidden safety holster. With the weapon in hand, he sprinted down the hall. He threw open her bedroom door—only to freeze.

Aspen's salt lamp cast a dim glow over the room...the seemingly *empty* room. Empty of anyone other than her. She lay in bed, chest rising and falling in slow succession. She was asleep.

So what the hell had he heard? Was he losing his mind?

His arm dropped, gaze once again scanning the room, searching for anything he'd missed the first time. Nothing.

He looked at her again. At the way her hair spread over the pillow. The hand beneath her cheek as she lay on her side.

Fuck, she was beautiful. And he was a creep for watching her while she slept.

He turned and had pulled the door half closed behind him when a soft whimper sounded. It was so quiet, he almost didn't hear it.

He stepped back into the room to see Aspen's eyes now scrunched, her chest moving faster, air whooshing in and out of her.

She was having a nightmare.

"*Stop.*"

His muscles tensed at her word. At the fear woven through her voice. He set the Glock onto the dresser and inched closer.

She rolled to her back, her chest moving faster again, breaths deep.

What was he supposed to do? Leave her? Wake her? Walking away when she was clearly in pain went against every protective instinct inside him.

"*No!*"

That single word…it was so filled with pain that it gutted him. It also propelled him forward. He perched on the edge of her bed. "Aspen."

Her eyes squeezed tight again, her breathing almost sounding like cries.

"Aspen!" He gripped her shoulders. "Wake up."

When she still didn't, he gave her a gentle shake.

One more scrunch of her eyes and they flickered open. But the second her gaze hit him, she screamed and swung her fist. He dodged it easily before lifting his hands up in defense.

"Whoa, Aspen, it's me, Jesse!"

Her brows flickered, breaths still too fast. "Jesse? I…I couldn't see you in the dark."

"It's me, honey. You're safe."

She turned her head to look around the room, as if needing confirmation of exactly where she was. "I'm in Amber Ridge."

"You are." He frowned. "Where were you in your nightmare?"

"Misty Peak."

"Do you have nightmares about Misty Peak often?"

"I…" She looked back at him and shook her head. "I'm sorry, what are you doing in my room?"

"I heard you."

Her brows shot up. "You heard me? From your room? Jesus, I'm a mess. What time is it?"

He hadn't actually checked the time. He hit the screen of her phone on the bedside table. "Three a.m."

"Three?" Her gaze moved down his bare chest. "You were

asleep, and I was so loud I woke you." She pushed up and ran her fingers through her hair.

"I'm a light sleeper."

She shook her head. "It shouldn't have happened at all."

"What were you dreaming about?"

Even though it was quiet, he didn't miss the sharp intake of air. "It was…"

A visible shudder rolled down her body, and all he wanted to do was hold her. Wrap her in his arms and chase the dream away.

"I don't remember," she whispered.

His frown deepened. She *did* remember. He could see it in her eyes. The way she was staring at a point across the room, as if reliving it in her head.

He cocked his head. "Want to talk about it?"

"No." The single word came quickly. And it was the proof he needed to know he was right. You didn't say no so quickly when you couldn't remember.

He glanced at the door, then back to her. He didn't want to leave. "I guess I should—"

"Wait." She swallowed. "Will you tell me a story? Anything. Help me fall back to sleep."

"I can do that." Right now, he'd do anything to wipe the fear from her eyes.

He shifted beside her so that his back leaned against the head-board. She lay back into her pillow, the warmth of her side against his.

"When Clara was ten, she convinced me and Becket to wake up early and help her bake a cake for Mom's birthday. Becket was the oldest at fourteen, and I was only twelve, and none of us had baked a cake before."

"What flavor?"

"Strawberry. It was Mom's favorite."

"Mm. Mine too."

He slotted that little bit of information into his memory for later. "The morning of her birthday, we all got up before her, and when I say we had no idea what we were doing, I mean, we had *no* idea what we were doing."

Aspen laughed, the sound soft and airy. "Who took the lead?"

"Clara. She'd been watching a few baking shows on TV, so she thought she knew how to do it. She didn't. But we gave it a really good go. We argued for the full hour. By the end of it, there was flour everywhere. And the cake, if you could call it that, resembled a charcoal brick."

"Mm. Sounds interesting." Aspen's voice was sleepy.

He looked down and found her eyes closed. "Interesting is one word for it."

"Did she like it?"

"Well, she ran in when the smoke alarm went off. Once she stopped it from beeping, she took one look around the kitchen, which was a disaster, then looked at our charcoal cake...and she smiled the biggest smile I've ever seen."

"That's nice. Did she eat it?"

"She did. And to this day, she still says it was the most memorable birthday surprise she's ever had."

"Mm, your mom's nice."

"The best."

He looked down to see her chest rising and falling in a steady rhythm. Eyes still closed and the look on her face...almost peaceful.

She was asleep. Good.

He didn't get up though, not right away. Instead, he stayed exactly where he was, his side pressed to hers. And he made a vow. To find out exactly what her nightmare had been about and destroy her ex...because Jesse was certain he was the culprit.

CHAPTER 5

*S*he'd manifested a good day today. It was *supposed to be* a good day. There'd been no nightmares last night. No embarrassing visits from Jesse. The blueberry jam and clotted cream on top of her scone at The Tea House was amazing. It had started *so* good.

But that good day had ended the second she'd pulled out her laptop.

She chopped the carrots with a bit more aggression.

There'd been no words written…again. Even bad words hadn't made it onto the page today.

She used to have so many ideas. Love stories and meet-cutes and funny little conversation starters…they'd all crowded her head, and she'd turned them into stories. *Good* stories.

What happened? Was she out of ideas? Would she never finish a book again?

The bad didn't end there though. She'd dropped and broken one of Mrs. Gerald's gorgeous teacups. She'd received half a dozen not-so-nice texts from her mother about the cost of mailing the things Aspen didn't want sent anyway. And the second she'd gotten home and taken off her shoes, she'd stubbed her toe. And, holy Hannah, did it hurt.

Now, all she wanted to do was make dinner…but she'd forgotten the pasta for her pasta casserole, which was kind of important.

The door opened and she didn't even look up. It would be Jesse. Perfect Jesse. Yesterday, he'd literally made her breakfast and a steaming-hot cup of coffee. Good coffee. It was like he'd *known* how much she needed it after the night she'd had. She'd wanted to fall at his feet and kiss them, she'd been so grateful. It was like he could do no wrong.

And he hadn't brought up the nightmare again. In fact, he was acting like it never happened…for which she was grateful.

"What did those carrots do to you?"

Her traitorous heart set off in a gallop at his deep, sexy voice. "I forgot the pasta for my pasta casserole and didn't want to walk back to the grocery store." Didn't really answer his question, but it was connected.

"I see. And is that the carrots' fault?"

"If I said yes, would you believe me?" Another far too aggressive chop of the carrot.

Suddenly he was right beside her, his hand covering hers, stilling her movements.

She sucked in a quick breath, her gaze stuck on his large hand on hers. When he touched her, it was like every other thought just dropped out of her head.

"You didn't get any words written today?" he asked gently.

She looked up. Mistake. Big mistake. His eyes were too close and too beautiful. "None."

Sympathy darkened his eyes as he removed his touch. Her skin suddenly felt cold. "Is that all that happened?"

How did he know? Was he really good at reading her, or was it just written all over her face? "My mother was messaging me."

"Okay, and what did she say?"

"Yesterday she called and insisted on sending me some of my stuff that I left at her place. Stuff that I don't want back. Stuff that *I told her* she could keep or throw away. But Karen Davies doesn't want to do that, because she doesn't like to respect other people's wishes. She knows best. So I gave her this address so she could mail the things I didn't need sent."

"What happened next?"

"Texts. Millions of texts, all in the span of an hour." Her words sped up. "It took her all morning, apparently. Hours to go through her house and make sure I hadn't left anything else there. Then it took her more time to take the stuff to the post office and package everything up. Oh, and it cost her a small fortune—her words, not mine. And when I reminded her that I did not need or want her to send any of it... Now I'm ungrateful. I'm irresponsible for leaving it all at her place. I'm also conniving, because I left the stuff there on purpose because I *wanted* to ruin her day and make her go broke. I'm one big—"

Jesse gripped her wrist. The wrist attached to the hand she hadn't realized was waving around the big kitchen knife. "I think I should take that." He slipped the knife from her fingers.

"I'm sorry." She scrubbed her hands over her face. "It's just been a frustrating day. She sent barrages of texts, and then she called and started verbally abusing me. I dropped Mrs. Gerald's teacup. Dylan also tried to call—"

"Dylan tried to call you?" Jesse's tone deepened, an edge to his voice.

"Yep. I swear he's the mistake that will haunt me for the rest of my life."

"What did he want?"

She shook her head. "I don't know. I didn't answer. I never answer. Then I blocked his number."

She'd come to Amber Ridge to escape it all, but her past just wouldn't leave her alone.

Jesse's frown was deep, anger darkening his eyes before he

seemed to visibly force it down. "Come to the bar with me tonight."

She straightened. "What?"

"I'm meeting my brother and sister. Join us. Have a night off from everything."

Go to the bar? With Jesse? All six foot four of him and his dimples? "I don't know. I had a pretty great night planned. It involved pasta casserole but without the pasta and some *Jerry Springer* reruns."

His lips twitched. "We can still finish the pasta-less casserole before we go, and *Jerry Springer* will still be here if the bar's a dud. Although, I think you'll have a good time. You haven't met my family yet. My sister's pretty awesome, and my brother will talk shit about me all night. You don't want to miss an opportunity like that."

She bit her bottom lip, and Jesse's gaze immediately lowered to her mouth. Air halted in her lungs.

You're not dating right now, Aspen. Look away. Look the heck away from the gorgeous man.

"The bar sounds good." Dammit, she sounded croaky. "I'll finish this and get changed."

She swung around and her elbow hit the cutting board which sent the carrots flying.

Jesse lunged for the board. He moved so quickly that she flinched. A big, thought-he-was-going-to-hit-her-even-though-she-knew-he-wouldn't-do-that flinch. The kind of flinch someone only did if they'd experienced a man's violence before.

Her heart stopped. *Shit, shit, shit.*

He frowned, looking at her so closely, it felt like he'd finally worked her out. "Aspen—"

"Actually, I might go get changed now. I need a shower." With a hurried step, she backed away, almost slipping on a carrot. He reached for her, but she took another quick step back. "I'm okay. I'll just go now."

Then she turned and walked, almost ran, to the sanctuary of her bedroom.

* * *

JESSE GOT out of the car, watching as Aspen climbed out of the passenger seat. She'd barely said two words to him since she'd run out of the kitchen. Hell, he'd barely *seen* her. She'd come out of her room so late, she hadn't eaten any of the casserole he'd finished.

He stepped beside her onto the sidewalk. "You sure you don't want to grab some food before we go in?"

"I'm okay."

He sighed as they headed toward the door of CJ's Bar.

His hand twitched to reach out and touch her. Put a palm on the small of her back. Or take her hand in his.

She wore high-rise jeans that hugged her curves and a tight black top that left nothing to the imagination. And her heels... fuck, they emphasized her sexy calves. How calves could be sexy, he had no idea. But hers were.

He fisted his hands as they stepped inside the bar. The smell of beer permeated the air, and the sounds of people talking and laughing were loud. The place was packed.

Aspen inched closer and, instinctively, he snaked an arm around her waist, grateful when she didn't pull away. He wove through the crowd, keeping her flush against his side.

The second he spotted his brother and sister standing at a table, a grin tugged at his mouth. Clara was whacking Becket on the shoulder and appeared to be scolding him, while Becket looked really fucking pleased with himself.

It was nothing new. Their five-foot-nothing sister enjoyed putting each of them in their places, while Becket liked to get a reaction out of people.

"What did Becket do this time?" Jesse asked as they stopped at the table.

One side of Becket's mouth lifted. "I said one innocent thing about my neighbor."

Clara rolled her eyes. "His neighbor is an acupuncture client of mine, and he was being an ass."

"Me? An ass?" Becket feigned disbelief.

"Yes, you," Clara said with a little shove at Becket's shoulder. His sister's gaze shifted to Aspen, then to the arm Jesse still had around her waist. Interest lit Clara's eyes. "Hi. You must be the new roommate we've been dying to meet. I'm Clara, the level-headed sister of these two knuckleheads."

Becket reached out a hand. "Becket, knucklehead number one."

Aspen chuckled as she took his hand. "Aspen."

Clara tilted her head. "You look familiar. Why?"

"You've probably seen me around town." She inched to the side, and Jesse's arm fell. Immediately, he wanted to tug her back.

"It's not that," Clara argued, squinting as if trying to figure out how she knew her.

"She's a writer," Jesse added, because he knew Aspen wouldn't.

Clara straightened. "I read. What do you—" She stopped, eyes widening. "Wait, are you Aspen Davies, the romance author?"

A small smile curved Aspen's lips. "I am."

"Oh my gosh, I *love* your books! I was sick a while ago, and reading was the only thing that got me through. I'm pretty sure I devoured everything you had out."

Jesse's chest ached at the memory of Clara's cancer, and he didn't miss Becket's fingers tightening around his beer.

His gaze immediately went to her glass. "What are you drinking?"

There was the smallest tensing in his sister's shoulders. Most wouldn't notice it. He did. She still suffered from chronic fatigue and alcohol made it worse.

"It's called none of your business." She looked back at Aspen. "Now, tell me, is my brother as overbearingly clean as he was growing up?"

Aspen leaned forward. "You could eat off his floor."

Clara threw her head back and laughed.

"There's nothing wrong with being clean." Jesus, most woman would love to live with a tidy guy. "Becket's clean too. It's drilled into us in the military."

Becket dipped his head. "It's true. It's just one of the reasons all the ladies love me."

"All except Sky," Clara said.

"Sky has issues."

"Is Sky your girl—"

"No." Becket cut Aspen off before she could finish. "She's my neighbor. My frustrating, seems-to-be-irritated-by-my-very-existence neighbor."

"She's also cute as heck and doesn't fall at Becket's feet like he expects the female population to do," Clara added.

Becket grabbed Clara playfully by the neck and scuffed her hair.

Jesus, could they not pretend to be normal for two seconds to meet a new person? He looked down at Aspen. "I'm sorry."

For the first time since leaving the kitchen, she met his eye, an almost envious look in hers. "It's sweet. I always wanted a sibling or two."

"You can have both of mine. I've endured them long enough."

A smile spread across her face.

He cleared his throat. "Aspen, in the kitchen—"

"Not tonight." Her words came quickly, almost desperately. "Can we just have a night off everything?"

He wanted to push. To ask about that flinch. Find out if what he suspected was true.

Instead, he dipped his head. "Sure. I'll get us a drink. Your usual amaretto sour?"

"Thanks."

He turned to his sister. "Anything for you?"

She shook her head.

"I'll come with you," Becket said, straightening. "I'm almost out."

Jesse and his brother headed back through the crowd.

"You know her usual?" Becket asked when they reached the bar.

"Yeah, we're friends. We went to the bar together a few times in Misty Peak."

Becket smirked. "You're not friends. You can lie to yourself, but you can't lie to me."

The bartender stopped in front of them, a young woman with purple hair. "What can I get you guys?"

"An amaretto sour and two of any of your tap beers."

"Sure." One side of her mouth lifted as she gave both of them a quick once-over, obvious interest in her eyes.

When she turned away, Becket nudged him. "If you're not interested in Aspen, you should give the bartender your number."

"I don't think so."

"Why not?"

"We're friends because *Aspen* wants to be friends."

Becket almost looked like he was biting back a laugh. "You lost your charm or something?"

"She just got out of a bad relationship."

Their drinks were set in front of them, and Jesse paid before turning back to his brother, his voice lowering, anger cutting through his words. "Today, I moved quickly to grab a chopping board that she knocked off the island, and she flinched."

The humor left Becket's eyes. "The fuck? You're thinking the ex?"

"Probably. Asshole's still contacting her even though she moved to the other side of the country. She had to block his number today."

Becket's fingers tightened on his bottle. They'd both been raised the same. To protect those around them, particularly the women in their lives. "Well, if he ever shows his face here in Amber Ridge—"

"He'll wish he hadn't."

CHAPTER 6

*A*spen threw back her head and laughed at something his sister said, and he couldn't take his eyes off her. The delicate curve of her neck. The lift of her lips.

She was beautiful. The kind of beauty he could stare at all day. And she was getting along really fucking well with his sister. It wasn't a surprise. His sister was friendly, and he hadn't met a single person who didn't like Aspen.

The only problem was, he wanted to go. He felt pretty damn uneasy about Aspen drinking on an empty stomach. How many times had he asked if she was ready to leave yet? Two? Three? Each time, she'd distracted him with that smile of hers. With little touches on his chest.

"Do you enjoy your job as an acupuncturist?" Aspen asked.

Clara's expression softened. "I love it. Being sick changed my perspective on everything. I wanted a slower lifestyle. A healing lifestyle. That's how I found acupuncture. Now I'm a crazy needle person who thinks acupuncture heals everything. Give me a problem and I'll tell you how needles can fix it. Got anxiety? Acupuncture can help. Fertility issues? Acupuncture."

The small smile on Aspen's face slipped. "I'm sorry you were sick."

"It was five years ago. I'm okay now."

"But you still need to rest," Jesse cut in.

Clara gave him a pointed look. "I know. And acupuncture is great for forcing rest because you stick the needles in and lie still. See, the solver of all problems."

Aspen laughed, but there wasn't much humor behind it. "Can it solve a crazy mother and a stalker ex?"

The beer paused halfway to Jesse's mouth. It was the first time Aspen had referred to Dylan as a stalker, and even though Jesse already knew it was true, hearing the words from her mouth made him even edgier.

"It can certainly help with stress," Clara said gently. While others would pry and try to get information, Clara wasn't like that. She was a listener, and eventually, people started sharing their problems with her just because they felt so comfortable. "Come by my place anytime," she added. "I work from a home studio."

"I might just take you up on that offer." Aspen took a big sip of her drink. It was her third one for the night.

Jesse leaned down so that his mouth was close to her ear. "Maybe we should go. Get some food."

She looked up at him, eyes slightly glazed. "You're always looking out for me."

"You look out for me too."

She snorted.

"You don't need looking after," she said. "You're big and strong and trained in a hundred and one ways to kill people."

"A hundred and two."

"Oh, sorry, missed one." She looked across the table at his brother and sister, who were now arguing about whether acupuncture could fix stupidity. "And you have an awesome brother and sister."

"My mom's pretty great too. You'll need to meet her soon."

Aspen put her elbow on the table and sat her chin on her palm. "While I have a crazy mother, no siblings and a dying career."

"Your career isn't dying."

"Try telling that to my forever-unfinished manuscript." She sipped her drink again. "How exactly does one become re-inspired?"

"When exactly did you lose inspiration?"

"One month into my relationship with Dylan." She cringed before frowning down at her drink. "You're right. I should stop drinking."

"What happened between you two?" He'd asked before, but she'd always deflected. And maybe it was unfair to ask while she was drinking, but, fuck, he needed her to tell him his suspicions were off. Way fucking off.

Her frown deepened. "He showed me who he truly was."

"And who was that?"

"Not you."

He held her gaze for long seconds, willing her to tell him more. To open up to him. *Trust him* with the information he needed.

The navy specks in her ocean-blue eyes bore into him. Gutting him. Distracting him just for a moment.

When the silence stretched, he inched closer, slipping an arm around her waist before lowering his head and whispering, "Let me in, A."

"Letting people in can be dangerous."

"Not with me." He lifted his head, those beautiful eyes once again holding him hostage. "You're safe with me."

Her chest rose and fell, her lips parting. For a moment, he thought—hoped and prayed—that she'd tell him something important. Then her lips snapped shut. She looked away, then immediately straightened and frowned.

He followed her gaze across the bar to a couple who appeared to be fighting beside a booth.

"Do you see the way he's standing over her?" Aspen asked quietly.

Yeah, the guy looked like an asshole. He was tall, towering over the woman, an angry scowl on his face. But she looked just as angry, as if she could give as good as she got.

Jesse looked back at Aspen. "He's not doing anything wrong, and she's not walking away. It's not our business."

Aspen's fingers curled.

"Jesse, will you tell Clara that my roast beef makes hers look like baked leather?"

Jesse turned to his siblings. "Both your roast beefs suck. Mine is obviously the best."

Clara's jaw dropped. "The last time you made me a roast, it was half raw."

"It was intentionally rare," he said, almost offended.

Becket shook his head. "You're delusional. You spent too long on those dangerous Ghost Ops missions, and they messed with your head. Your roast beef is the worst in the family."

"Hey, I—"

Jesse stopped when Aspen left the table and marched across the bar, right toward the couple. He looked at the guy who'd been towering over the woman, and he now had a firm grip on her arm as he yelled into her face.

Fuck.

He took off after her. "Aspen."

She didn't stop or turn. When she reached the couple, she grabbed the guy's arm and yanked. "Get the hell off her!"

Now the guy turned and towered over *Aspen*. "Why the fuck are you touching me, bitch?"

"Bitch?" Aspen stepped closer. "You're lucky touching your arm is all I'm doing. I should kick you in the balls for grabbing a woman like that."

Red darkened the guy's cheeks, and he reached for her, but Jesse pushed between them before he could touch her and shoved his chest. "What the hell are you doing?"

"What am *I* doing? This bitch—"

Jesse grabbed his arm and twisted it back, shoving him down so he was bent over the table, ignoring the gasps around him. "You *do not* call her that. And while I'm here, you don't grab women like that. Do you understand?"

"Get the fuck off me!" the guy yelled, attempting to shove back into Jesse, but he didn't move an inch.

"I will," Jesse said between gritted teeth. "Once you tell me you understand."

The asshole struggled for another second before clearly realizing he wasn't getting out of this until Jesse let him up.

"Fine," he growled. "I *understand.*"

Jesse released him and stepped back, making sure he remained between the jerk and Aspen. "Now get out."

The guy's brows rose. "You can't tell me to—"

"I just did."

"So did I," CJ, the older bartender, said as he came up behind Jesse.

The asshole's chest rose and fell as he looked down at the woman he'd grabbed. "Come on. We're leaving this shithole."

The woman glanced at Aspen, holding her gaze for a beat before looking back at him. "No."

His hands fisted, and Jesse's muscles twitched, preparing to grab the guy a second time. But he was obviously smarter than he looked, because he turned and stormed out of the bar.

Good.

Jesse turned to see Becket standing close by. He had no doubt his brother would have backed him up if he'd needed it.

He looked down at Aspen.

"Thank you, I—"

"What the hell were you thinking?" he interrupted, his voice almost a shout.

Her brows rose. "What was *I* thinking? Um, that he was an asshole."

"So, what? You grab him? A guy who's over six feet tall and clearly aggressive?"

"If he has a hand on a woman, yes, I grab him."

Jesus Christ. "No. You get me, and *I* grab him. We're going."

"I don't think so. Not after you shouted at me like that."

"*Yes*, we are. We're done here."

"Stop telling me what to do."

He lowered his head. "Aspen, I'm this fucking close to losing the slim hold I have on my self-control. Either you walk to the door with me, or I throw you over my shoulder and carry you out."

Her eyes narrowed. "I'm *not* going."

"Fine." He bent and threw her over his shoulder.

She screeched. "What the hell are you doing?"

"I'm taking you home before you piss off the next asshole and get yourself hurt." He passed his brother and sister. Clara was looking at them wide-eyed, while his brother was visibly biting back a grin. "I'll see you guys later."

Aspen pounded his back. "Let me go, you big bully!"

"No." He stepped outside and walked to his car.

"Put me down. *Now*."

He slid her down his body beside the car.

The second her feet were on the ground, she shoved him. "I can't believe you did that. And why the hell didn't anyone stop you?"

"People in this town like me."

"Yeah, well, they see you kidnapping a woman from the bar and that should change."

He opened the passenger door. "Get in, Aspen."

"No." She crossed her arms.

Jesus. He forced his voice to soften. "Aspen, I'm on edge because you were a second away from getting hurt in that bar. I'm easygoing until I'm not anymore. Now will you please get in the car?"

She swallowed as her chest rose on a deep inhale. "Look, I know I put myself in harm's way, but I did it for a good reason. I didn't *want* to cause a scene, and I didn't want *you* to have to lay hands on anyone. But you *still* shouldn't have shouted at me." She was about to turn when she added. "And the next time you throw me over your shoulder, I'm going to kick you in the balls."

Then she lowered into the car and slammed the door.

Even though he was still mad about what she'd done, he couldn't stop the wide ass smile from crossing his face. Even after all that she still threw that shit at him.

He rounded the vehicle and got in, then gave her a few seconds to put on her seat belt. But when she sat there too long with her arms crossed, he reached for it himself.

"What are you—"

He pulled the belt across her body, ignoring the way his arm grazed her chest, and the way her breath brushed his cheek.

Yeah, his heart fucking sped up, and he hated that.

On the way home, neither of them spoke, and the silence was tense. It was probably the longest he'd ever witnessed Aspen not speak before.

They were almost home when he shot a glance her way. "You're not talking to me now?"

She leaned her head back. "I'm tired, Jesse."

When he pulled into his driveway, he turned off the car and looked at her, only to see the even rise and fall of her chest.

"Aspen?"

Silence. She was asleep.

He reached over and slipped a lock of hair behind her ear, grazing the smooth skin of her cheek. A small hum slipped from her lips, and the sound shot right into his gut.

With tight muscles, he climbed out of the car and crossed over to her side.

She was soft in his arms as he carried her inside. And warm. And she kept making those sexy little humming sounds.

It was killing him. All of it.

He went straight to her room. A room that had been empty a couple months ago, but now there were pink bed linens, a fluffy purple clock, photos... It was all Aspen.

Gently, he laid her in bed and removed her heels before pulling the covers up.

Her eyes opened, a small frown on her brow. "Hey."

"Hey, yourself."

She rolled to the side, pulling the sheets over her body. "You still mad at me?"

"I could never be mad at you."

She gave a soft laugh, holding up two fingers and showing the smallest gap. "You were a little mad. I forgive you too."

"Good. I wouldn't have been able to sleep otherwise." Then he did something stupid. He leaned down and kissed her temple. He even let his lips linger. "Good night, Aspen."

There was a slight shift in her breathing before she whispered, "Good night, Jesse."

Without looking back, he left the room, almost damn well running to get away from her.

CHAPTER 7

*A*spen's stomach rolled and her eyes shot open.

She was going to be sick.

She slid out of bed, almost falling on her face in the process, and on her first step, stubbed her toe on the bedside table.

She cried out and scrunched her eyes, hopping and grabbing her toe.

Jesus freaking Christ.

Her belly rolled a second time, and she ran, ignoring the pain in her foot.

Damn her bedroom for not having an attached bathroom.

She'd almost made it to the bathroom when a very large, dark shadow appeared from seemingly nowhere, stopping in front of her.

She screamed, her heart thrashing in her chest.

His face came into focus and she gasped in air. Jesse. It was just Jesse.

His gaze moved around the hall before he searched her face. "Are you okay? I heard you cry out."

She looked down at his hand. "You've got a gun?"

"Of course I have a gun. I thought you screamed."

"I—" The bile crawled up her throat, cutting off her words.

Oh no...not in front of Jesse. She turned into the bathroom and dropped beside the toilet. She didn't even have time to kick the door closed before every drink she'd consumed that night came back up.

Footsteps sounded behind her.

He was right here. Inside the bathroom. Jesus Christ Almighty, someone kill her.

"Can you close the door?" she gasped when her stomach finally stilled. She dropped her forehead into her palms and closed her eyes.

The door didn't close. In fact, she heard footsteps moving even closer.

No, no, no.

She wanted to tell him—*scream* at him—to leave before she died of embarrassment. But before any words could leave her throat, another wave of nausea hit and she started throwing up a second time.

Warm fingers brushed the back of her neck as her hair was pulled up. She opened her mouth to tell him to leave, but then he started to rub circles on her back. Warm, soothing circles that almost distracted her from her swirling belly and head.

The words died on her lips, and she leaned into his touch.

Dumb. She'd been so dumb tonight. Or last night. She had no idea what the time was.

"I should have listened to you," she groaned, finally flushing the toilet and backing away, Jesse's hand replaced by the cool tiled wall.

His brown eyes darkened with concern. "I should have made sure you ate something before you went to bed. I'm sorry."

"Believe it or not, I am a fully grown woman and know better than to drink on an empty stomach." She tilted her head. "I'm sorry you got a front-row seat to my stupidity."

"I just want to make sure you're okay." His frown deepened. "*Are* you okay?"

Right now? Or in general? It probably didn't matter—both answers would be the same. "I'm not sure."

His beautiful eyes flickered between hers. "What can I do?"

"Try not to be so perfect."

He chuckled, and it transformed his entire face. "I'm far from perfect."

"Liar." She swallowed, breathing through some of the nausea. But she didn't just feel sick. It was something deeper. "Can I tell you something?" she asked quietly.

"Anything."

"I kind of don't like who I've become."

His eyes darkened. "Aspen—"

"No, it's just... I used to think I was such a strong person. I used to pride myself on it. Now, I'm not sure that was ever true. I think I just never *had* to be strong."

He seemed to think about that for a moment. "Do you know what I first thought when I met you?"

"That I was a mess?"

His lips didn't so much as twitch. "That you were someone I wanted to get to know. You looked interesting and deep and *brave*."

"You can't tell any of those things about someone when you just meet them."

"I can."

"How?"

"It's in the eyes. And your eyes tell me a lot. Even the things I have a feeling you wish I didn't know."

"Do you still think I'm brave?"

"You have to be. You moved across the country, away from the only home you've ever known. You left your best friend. All to break away from your mother and ex."

One deep breath. "There you go again, being perfect."

"Is that so bad?"

"Yes." A huge, gigantic yes. Because it tested every ounce of self-control she had. "It makes me want something I shouldn't want...you."

* * *

JESSE COULDN'T BREATHE when she looked at him like that. With eyes so sad that all he wanted to do was sweep her up. Shield her from whatever demons were in her head.

"You could," he said softly. "Want me."

"I got burned the last time I wanted someone, and I still haven't recovered."

A muscle ticked in his jaw. "I hate that he hurt you."

"I hate that I *let* him hurt me." A sad smile curved her lips. "You know, I used to believe in this magical kind of love. The kind that just hit you in the face and changed the world around you."

"And now?"

"Now I know the truth...there is no magic."

Anger pulsed through his veins that her asshole ex had done this. "I believe in magic."

She scoffed. "You do not."

"I do. But not a hit-you-in-the-face kind. The magic is when you feel safe with someone, physically and emotionally. It's trusting them with your entire self, even the parts you think they'll run from. It's wanting to see someone, talk to them, every day."

Her brows flickered, her voice softening. "That sounds pretty magical."

"Maybe I'll turn you back into a believer."

"Maybe." But the smile was still sad, as if she was thinking of *him* again.

"You know if I ever see him, I'm going to kill him, right?" The words fell from his mouth completely uncensored.

"Let me have the first swing."

Hell no. She wasn't going anywhere near him. "Come on. Let me help you get back to bed." He tried to lift her, but she pressed her hands to his chest.

"Absolutely not."

"Why not?"

She glanced at his bare chest and swallowed before snatching her hands back. "I need to shower and brush my teeth…try to feel semi-human again."

"I don't want to leave you alone while you're sick."

"I'll be okay."

But would *he*?

She started to push up from the floor, and he gripped her upper arms to help her. The second they were both on their feet, they stood far too close. Her warm breath brushed against his bare chest, and every inhale almost had them touching.

Like his hand had a mind of its own, it cupped her cheek. "Call out if you need anything."

Was it him, or did she lean her face into his palm?

"I will."

He swallowed, and it took far too much willpower to drop his hand. To turn and step away from her.

He'd just reached the door when she called to him.

"Jesse."

One deep inhale and he turned. "Yeah."

"Thank you. Not just for tonight. Thank you for being my friend when I really needed one."

"I will be whatever you need me to be, for as long as you need." Even if it killed him.

CHAPTER 8

*J*esse pulled up in the parking lot of the Chinese restaurant.

It had been a long-ass day. Hell, it had been a long *week*. Too many people doing the wrong thing and a hell of a lot of paperwork. But work issues felt trivial compared to Aspen.

His feelings for her were growing every day. She wasn't in a place to be anything more than friends. He knew that. But when they were together, it didn't matter. When he spoke to her, *touched her,* all he could think about was how right they felt together. How right *she* felt.

Did she feel it too? Sometimes, he swore he saw it in her eyes. Felt it in her touch.

With a long sigh, he climbed out of the car and slammed the door behind him. The entire situation was driving him crazy. But at the same time, if he had the chance, he wouldn't go back and take away the offer for her to have his spare room. Because having her close without being with her was a lot better than not having her at all.

He crossed the parking lot and pushed into the restaurant, but one glance told him Luke wasn't here yet.

"Hi. Do you have a reservation?"

He looked at the waitress. "Possibly. Is there something for two people under Luke?"

The woman looked at her computer and nodded. "Yes. Follow me."

He trailed behind the woman to a two-person corner table.

He'd just sat when a text came through.

Luke: Running a bit late. But I forgot to tell you that I invited my friend April.

The fuck?

"Hi!"

He looked up to see a young woman with long brunette hair and a tight red dress standing beside the table.

"I'm April, Luke's friend. May I?" Before he could respond, she lowered into the seat opposite him. "Jesse, right? Luke's told me a lot about you."

"He has?"

"Yeah. You've just been promoted to sheriff, right? After retiring from the military?"

What the hell was going on? He eyed his phone suspiciously before looking back to the woman. "And how do you know Luke?"

"Yoga."

Jesus Christ. "Excuse me while I respond to a text message." He lifted his phone.

Jesse: You're not coming, are you?

Luke: Shit, man, I've gotten caught up helping my sister with something. Stay though, have a meal with April. She's lovely. And very...bendy.

Asshole. He knew how Jesse felt about Aspen. Did he think he was doing Jesse a favor? He wasn't. Jesse was gonna kill the guy. Murder him with his bare hands.

"Luke's not coming."

April frowned. "Oh, I know. This is...I mean, it's a date for you and me. Why would Luke come?"

So Jesse was the only one who'd been out of the loop.

She lifted the menu. "Have you been here before? I'm not big on Chinese, but Luke said it's your favorite."

Of course he did. "It's better than pizza."

She laughed, and all he could think was that it wasn't Aspen's laugh.

He cleared his throat and leaned forward. "Look, April, this is nice, but if you're not into it, we don't need to—"

"You don't like me."

Shit. "No, it's not that."

"Am I not what you thought I'd be?" She started touching her hair as she looked down at her dress like there was a problem with her looks.

He was an asshole. "No. You're beautiful." The small smile returned to her face. "It's just, I didn't realize this was a date. I thought I was meeting Luke tonight."

She frowned. "He didn't tell you?"

"No. And I don't like surprises."

Her brows flickered. "Okay. But we can still have a nice night, can't we? I mean, we're both here, and we're hungry. You don't look like terrible company, and I can assure you that I'm not either."

He scrubbed a hand over his face. He clearly took too long to answer, because red tinged her cheeks like she was embarrassed, and she started to push her seat back.

He reached over the table to touch her wrist. "Hey. Wait. I'm sorry. I didn't mean to offend you, I just...I'm interested in someone else."

"Someone else?"

"Yeah, and Luke knows that, so he never should have set this up. And trust me, when I see him, I'm going to kick his ass."

"Oh. That's a shame. But I get it."

He was still holding her wrist when the restaurant door opened and Aspen stepped in.

* * *

"It's not that embarrassing."

Aspen's fingers tightened around the phone. "Callie, did you not hear the part where he held my hair and rubbed my back while I threw up?"

She opened the fridge. Nothing. No food in sight. Well, nothing she'd made, anyway. There was plenty of Jesse's food. Food she was sure he wouldn't mind if she ate. Food she *wouldn't* eat. He was already giving her ridiculously cheap rent. She didn't like taking his food too.

Callie sighed. "That was really sweet of him."

"I know. He *is* sweet. And cute and protective and a million other things." She still got goose bumps when she thought about how he'd handled the guy at the bar, even if they had fought about it after.

She stepped into the pantry. There was rice. She could have that for dinner. Maybe add some tuna and soy sauce.

"You know," Callie started, "you could always—"

"Don't say it," Aspen cut her friend off. "He and I are *friends*. He offered me the room in his house as a friend, and even if I did a complete one-eighty and decided I wanted more—flower girl."

"Flower girl?"

"You can't have forgotten. He bought someone roses." And she was grabbing on to that excuse with both hands to stay away from him.

"We still don't know that they were for a girl."

"Of course they were." She lifted the can of tuna and wrinkled her nose. She'd been living off rice and tuna for the last week. Why? Because it was cheap, and she was trying to be smart with her money while she hadn't released a new book for a while.

"I saw your mom the other day, by the way."

Aspen put the tuna back onto the shelf, trying not to tense at the mention of her mother. "Where?"

"In the grocery store. She was arguing with one of the managers. I think I heard her say she was going to sue."

Aspen rolled her eyes. How many people had the woman threatened to sue in her lifetime? So many she'd lost count.

"Sounds like Mom." She lifted a packet of noodles. She could cook those with an egg.

"I saw Dylan the other day too."

The noodles slipped from her fingers. "Really? Where?"

"He walked past Sugar and Spice and glared at me through the glass. Lock was a step away from getting up and going after him."

She shuddered. Even thinking about the guy made a sick feeling swirl around her belly. "It makes The Tea House sound a bit better."

"The Tea House?"

"I've been going there almost every day. The coffee's terrible, but the coffee's terrible everywhere in Amber Ridge. And I really like Mrs. Gerald, the older English woman who runs the place. She kind of feels like the grandmother I never had." They talked every day. About little things. Big things. Work. She'd even mentioned her rocky relationship with her mother.

"It sounds nice," Callie said.

"I'm kind of liking tea now, too."

"You are not."

"I am. I've tried a dozen different types, but I think Earl Grey is my favorite."

"Who are you and what have you done with my best friend?"

"I'm a tea-drinking Amber Ridge woman now."

Callie chuckled, but that chuckle became a sigh. "I miss you."

"I miss you more."

"All right, Lock's calling me for dinner. Chat tomorrow?"

"Obviously." She hung up and opened the fridge again, the same food staring back at her.

Oh, screw it, she was getting takeout. Cheap Chinese takeout, but that was still takeout. Pizza would be cheaper, but she'd been warned off Burt's Pizzeria, and that was too far to walk.

She called and ordered. As she grabbed her house keys, her gaze flicked to Jesse's closed bedroom door. Where was he tonight? Was he working late? He'd been working a lot since taking up the role of sheriff. And maybe a teeny tiny part of her missed him. But just as he was working a lot, she was out writing a lot. Or...trying to write.

With a deep sigh, she headed outside. The Chinese place was only about a twenty-minute walk, and thankfully, it wasn't dark yet. She really shouldn't be eating takeout, but man, did it sound better than plain steamed rice and tuna.

As she walked, a text came through on her phone.

Mom: I spoke to Dylan today. You need to call him. He misses you.

All the fine hairs on her arms stood on end, and for a moment, she just stared at the text as if hoping the words would dissolve in front of her.

She'd told her mother things hadn't ended well. Why was she talking to Dylan? Why was she trying to convince *her* to talk to Dylan?

She clicked out of the message and walked faster. When she entered the Chinese restaurant, the scent of Asian spices surrounded her. *So* much better than rice and tuna.

She was just stepping up to the counter when two people across the room caught her attention—and one of them was Jesse.

He sat at an intimate corner table with a woman.

"Flower girl." The whispered words slipped from her lips.

She wore a tight red dress that exposed her shoulders. Aspen had never thought of shoulders as sexy before, but on that woman…yeah, they were definitely sexy. Jesse was leaning forward and touching her arm. It looked…intimate.

He was on a date. Jesse Hayes, her roommate, the man she was in complete denial about her infatuation with, was on a date.

His gaze collided with hers, and she gasped and looked away.

Shit. Wrong move. She looked back at him and gave a forced, awkward, I-don't-care-that-your-date's-gorgeous smile.

Good job, Aspen. You were about as convincing as a two-year-old saying they hate chocolate.

She switched her focus to the lady on the other side of the counter. "Hi. I have a phone order for Aspen."

"Sure. I'll go get it."

When the woman turned, so did Aspen—right into a big, broad chest.

"Jesse. How the heck did you get over here so quickly?"

"I walked."

Oh, so he was a funny man as well as the date of a beautiful goddess tonight. "How, um, how's your date going?"

"It's not a date."

Yeah, and she was the Queen of Poland. "It's okay. You're free to date whoever you like, just like you're free to send flowers to whoever you like."

"Flowers?"

Shit. Stop talking, Aspen.

She shook her head. "Nothing. I should…"

He inched closer, and the words just died on her lips. Because he was right there. Right freaking there and he smelled *so good*.

"It's not a date," he repeated.

Her mouth opened and closed. "I didn't…I mean, that's your business."

"I know. But I want you to understand my position."

"Your position?"

"I'm not dating her or anyone else, because there's someone I'm interested in."

Her pulse picked up speed. She needed to get out. She needed a freaking bullet train out of here. "Well, that's, um, that's lovely for you. And totally your business." She stepped back, and her legs hit the counter behind her. "I—"

"Here you go."

Thank God. She paid for her food and grabbed the bag. She actually held it in front of her like a shield; any small barrier between her and Jesse had to be a good thing. "I should go. You enjoy your...not date."

"Did you walk?"

"What?"

"Did you walk here?"

"Yes."

"I'll drive you home."

"No." Well, that came out way too fast. But really, even a two-minute drive in such close quarters with him felt too much. "I mean, I really enjoyed the walk and it's still light outside." Kind of light.

"Aspen—"

"Really. I'm fine. You finish your...whatever it is, and I'll see you at home."

Then she ran out of there like the place was on freaking fire.

CHAPTER 9

*A*spen stared at her blank laptop screen, her tea cooling beside her. It was so blank that the white was blinding her.

Maybe she needed to change genre. Maybe romance just wasn't her jam anymore. She could try horror. That would be a nice one-eighty from romance. Or maybe a good crime mystery where the woman murders her ex for doing something really terrible. She'd get away with it, of course. In fact, she'd outsmart everyone and live off his life insurance on a beach in Hawaii.

A small smile played at Aspen's lips. Now *that* was a story she felt motivated to write.

Although she'd need to find an entirely new reader base because she wasn't sure her current romance-loving fans would want to read about a murderous feminist. And she didn't actually know a lot about the genre, so she'd need a whole new marketing plan.

She dropped her head onto the table. This sucked. Big gonna-need-to-find-a-new-job-soon kind of suck.

"Still having trouble with the story, honey?"

She shot up to see Mrs. Gerald beside the table. God, she'd complained so much to the café owner, the woman was basically her therapist. "I think I'm having a midlife crisis."

"You're too young for that." She set a slice of pie beside Aspen's laptop. "I brought you some apple pie, on the house, because you look like you need it."

Oh, she definitely needed pie. It smelled good too. And that lightly browned pastry with the side of cream kind of made her salivate. She'd been meaning to try the pie since first stepping into this place.

"Thank you. But I'm not even sure pie can fix this one."

"If there's anything I've learned in my seventy years, it's that very few things are so dire they can't be fixed with pie. Maybe the sugar hit will help you get some words on the page."

"Good words?"

"The best ones you've written."

She gave a small smile. "I hope you're right. Thank you again for the pie, but I *am* paying for it."

"Absolutely not. Besides, I don't know how much longer my little shop will be in business."

Aspen straightened. "Why's that?"

"Not *enough* business. Unless things pick up, I'm afraid I'm down to my last few months."

Aspen's heart gave a sad little kick. "What can I do?"

"You're already doing it by coming and drinking my tea every day." The older woman gave her a small smile before heading away from the table.

There were a couple of people at The Tea House today. An elderly man at the counter and an elderly couple in the booth by the window, having what looked like a high tea. No one remotely close to her age.

This was probably the busiest Aspen had seen it, so she shouldn't be surprised Mrs. Gerald might need to close. But it still hurt. She came here almost every day. It had become her sanctuary, and Mrs. Gerald her sounding board.

She sipped her tea. She'd chosen wild lavender today. It wasn't too bad. It did kind of taste like she was drinking a flower, but it beat the coffee.

She lifted the fork. Lordy lordy, the pie looked and smelled delicious. Or maybe that was her starving belly talking. She'd run out of the house so fast this morning she hadn't grabbed anything to eat.

The starving belly was worth it though, to save her from running into Jesse and having the awkward "how was the date?" conversation.

A date. He'd been on a *date*. Why was that so hard to accept? He was young, fit, with the best dimples she'd ever seen. Of course he was dating.

He'd gotten home shortly after her and insisted again that it hadn't been a date. Something about a guy from work setting him up with a woman from yoga? Honestly, even if he had been set up, the woman was gorgeous. Exactly the kind of woman someone like him should date.

Plus, as Aspen had told him, *she* wasn't ready to date. And she'd never expect him to wait for her. That would be silly and selfish.

So why did the image of him sitting at an intimate corner table with a beautiful woman *still* make her want to scratch her own eyes out?

She put a huge forkful of pie into her mouth.

Holy hell in a handbasket. It was phenomenal. An explosion of flavors in her mouth and easily the best pie she'd ever had. A mixture of blueberries and apple. And the pastry...it was buttery soft, like a small drop of heaven on her tongue.

Mrs. Gerald was marketing this place all wrong. It shouldn't be The Tea House. It should be The Best Pies in Montana House. Heck, the best in America.

She shoved another gigantic forkful of pie into her mouth as a shadow suddenly loomed over her table. A huge shadow.

"Hungry?"

She looked way up into Jesse's chocolate-brown eyes and almost choked on the food in her mouth. "What are you doing here?" Or that was what she'd tried to say, but the words were mashed up between dough and apple.

Jesse chuckled as he lowered into the booth opposite her. "I'm not due to start my shift for another hour, and this place was on the way, so thought I'd pop in and check on you. I missed you this morning."

Missed her as in didn't see her? Or *missed her*, missed her?

She swallowed the pie. "I wanted to get an early start."

He nodded, looking at her laptop. "How's it going?"

Oh, about as well as a steam train with a broken motor. "Good. I think I'm really going to make some progress today."

Liar.

He gave her one of those knowing smiles. Yeah, he totally knew she was lying.

"So…last night—"

"We already spoke about your date. We don't need to rehash it. It's your business."

"I told you it wasn't a date."

She lifted a brow. "Intimate corner table at a restaurant with a beautiful woman in a sexy dress? That's a date, regardless of who set it up."

Mrs. Gerald stopped beside their table. "Cappuccino."

Jesse smiled up at her. "Thank you."

"Are you sure you don't want a slice of pie with it? I have some fresh apple and blueberry this morning."

Jesse put a hand over his flat stomach. "Just ate. But thank you."

The second Mrs. Gerald left, Aspen leaned forward and hissed, "You got coffee?"

"Yeah, I don't drink tea, and I haven't tried the coffee here before. Maybe this will be the first good cup in Amber Ridge."

"I wouldn't—"

He choked on his first sip. "Oh, God, what is this? It tastes like battery acid."

"Yeah, it's bad. Worse than everywhere else in this town, which is saying something. I'm becoming quite accustomed to tea."

He wrinkled his nose.

She pushed the pie across the table. "Here, try this. It will cleanse your palate."

"I'm not—"

"Try it. Trust me."

He held her gaze for a full second before lifting her fork and scooping some pie into his mouth.

Her lower belly did a little flutter. Why was that so hot? Because he'd used *her* fork? Or because there was something incredibly sexy about his mouth?

Probably both.

His gaze shot to the pie. "Jesus, that's good."

"*Right*? It's amazing." She took the fork from his fingers and ate some more.

"So…last night."

Oh man, were they still on that?

"I was supposed to be meeting Luke from work," Jesse continued. "He sent her instead."

"I know. You told me. I still don't understand why."

"Because he's an interfering asshole."

She lowered her gaze to the pie. "She was pretty."

"She was."

Aspen's stomach dropped, even though there shouldn't be any reason for it to do so.

"But the person I'm interested in is *beautiful*."

Her gaze flew up, every inch of her skin tingling.

"You should date whoever you want," she said quickly.

"It's not her."

Her skin went from cool to hot and clammy in a matter of seconds.

Not dating, Aspen. Not. Dating.

Jesse lifted his coffee and cringed on his second sip. "Christ, it just keeps getting worse."

"Yeah, there's a real aftertaste there."

She wet her lips, and his gaze immediately lowered.

She drew in a shaky breath. "Okay, well...I should work. I'm determined to have a good writing day today." She was just lowering her gaze to the screen when her phone lit up from the table. She lifted it and cringed.

Jesse leaned forward. "Who is it?"

"No one."

"Is it him? I thought you blocked him."

"I did. It's Mom. She wants me to talk to him. She's decided he can't possibly be the bad guy in all this, that it must be me." She shook her head. "It's nothing."

Jesse's eyes narrowed. Because he knew it was another lie. It wasn't nothing. She'd blocked his number and now her mother was texting. And every text was like a little reminder from the universe that she'd chosen wrong with Dylan. That sometimes people made you think they were right for you when they really, *really* weren't.

* * *

JESSE PULLED into the parking lot outside the sheriff's station. His fingers were tight around the wheel, but he couldn't loosen them.

That asshole ex of hers was still trying to connect to her, this time through her mother.

Images of him grabbing her arm and dragging her out of the bar in Misty Peak made his back teeth grind together. Obviously,

Dylan hadn't gotten the damn message when she'd moved to the other side of the country.

He climbed out of the car and slammed the door.

When he stepped into the station, Bea looked up from the front desk. "Hi, Jesse. Everything okay?"

"Yeah, I just need some good coffee." Why no business in this town could sell a good cup of coffee, he had no idea.

He headed down the hall. In the kitchen, Luke looked up from the table, a huge fucking grin spreading across his face that did nothing to improve Jesse's mood.

"Morning, stud. Have a good night with April?"

Jesse loaded coffee into the coffee machine. "You're an asshole."

Luke's smile fell. "Most men would be dropping to their knees and worshiping me for setting them up with a woman like her."

"I told you I didn't want to be set up on a date."

"Yeah, but that was before you saw her."

"I saw her. I still don't want to date her." He opened the cupboard. One clean mug left...the fucking breasts mug.

Goddammit.

He slammed it closed, grabbed a dirty mug from the dishwasher and washed it in the sink.

Luke's chair scraped against the floor. "Whoa. Someone's grumpy. Let me guess, she didn't put out."

"How old are you?"

"Old enough to know that one night with her and you'd be a lot happier."

"Yeah, and *I'm* old enough to tell *you* that if you ever pull shit like that again, you'll be on desk duty for a month."

Luke straightened. "You can't mix business with pleasure."

"Try me."

Luke's eyes narrowed. "You know what? I think your roommate's holding out on you and you're taking your frustrations out on me."

When his coffee was ready, he lifted the mug and headed toward the door. "Nope. But I *am* frustrated with you."

Luke muttered something, but Jesse ignored it. He reached his office and settled behind the desk. On his first sip of coffee, his eyes closed.

Shit, that was good. And necessary.

He was about to log onto his computer when his cell rang, the name of his best friend—also his former Ghost Ops teammate—on the screen.

A smile curved his lips as he pressed the phone to his ear. "Holden. It's been too long."

"It has. Thought I'd check in on how everything's going being the big guy around town."

"You mean sheriff? Not too glamorous, I'm afraid. Usually, I'm snowed under in emails and paperwork."

"Lucky you love being stuck at a desk."

His friend knew he hated that. "Trouble usually hits at some point."

"Trouble? In the small town of Amber Ridge? Ah, you mean stopping Mrs. Allen from clubbing poor Pete over the head with her walking stick for driving too fast."

Jesse's lips twitched because it was so damn accurate. Pete was Burt's nephew, and also the pizzeria delivery driver. He was notorious for zipping around town and breaking the speed limit. Mrs. Allen was notorious for clubbing people with her walking stick when she got angry...which was often.

Holden knew all of that because he'd spent a lot of holidays here with his family.

"I'd take that over paperwork right now," Jesse finally said.

Holden laughed.

"When are you coming down here next?"

Holden cleared his throat. "Actually, that's kind of what I'm calling about. I want to run an idea by you."

"Shoot."

"How would you feel about me moving to Amber Ridge?"

Jesse's brows shot up. "Uh...I'd fucking love it."

"Good. Because Minnesota's not really feeling like home anymore, and I can do my woodwork anywhere."

Jesse grinned. "Get your ass over here then."

"Great. Plus, I'm missing your mom's cooking."

"And my pretty face?"

"Every damn day."

Jesse chuckled. "Remember though, the coffee's shit."

"Oh, I remember. I'll keep you updated then."

"Sounds good."

Jesse hung up, the first real smile stretching his mouth since leaving The Tea House.

Even though he'd been close to his entire Ghost Ops team, he and Holden had always been closest. It would be good to have him here.

He logged on to his computer to see what he'd missed from the night shift. A couple of noise complaints. A domestic dispute. That was it.

He spent the next hour trying to concentrate and get his head into what he was doing. It didn't work. All he could think about was Aspen. About that text she'd received about Dylan. A text she wouldn't read to him.

Ten more minutes, and he still couldn't get his head into work.

Fuck it.

He lifted his phone and sent a text to Aspen.

Jesse: What's his last name?

The three dots appeared almost immediately, then her text.

Aspen: What are you talking about? Did that coffee mess with your brain cells?

Jesse: Dylan. What's his last name?

There was a pause. Then the three dots popped up and disappeared. Then they popped up again and disappeared. That happened three times before her text finally came through.

Aspen: Why?

Jesse: Because I want to do a background check on him.

Aspen: Are you allowed to do that?

Jesse: Just tell me his last name. Please.

Aspen: No.

Jesse: Why?

Aspen: Because he's on the other side of the country, so there's no point.

Jesse: It doesn't matter if I look into him then.

Another pause in replies.

Jesse: Please. I promise, all I'm going to do is a background check.

Aspen: Will he know?

Why did she care about that? What did she think he'd do if he found out?

Jesse: No.

Aspen: Bollard. His name is Dylan Bollard.

Jesse: Thank you. Now go back to your writing.

Aspen: And you go back to sheriffing this town instead of looking up random guys.

Dylan wasn't random. He was an ex who couldn't move the fuck on.

Jesse looked up just as Claudia was passing his office.

Perfect timing.

"Claudia," he called. She was a deputy, and the best they had at digging up information.

She turned back and stepped inside. "Hey, Sheriff."

"Just Jesse. I need you to do a background check on someone for me."

"Sure."

Jesse wrote down Dylan's name and the town he lived in. If there was something to find, Claudia would find it. "Thanks."

She took the paper. "No problem. I'll let you know when I have any information."

She left the office, and a part of him hoped she didn't find anything. That Dylan turned out to be a normal guy who had a problem letting go of his ex and who'd disappear soon enough.

But another part of him had a strong fucking feeling that wasn't going to happen.

CHAPTER 10

*J*esse stepped out of the shower and pulled a towel around his waist. It had been a cold shower. Stone fucking cold. He'd had a few of them lately, living in the same house as Aspen.

The other morning, *she'd* stepped out of the bathroom in a towel. Just…a towel.

His dick twitched at the memory of water droplets on her shoulders. At the way the towel had squeezed her breasts. And he'd been so damn aware that she was naked beneath that cloth.

Shit, he was losing his goddamn mind and it was no one's fault but his own.

He stepped into his bedroom and had just pulled on some briefs when he stopped.

What was that sound? Was Aspen…singing? It couldn't be. It was seven in the morning, and Aspen was *not* an early riser. Well, unless she was trying to leave before he woke up.

Then the distant clatter of pots and pans hitting counters had him frowning.

Was she cooking? She rarely ate breakfast, and when she did, it was cereal.

He pulled on his uniform and stepped out of his room. His feet ground to a halt in the living room at the sight of Aspen in the kitchen.

She had her back toward him as she leaned over the counter to watch something on her laptop. Her hair was pulled up in a messy bun, she wore denim overalls, and she was singing "Love Shack" by the B-52s.

And Jesus Christ, was she out of tune. He'd never heard someone sing so off-key, and somehow the sound was cute as hell.

She stepped back from the counter and opened an overhead cabinet.

His gaze shifted to the laptop. A baking show? What was she baking so early?

He'd started crossing the space between them when Aspen climbed onto the counter.

What the hell was she doing?

She reached up for something on the top shelf, and he saw it before it happened. Her foot landed in some spilled milk and slid.

Shit.

Jesse lunged across the kitchen as she screamed and fell. He caught her a split second before she hit the hard counter.

Her scrunched eyes popped open, and she stared up at him, surprise lifting her brows. "Jesse."

"What the hell are you doing, Aspen?" Anger wove into his words, because fuck, if he hadn't been here to catch her, she could have cracked her damn skull open.

"What the hell I was doing was getting the muffin tray down, because *you* put it in a ridiculously hard-to-reach place."

She pushed at his chest, and he set her on her feet.

"Next time, ask me." He reached up and grabbed the tray before setting it on the counter. "You're baking?"

She frowned. "Why do you ask like that?"

"Like what? A question?"

She rolled her eyes and went to the fridge and grabbed the butter. "Like you're shocked."

"I just haven't seen you bake before." And definitely not at seven in the morning.

"I'm changing my main character's profession to a baker, but I haven't baked much before, so I thought I should at least learn how to make muffins before I write about her doing it."

Jesse leaned against the island. "What was her profession before?"

"An accountant. But it didn't suit her. She's not analytical enough for that. She's messy and erratic and creative."

"What does the guy in your book do?"

Her eyes flew up and flared before going back to the counter. "He's in…law enforcement."

The corners of Jesse's mouth twitched. "Really?"

"Don't read too much into it. Heroes in law enforcement are popular."

"Is that because a man in a uniform's sexy?"

"I suppose some people find them sexy."

"Do you?" He was being direct, but he couldn't bring himself to care.

Her throat bobbed. "I'm impartial."

He almost laughed, and the sudden need to test her had him stepping closer. He lowered his head, touching a hand to the small of her back as he whispered into her ear, "So falling into my arms did nothing for you?"

A shudder rolled down her spine, one he felt with every muscle in his body. "Maybe for a small fraction of a second, I was a little bit affected." She looked up. "But then you spoke."

"Ouch."

Her lips twitched, and she went to step away, but he snaked an arm around her waist and tugged her back. "Aspen. I'm sorry I got angry. I was scared about what could have happened if I hadn't caught you."

She looked up, and the second her gaze collided with his, his heart shot into his fucking throat.

Damn, she was beautiful. A natural kind of beauty. Effortless.

And standing this close, with her mouth an inch from his, her scent everywhere...all he wanted to do was kiss her. The voice in his head pushed him—*screamed at him*—to do just that. To lower his head and see if her lips were as soft as they looked.

"Thank you for catching me," she whispered. Her eyes dropped to his lips.

It was too damn much to resist. He started to lower his head. She didn't pull away. He was almost touching her lips, could feel her breath on his mouth...

When the ringing of the doorbell cut through the silence.

Jesus fucking Christ.

Aspen's spine straightened and she took a hurried step back.

He was gonna kill them. It didn't matter if it was family or a friend or a neighbor, whoever was at the door was about to breathe their last breath.

He crossed to the front door and tugged it open. An older woman with short, graying hair and familiar blue eyes stood in front of him. *Aspen's* eyes.

A gasp sounded behind him, then Aspen whispered, "Mom."

* * *

HER MOTHER WAS HERE, in Amber Ridge, the same town she'd run to, in part, to get away from her.

At least it was the happy version of her mother. The version that wanted to have coffee and chat and bond.

Plus, her mother had good timing, interrupting an almost-kiss with Jesse. What had she been thinking?

Just because he smelled good—okay, not good, fan-freak-ing-tastic—and he had the strongest arms that had ever wrapped around her, *did not* mean kissing his beautiful lips was a good idea. In fact, it was the *opposite* of a good idea. Because he had the kind of lips she could become addicted to.

"Jesse's still cute, I see."

She dropped the napkin she'd been fiddling with, and it fell to the diner table. She never came to the diner. But she didn't want to take her mother to The Tea House. That was *her* place, and she didn't want her mother to tarnish it in case she had a sudden change of mood.

Aspen leaned forward. "What are you doing here, Mom?"

At seven in the morning, no less.

Misty Peak didn't have a big airport, which meant no direct flights, so she'd probably taken at least one connecting flight... that was about a six-hour trip. So she'd have to have left in the middle of the night. Either that or spent the night somewhere last night.

"I told you, I missed you and wanted to see you."

Her mother didn't have many people in her life—mostly because she struggled to maintain healthy relationships—which was why Aspen had always tried to maintain *their* relationship... until it had become too much.

"You shouldn't be spending the kind of money coming here must've cost."

"I worked it out because I wanted to see you. You just up and left me. No warning, just a text."

Yeah, because if she'd given her mother an in-person warning, she would have spiraled and harassed Aspen, guilting her into staying. Leaving without notice had been her only option.

"I needed to get out for my sanity," Aspen said gently.

"Because of Dylan."

Among other things. "Yes."

"I don't understand what happened between you two. I thought you made such a good couple."

Yeah, because Dylan could be charming when he wanted...

and just like her mother, she'd fallen for it, hook, line and sinker. "He wasn't a good guy."

"Wasn't a good guy how?"

Oh, there was no way she was going into the finer details with her mother while in a diner. "I just need you to take my word for it. I can't ever have him in my life again."

Her mother gave a little *humph*, like she was offended Aspen wasn't giving her all the sordid details of the worst relationship of her life.

Aspen softened her smile. "Let's change the subject. Where are you staying?"

"Oh, I rented the most gorgeous little Airbnb. I got in last night. You need to visit. It's so charming. And the owner has said I can have it for as long as I want because he hasn't got any bookings for a few months."

"How are you paying for it?" How was she paying for the entire trip? She barely worked because she could never hold down a job. Her last job had been an after-hours office cleaning gig, but she was fired when she'd started threatening to sue for underpayment, even though Aspen was sure her mother had been paid the agreed-upon amount.

Her mother waved her hand. "You don't worry about that. I've got it all taken care of."

Aspen frowned at the sparkly silver bracelet on her wrist. "Where'd you get that?"

"Oh, do you like it? It was a gift."

It looked expensive. "Who—"

"One croissant with jam, and a plate of toast and eggs."

Aspen smiled at the waiter as he set down the food. What she really wanted was a big steaming cup of coffee, but the coffee here was almost on par with The Tea House. Instant and watery and just bad.

The waiter left, and her mother leaned across the table. "He's cute."

"Who?"

"The waiter. Do you think he was looking at me?"

"He had to look at you to give you your food."

Her mother rolled her eyes. "Okay, but do you think his gaze lingered?"

"Mom—"

"Aspen, hi!"

Oh, thank God.

She looked up to see Jesse's sister Clara standing by the table, an older woman with graying hair and a kind smile beside her. "Hi, Clara."

"It's good to see you again. Have you met my mother?"

"No, I haven't."

"Mom, this is Aspen, Jesse's roommate. Aspen, this is my mother, Pam."

Pam reached out a hand. "It's so nice to finally meet you. I've heard so much about you."

She had? Good things? Aspen was too afraid to ask. "It's nice to meet you too." She looked across the table. "And this is my mother, Karen. Mom, this is Jesse's sister and mother."

"It's nice to meet you both," her mother said politely. "Would you like to join us?"

Aspen's spine stiffened. *Please, say no.* Her mother was fine right now, but that could change in a split second.

"That's kind of you to offer," said Clara, "but we're running late for an appointment. I just saw Aspen and thought I'd pop by the table and say hi. Rain check?"

Absolutely not. Or at least, not with her mother in tow. "Sure."

Pam touched her shoulder. "We'll hopefully see more of each other. Thank you for keeping my son company. He needs someone with him."

"Trust me, he's helping me a lot more than I'm helping him."

The memory of him catching her that morning and saving her

a broken neck flashed in her mind. Yep, huge, gigantic helping happening.

"That's my son, always wanting to help." Pam's smile widened. "Have a lovely day."

Aspen noticed her mother frowning as they left the table.

"Everything okay over there?" Aspen asked, once Pam and Clara were gone.

Her mother blinked and shifted her attention back to Aspen. "Of course. They seem friendly."

"Everyone in this town is friendly." Which was saying something, seeing as she'd lived her entire life in the small town of Misty Peak, where the locals resembled the cast from *Gilmore Girls*.

Her mother cut into her croissant. "Oh, I meant to tell you, I read your last book."

Aspen paused, toast halfway to her mouth. "You did?" Her mother never read her stuff. Not a single word.

Her mother nodded. "It was just wonderful. My favorite part was when Darren took Kathryn to the ball, and they finally put their differences behind them. It was a beautiful ending."

Aspen looked at her mother like she'd grown two heads. She *had* read it.

"I was so sad when I finished," her mother continued, "that I ordered three other books from your backlist."

Okay, who was this sweet, supportive woman and what had she done with her mother? "You really read my book?"

Her mother lifted her gaze from her croissant and frowned. "I'm your mother. I want to support you. I'm looking forward to the next one."

Aspen's heart gave a little kick. Was it possible her mother was actually getting better?

She almost didn't want to get her hopes up. She'd always craved a normal mother-daughter relationship, but it had never been possible. Could that change?

CHAPTER 11

*J*esse leaned back in his seat. He was almost done. The day had been filled with speeding fines, warnings for minor offenses, and a house call to check on an elderly couple who hadn't stepped outside in a few days. It hadn't been a bad day—he was just ready to get home.

It was late, so Aspen should be home from spending time with her mother.

He was about to stand when his cell rang, his mother's name on the screen. "Hey, Mom."

"Jesse, honey, I hope I haven't caught you at a bad time."

"Not at all. I'm just about to leave work."

"Oh, your job worries me, honey. Are you keeping safe?"

She worried a lot. The day he'd told his mother he was joining a Ghost Ops team, she'd almost fainted, and that was *after* Becket had become a SEAL.

"There's not a lot of danger in Amber Ridge."

"Don't jinx it. Not while you're sheriff and Becket's fire chief. At least Clara has a nice, safe job."

"I would argue that jabbing people with needles could put her in more danger than me."

His mother chuckled.

"Are you doing okay, Mom?"

"Better than okay. I just called to tell you that I met Aspen today."

Something buzzed in his gut at the mention of her name. The sheer fucking mention. That was what she did to him. "Yeah? Where'd you meet her?"

"Clara and I were in the diner, and so were she and her mother." There was a brief pause. "She's pretty."

He bit back a laugh. She wasn't pretty. She was beautiful. "Yeah, she is."

"And that smile of hers...you know, you can tell a lot about a person by their smile."

"Is that right?" He rose and started to clear his desk.

"Absolutely. Her smile told me that she's kind. Smart. Maybe has a bit of fire to her, which is exactly what you need in your life."

His lips twitched. "You read all that in one smile?"

"I did. Now, I'd like to have her over for dinner soon."

He should have seen that coming. "Mom, she just got to town—"

"No, she didn't. She's been here for months. Can I trust you to ask her and come back to me with a date?"

He'd understand it if they were dating, but they weren't. "She's just renting a room from me."

"Which means she's close to you, so I want to get to know her a little better. Now I have to go, but you'll get me that date, won't you? I'll make my pot roast."

He loved his mother's pot roast. And he loved his mother. But *she* loved to meddle. "I'll talk to her."

"Thank you. Drive home safely, okay?"

"Always. I love you, Mom."

"I love you too, honey."

He hung up and slid his phone into his pocket. He was so

aware of how lucky he was to have the family that he had. Aspen deserved more from her own mother. Hopefully, she'd gotten more from her today.

A knock sounded at the door, and he looked up to see Claudia poking her head in. "Can I come in?"

"Of course."

She stepped inside and his gaze lowered to the folder in her hands, then back up to her face.

And immediately, he knew...he just fucking *knew* what it was without being told. "That's information on Dylan Bollard."

She nodded, and by the look on her face, it wasn't good.

Shit. "Tell me."

"He doesn't have a criminal record, but I dug a little deeper into his past and found something you might be interested in. He used to live in Billings, and he had a fiancée."

Jesse frowned. "What does that—"

"Her name is Lilly Spawn, and she almost died."

Every muscle in his body pulled so fucking tight that they could have snapped. "How?"

"She was beaten so badly, she ended up in a coma."

He wanted to punch something. A wall. A desk. *Anything.* "He did it."

"Not according to the police report. She told them it was a home invasion, but police never found evidence of anyone else being there. Then, two months later, she left town and there's been no sign of her since. She disappeared."

A vein throbbed in Jesse's temple. "He almost killed her, and she either ran from him or..."

"He made her disappear." She held out the folder. "This is the report. It includes photos of what he did to her."

He almost didn't want to take it. He forced his hand to stretch out and his fingers to wrap around the folder. Then he opened it.

Fuck.

The woman was black and blue with bruises. Her eye was

almost swollen shut, her lip was split and she had bandages everywhere.

He turned the page and read over her injuries. Broken ribs. Concussion. Internal fucking bleeding.

He slammed the folder shut. "I have to know where he is."

He wasn't sure if the words were for Claudia or himself. There was nothing Claudia could do...nothing legal anyway. They needed legal recourse to access things like his vehicle or his phone number, both of which could be used to track him.

Claudia glanced over her shoulder before closing the door. "I know someone."

Jesse frowned. "Someone?"

"Don't ask me how, but I might be able to get you the information you need."

His frown deepened. "I don't want you getting into trouble for me."

"Maybe I like living in the gray area. I'll let you know when I get something."

She left his office and Jesse packed up his stuff. His muscles were tense the entire way home, his fingers curled too tightly around the wheel. He drove over the speed limit, and it still didn't feel fast enough.

The second he stepped inside his house, he was greeted by an eerie silence and not a single light on. Was she not home? It was almost dark, and she didn't have a car.

"Aspen?"

Nothing.

He checked the kitchen and living room, then went down the hall to her bedroom. He wanted to walk straight in but forced himself to stop and knock.

Again, no response.

He stepped inside and, just like the rest of the house, the room was cloaked in darkness and empty.

She wasn't home. Where was she?

He pulled out his phone and dialed her number. Straight to voicemail.

Goddammit.

He marched over to the door and yanked it open—only to stop at the sight of her standing on the porch, key raised.

She frowned. "Jesse...is everything okay?"

* * *

ASPEN FELT LIGHT. And cautiously happy. She'd had a good day with her mother. A really good day. They hadn't fought once. There'd been no big mood changes. Her mother had been kind and funny and had taken an interest in her life. A real interest.

One good day didn't erase the lifetime of trouble her mother had caused. But they hadn't had a day like today in... heck, ever.

She climbed up the front steps and had just lifted her key when the door opened and Jesse stood in front of her. Only he wasn't wearing his usual smile.

She frowned. "Jesse...is everything okay?"

He studied her face before sweeping his gaze down her body and back up.

A shiver ran down her spine.

"*You're* okay?" he asked.

"I'm fine." What was going on? She slipped past him and dropped her bag onto the hall table before facing him. "What's wrong?"

"I was worried. It's late."

Her brows shot up. "You were worried about me because it's late?"

"I don't like you walking home after dark. You should have called. I would have picked you up."

Why did it feel like more than that?

She walked into the kitchen and pulled some containers of

leftover Chinese takeout from the fridge. "You know, this is Amber Ridge. It's pretty safe here."

"Funny you should say that. I just told my mom the same thing."

"Oh, did she tell you we met?"

"She did. She wants to have you over for dinner."

Aspen paused in the middle of pulling a fork from the drawer. "Really? Why?"

One side of Jesse's mouth lifted. "I guess she likes you."

"Two moms in one day. I'm on a roll." She tipped the Chinese into bowls, just assuming Jesse would have some too, before putting them into the microwave.

"I take it you had a good day with your mom?"

She set the microwave timer. "I did actually. We went to the diner, we walked, we talked. We haven't spent a whole day together since I was a kid, and we've certainly never spent so much time together without arguing. I kept waiting for the switch to flip and for her to say something horrible to me, but it never happened."

Jesse leaned a hip against the island. "Maybe the distance has done the relationship some good."

"Maybe. I mean, I hope so. I was almost wondering if she's actually sought some help from a therapist or something, but I was too scared to ask." Mentions of her mother's mental health had never gone well in the past.

She grabbed the Chinese from the microwave and handed one bowl to Jesse.

He slipped it from her fingers. "Thanks."

"So, you gonna tell me why you got weird about me coming home late?"

His frown deepened, and his fork paused its stirring. "Not right now. You've had a good day. We should keep it that way."

She cocked her head. Did he have something to tell her that would ruin her day? She opened her mouth to ask, then stopped.

He was right. She *was* having a good day, and she didn't want to ruin it.

She cleared her throat. "Did you arrest anyone today?"

Jesse laughed, and the deep timbre made all the fine hairs on her arms stand on end. "I cuffed someone. Does that count?"

"Absolutely."

They spent the rest of the evening talking and laughing about anything and everything while eating two-day-old Chinese food and finishing it off with ice cream. It felt good. Easy. But then, conversation with Jesse had always felt easy.

When they were both done, Jesse took her bowl and popped it into the dishwasher. "I may check the locks and head to bed now."

"Did I wear you out?" She grinned, but that grin slipped when he lowered his head and his lips brushed her ear.

"Nope. With you, I could go all night."

Her belly rolled, a tingle slipping over every inch of her skin. Then she swallowed as she watched him leave the room, her gaze fixed on his broad shoulders. The muscles in his back contracting beneath his shirt as he moved.

Man, he was a temptation she rarely felt strong enough to resist.

She was still smiling when her phone beeped with a text. She pulled it from her pocket to see it was her mother. The smile dropped the second she read over the words.

Mom: Did you say something to him?

Aspen: Who?

Mom: The waiter at the diner...did you say something to him?

Aspen: Like what?

Her phone rang, and she had to work up the strength to answer it because she knew the second she did, the great day would be tarnished.

One breath, and she put the cell to her ear. "Mom—"

"I went back to the diner this evening to talk to him, and he didn't want anything to do with me."

"How does this involve *me*?"

"I *saw you* talking to him on your way back from the bathroom today. Did you tell him lies about me? Is it because you want him for yourself?"

Aspen dropped her head into her hand. She could almost hear the pop of the bubble that had been her magical day. For a split second, she'd thought she and her mother might be able to have a semblance of a normal relationship…now that second had ended, and reality was hitting her smack in the face.

"No, Mom. He asked me if we'd like any cake for the table before he sold the last piece, and I said no."

"You're lying."

Deep breaths, Aspen. "No, I'm not. But I *am* hanging up."

"Don't even think about—"

She ended the call, tipped her head back, and closed her eyes. It would be easy to cry right now. But she didn't want to cry. She wanted to rage at the unfairness of it all. That she had to deal with this while others didn't.

Yeah, anger. That felt safer. Anger at her mother for not seeking help for her mental health when Aspen had suggested it so many times. Anger at the universe for giving her a mother who was so mentally unstable.

Her phone beeped with another text.

Mom: You're a slut! You know that?

The tears once again pushed at her eyes.

With fast steps, she marched toward the front door, tugged it open and threw her cell outside. When the door closed, she laid her head against the wood.

It was always going to be like this. Her mother was always going to be mentally ill, and Aspen would never have the relationship with her that she craved. She just had to accept it and move on. To stop wanting better.

A few deep, calming breaths later, she pulled the door open, crossed the lawn and lifted her phone. Once back inside, she wanted to slam the door closed after her. She didn't. Because then Jesse would come find her. He'd want to know what was wrong. And for some reason, she felt embarrassed about her mother. Maybe because he had such a perfect family. Maybe because she'd just told him what a great day she'd had and now felt like an idiot.

She closed the door quietly, then headed to her room, promising herself she'd never make the mistake of trusting her mother again.

Once she was in bed, she lay there staring at the ceiling, emotions rolling through her. Frustration. Sadness. And anger. But mostly anger at herself for thinking things could be different.

It took her a long time to fall asleep. Too long. She was just drifting off when a hand suddenly covered her mouth, causing her eyes to pop open to the outline of a large male figure standing over her.

CHAPTER 12

*A*spen's heart crashed into her throat as a scream built in her chest. She was a second away from kicking the sheets back and clawing at the man's eyes when he spoke.

"It's me."

Jesse? It was just Jesse. The air rushed from her chest. She wasn't being attacked. She was safe.

His head lowered, his face finally coming into view. "There's someone in the house."

Her skin chilled, her pulse once again speeding up.

"I'm going to remove my hand," he whispered. "But I need you to not make a sound."

She nodded, but the move was jerky and stiff.

Slowly, he lifted his hand from her mouth.

"Who?" she whispered, as soon as she had a chance.

"I don't know. But I'm going to find out. I need you to promise me that you'll stay here, regardless of what you hear."

Her brows flickered, a new fear spidering through her veins. Fear for Jesse. That he was about to face an unknown threat.

Then she saw the glint of the gun in his hand.

"I don't want you to go out there." The words rushed from her throat. "Call someone."

"I'm the sheriff, Aspen. I'm the person people call. I'm well trained. I'll be okay."

She didn't care if he was the sheriff or if he'd spent his entire life training for this very moment; she wanted someone else to put themselves at risk. She opened her mouth to tell him that, but he spoke first.

"Please, Aspen. Promise me you'll close the door after me and stay exactly where you are."

She swallowed. It was the last thing she wanted to do. But his eyes...they pleaded with her, almost looking desperate. "I'll stay."

Relief washed over his features. "Thank you."

She climbed out of bed and rose with him. He was about to open her bedroom door when she grabbed his arm. "Jesse..." He stopped and turned. "Be careful."

"Always." He pressed a quick kiss to her forehead, then he was gone.

Oh God, oh God, oh God. Who was out there? And how had they gotten in?

Her heart stopped. The front door. Had she locked it after grabbing her phone? She'd been so angry that she couldn't remember. What if she hadn't?

Stupid. So stupid! It was her fault someone was here. And if Jesse got hurt, *that* would be her fault too.

No. He wouldn't get hurt. He *was* well trained. One of the best-trained soldiers in the country. If anyone should be scared, it was the intruder.

She laid her head on the door and waited, flinching when she heard Jesse's deep voice as he yelled at the person. She couldn't make out his words through the door, but he was angry.

When the second voice sounded, it was muffled, but it had Aspen's spine going ramrod straight.

No... It couldn't be.

They spoke again, and the familiar muffled voice had Aspen yanking open the door and sprinting into the living room.

"One more chance to stop, or I will restrain you," Jesse yelled.

Aspen stepped into the room to see her mother pulling it apart. Drawers were pulled out, their contents on the floor. Little knickknacks that had been sitting on end tables had been swiped off.

"Mom!" Aspen gasped, drawing the attention of both her and Jesse. "What are you doing?"

Jesse growled. "I told you to stay in the bedroom."

That was never going to happen with her mother here.

Karen Davies stepped forward. Her hair was a mess, the scowl on her face murderous. "You took it. Where'd you put it?"

"Put what?"

"*My bracelet.* Where'd you put my bracelet?"

"I haven't touched it."

Her mother's eyes spat fire. "Don't lie to me. I saw the way you looked at it today. You were jealous and wanted it for yourself."

No...not here. Not in front of Jesse. "I didn't—"

"First you turn the waiter against me. Now this. You're an ungrateful little—"

"Don't even *think* about finishing that sentence, Karen," Jesse growled.

Her mother's gaze shot to him. "Of course you're defending her. Are you in on this too? You gonna sell my bracelet and split the profits?"

She was out of her mind. "Mom, you need to leave." There was no anger in her voice, just an awful mix of disappointment and embarrassment and exhaustion. God was she tired. Physically. Emotionally. In every way a person could be tired.

"Aspen—"

"*Now*, Mom. I will not have you follow me across the country and pull the same shit you always pull." Aspen crossed over to the door and pulled it open. "I do not have to put up with this behavior if you refuse to seek help for your mental health."

Her mother's cheeks reddened. "I do not need—"

"You do. And until you get that help, we can't have a healthy relationship...or any relationship at all. Now leave, before Jesse calls his deputies to arrest you."

"You wouldn't—"

"I would," he cut in. Then, as if to prove his point, he lifted his phone and moved to stand beside Aspen.

Her mother huffed. "Fine. I'll leave this house, but I'm *not* leaving town until you return my bracelet. You hear me? *I'll* press charges if you don't."

Her mother stormed toward the door, and Jesse inched in front of Aspen. Which was fair. Her mother had never physically assaulted her but she was unstable, so it wasn't out of the realm of possibilities.

The second her mother stepped outside, Aspen closed the door, making sure she turned the lock this time. Then she leaned her head against the wood, and for the second time that night, she wanted to cry. She tried to hold back the tears. Lord knew she'd been embarrassed enough already.

But then Jesse's warm fingers curved over her shoulder, and he turned her. Without a word, he tugged her against his bare chest and held her.

Finally, she let the first tears fall.

She let out the anger that her own mother would treat her like that. The frustration at the unfairness of it all. And the disappointment because, once again, she'd been let down by the person who was supposed to love her most.

* * *

JESSE LOOKED from the coffee he was preparing to Aspen on the couch. Her eyes were red and puffy, and she looked so sad, all he wanted to do was fix this. Make it better.

But he couldn't.

His muscles tightened as he poured milk into the mugs. Fuck, he was angry. The anger crawled up his chest, burning his throat. But he was trying to keep it off his face. She didn't need his anger right now.

He carried the coffees to the living room and handed one to her.

She slipped it from his fingers. "Thank you."

She didn't even sound like herself. She was too quiet, her voice too sad.

He sat beside her on the couch. "What are you thinking?"

"That I should have locked the door." She half laughed, but there was no humor behind it.

Jesse didn't so much as crack a smile. Another thing he was pissed as hell about. He usually checked every lock in the house *after* she went to bed. Tonight, he hadn't.

He wanted to kick his own ass.

"Can I ask you something?" he asked.

Her gaze lifted, apprehension skittering through her eyes. "Sure."

"Why haven't you cut her off completely? What she did tonight wasn't an isolated incident. And the way she spoke to you... You deserve better."

Aspen lifted a shoulder. "Because she's my mom. She's the only family I have, and there are moments like today where, just for a second, I feel like I have a real parent." She shook her head. "After tonight, that probably sounds stupid."

"It doesn't. It sounds like you look for the good in her and hope that the good sticks." Which made it even worse that the woman couldn't be what Aspen needed.

She frowned at her coffee. "I was twelve when I realized she needed help. We were learning about mental health at school. Borderline personality disorder came up, and she displayed every symptom. But she also fit about three other mental illnesses. I was so happy because, in my mind, the mystery of why she behaved the way she did was solved. And if we knew the why behind her behavior, she could get help."

A pit formed in his stomach. "What happened?"

"I ran home and told her. Mistake. *Big* mistake. She was so angry. Angrier than I'd ever seen her before. Screaming that there was nothing wrong with her. Throwing things at me." Aspen pulled down the shoulder of her pajama top and pointed to a small scar. "This is the result of a framed photo hitting me in the shoulder."

The anger returned, squeezing his chest. "Why didn't anyone do anything? Teachers? Neighbors?"

"Everyone knew something wasn't right with her. I used to hear kids at school gossiping about it all the time. I'm still scarred from that too. But she never did anything in front of anyone. Nothing serious enough to warrant being reported."

Jesus, his heart hurt for her. "I'm sorry."

"I thought by coming here that I'd finally gotten away. And then I do something stupid like give her my address."

"You didn't know she'd come."

"I should have." She tilted her head, the first small smile since her mother had left tilting her lips. "Thank you for having my back tonight."

"I'll always have your back."

Something flashed through her eyes. An emotion that came and went so quickly, he couldn't place it.

"Okay." She straightened. "I'm ready for you to tell me the real reason you were so freaked out when I got home late tonight."

"I told you—"

"No. You left something out. And at the time, I was so blissfully happy with the illusion of having a normal mother that I didn't ask, because I didn't want to pop the bubble. But the bubble has well and truly exploded, so now I'm asking."

Shit. Telling her about Dylan felt like kicking her while she was down. But he couldn't avoid the truth a second time. "Did you know Dylan was engaged?"

"Yeah, when he lived in Billings. Her name was Lilly."

Jesse dipped his head. "Correct. But did you also know she was beaten so badly, she ended up in a coma?"

Aspen flinched. "A coma?"

"Yes. She said it was a home invasion, but police never found any evidence of anyone else being in the house."

The color drained from Aspen's face.

He set his coffee on the table and closed the small distance between them. Then he placed a hand on her thigh. "You left him. You did everything right."

"Not everything. I should have left sooner." She kept her eyes on his.

He cupped her cheek. "But you *did* leave."

She frowned. "I wish I'd met you first." Then, without a word, she lay her head on his shoulder.

Warmth bloomed in his chest. He slipped the mug from her fingers, set it on the coffee table and wrapped his arms around her. She fit so perfectly against him. Like this was exactly where she was meant to be.

"Thank you for looking out for me," she whispered.

He tightened his arms. "Always."

And he meant that. He might not have known her for long, but she'd worked her way into his life, making herself something he couldn't live without.

He wasn't sure how long they sat there, but at some point, her chest relaxed with deep, even breaths. She was asleep. Still, he didn't move, not for a long time. Because being with her felt good. *Holding her* felt good.

Eventually, he slipped an arm under her legs, rose and carried her to her room. He'd just eased her beneath the covers when she grabbed his arm.

"Jesse…" Her eyes were still closed, voice half asleep. "Lie with me. Just for a bit."

Fire laced his veins. The idea of holding her in bed…it did things to him.

"Please," she added softly.

Usually, he liked to think of himself as a strong person. But right now, every part of him felt weak. Far too weak to say no to her. He slid beneath the covers, and immediately, she nestled her head on his chest and her breaths evened out once more.

Jesse lay there, holding her, wondering how the hell he was ever supposed to let go.

CHAPTER 13

Mmm. Aspen was warm. So warm, she didn't want to get up. But why was her pillow hard? And why was it moving? It was rising and falling...and there was a dull thud beneath her ear.

Her eyes popped open. Not a pillow, a chest. She was lying on a chest. *Jesse's* chest.

Shit. They'd *slept* together. He was in her bed...because she'd asked him to get in with her.

She winced. *Stupid.* What was she thinking?

But she knew what she'd been thinking. That she was sad and didn't want to be alone, and beautiful Jesse could fix all that.

It was fine. This was fine. She could get out of bed without waking him. Avoid the awkward "good morning, thanks for letting me cry on your chest and use you as a pillow" conversation.

She did a quick body scan. His hand was on her back, but no biggie, it would drop when she slid off the mattress. And her leg was tangled between his, but that should be a simple lift-and-roll situation.

Now she just needed to move.

But what if she woke him?

Possible. Very possible. But the longer she waited, the more chance there was of him waking.

Slowly—so slowly she swore an entire minute passed—she lifted her leg.

Good. Next, she needed to lift her head and arm, then roll away.

She raised her head and the arm wrapped around his stomach, then went to roll, but the arm around *her* waist tightened.

She froze.

"Running away?"

Her head shot up to see Jesse staring at her. A very sexy, *very awake* Jesse. "You've been awake this whole time?"

"During your grand exit? Yes, I have."

She whacked him.

"Ow." He grabbed at his chest.

"Why didn't you say anything?"

"Because I liked watching you try to be all stealthy."

Stealthy? Ha. That wasn't a word that had ever been used in reference to her before, and it certainly didn't apply now.

He shifted a leg, and his muscled thigh rubbed against her, making her lower belly tingle. And suddenly her attention was brought back to his chest beneath her. His very *bare* chest. And his face...it was so close to hers she could feel his breath on her cheek.

She swallowed. "I should get up."

"Why?"

Why? Had he lost his mind? "Because we're in bed together."

"I don't have a problem with that." His thumb swiped her bare hip where her top had risen.

She jolted.

Get out, Aspen. Get out before you do something stupid. Like touch his sexy day-old stubble or kiss his oh-so-kissable lips.

She threw off the covers and, in her haste to stand, almost fell straight back on top of him.

"Whoa, darlin'."

He tried to touch her, but she lurched away from the bed so fast that she stumbled. "I have to go."

Humor danced in his eyes. "Where?"

"Shower."

She turned and speed-walked out of the room so fast that it was basically a sprint. The bathroom door closed behind her with a thud, and it wasn't until she was locked in that she took her first full breath.

Oh, God. Why did the man have to be so…everything? Sexy. Funny. Chiseled. And she'd *slept* with him. All freaking night.

She stripped off her clothes and stepped into the shower. The water was far cooler than she usually made it, but she needed a bit of cool right now.

She should be focused on everything that happened last night. Her mother trashing the living room and accusing her of stealing. The information she'd learned about Dylan.

Dylan. The memory slapped her in the face. Had he really almost killed a woman? If *she'd* stayed, would that have been her?

She touched her cheek, closing her eyes and remembering the first time he'd hit her.

"You can't tell me what to do, Dylan. If I want to go to Meridian with Callie, then I'm going to Meridian with Callie."

His hand moved so fast, she didn't see it coming, slapping her across the face and whipping her head around. Pain ricocheted through her skull, and she fell back onto the floor.

For a moment she was still, shock and fear and disbelief clogging her throat and stealing any words.

Then she looked up, way up, into Dylan's hate-filled eyes.

She closed her eyes, forcing the memory away. But that wasn't the worst part. The worst part was that he'd apologized the next day, *begged* for her forgiveness. And stupid, weak Aspen had given it to him.

Self-loathing clenched her hands into fists. She hated herself for that. Deep down, she knew he was the reason she couldn't write, because a part of her had fallen out of love with men that day. Or the idea of men being protectors, at least. And maybe even the idea of love itself.

But she was here now, with Jesse, a man so beautiful he made her want to believe in love again. And romance and happily ever afters.

The problem was that her greatest loss after dating Dylan was her trust in her own judgment. In her ability to separate the good guys from the bad. Dylan had *seemed* good...until he'd proven he wasn't.

She stayed in the shower so long that her skin wrinkled. When she finally stepped out, she wrapped a towel around her chest and cursed.

Dammit. She'd been in such a rush to leave her bedroom, she'd forgotten her clothes. She always took a set in with her so she didn't have to walk into the hall and risk running into Jesse half naked. It had happened the other day, and the way he'd looked at her...she'd almost turned into a puddle on the floor.

After a deep, closed-eyes breath, she unlocked the bathroom door and stuck her head into the hall.

Empty. Good.

She raced to her room like she was being chased by a herd of wild elephants. The door slammed closed behind her.

She'd made it. Thank God.

She turned to see that her bed was already made. He'd made her bed? And the room smelled of him. How on earth could it smell of him after one night?

With a groan, she dropped the towel and got dressed. She took her time getting ready, and only when she couldn't hide any longer did she finally make her way into the kitchen. But that room was also empty. On the counter, she found a mug of coffee beside a note.

She frowned as her gaze slid over Jesse's masculine hand-writing.

I made you a coffee. Hopefully you didn't hide from me for so long that it's gone cold. I'm meeting Becket and Clara at the diner for break-fast. You're welcome to join us. J.

Her heart gave a little pitter-patter, and she wasn't sure if she was relieved or disappointed that he wasn't here.

She lifted the coffee and took a sip.

How did he always make it so freaking good?

She could meet him at the diner. They had good bacon there.

Her gaze caught on her laptop on the coffee table. She frowned. Did she actually feel like writing? Her fingers itched to move across the keys, and words and storylines whispered in her head.

Would it all disappear when the screen was in front of her eyes?

Only one way to find out.

Still holding her coffee, she crossed the room and opened her laptop.

As soon as she opened her manuscript, her fingers started moving. Full sentences formed on the screen in front of her. Good sentences. And for the first time in a long time, she felt inspired.

* * *

JESSE PULLED into the diner's parking lot. The place was called Rob's Diner, because a guy named Rob had opened it. But he'd sold it years ago, and the name remained even though it no longer fit, so most locals just called it the diner.

He climbed out of his car. The place had changed hands a few times, and every time someone new took over, he hoped they'd make better coffee.

Nope. Hadn't happened yet. Everyone seemed just fine with

the awful pots of instant shit.

His mind shifted to Aspen. To the way she'd slept half on top of him last night. He hadn't meant to fall asleep. He'd planned on getting up and going back to his own bed. But she'd been so soft and warm against him, he hadn't been able to keep his eyes open.

A part of him hoped she'd join him this morning. But another part of him knew that too much Aspen could be a dangerous thing when she didn't want more than friendship.

She was afraid to date him. Maybe afraid to trust him? Maybe even of trusting herself?

He was about to step into the diner when the door opened and Mrs. Allen stepped out, walking stick in hand. Her gaze immediately pinned to him.

Great. It was bad enough he had to deal with the woman at work, he didn't need to see her when he was off duty too.

She was the angriest woman he'd ever met. Everything made her rage, and that walking stick was more of a weapon than an aid.

"Sheriff."

His chest rose on a deep inhale. "Mrs. Allen. Having a nice morning?"

"No. That ratbag pizza delivery boy almost ran me down yesterday. I thought you were going to do something about him."

"We've had a chat with him."

"A chat?" She lifted her stick and pointed. "He doesn't need a chat. He needs a—"

Jesse grabbed the end of the stick the second it started waving in the air. "I need you to keep your cane on the ground."

"But that kid—"

"Has been spoken to, and I can speak to him again if you'd like. But I need *you* to make sure you're not assaulting people."

"Assault? I don't assault people!"

How many times had they had this conversation? "Hitting people with your cane is assault, Mrs. Allen."

Her eyes narrowed. "Back in my day, it was called discipline. Do your job before I become roadkill." Then she walked away, muttering something about no-good, unruly kids.

Jesus Christ.

He stepped into the diner to see Becket and Clara sitting in a booth by the window, humor in their eyes.

"I take it you saw," Jesse muttered as he lowered to the bench opposite them.

"I got really excited when she started waving that stick," Clara said, tilting her head. "I thought she was going to hit you."

"I wouldn't put it past her."

"I would pay good money to see that," Becket said with a chuckle. "We ordered your usual. You didn't bring Aspen."

"I didn't." And he didn't want to go into why either.

Clara frowned. "What's going on between you two?"

"I'm not sure." He knew what he *wanted* to go on between them.

Her lips pursed like she was thinking. "I think with a bit of time, she'll come around."

How did she even know Aspen was hesitant?

Becket's gaze went to the counter, a half smile stretching his lips.

Jesse followed his gaze to a woman with long brown hair pulled up in a multicolored scrunchie. She wore leggings and a white T-shirt that said Easily Distracted by Dogs.

She caught Becket's gaze and immediately rolled her eyes.

Jesse bit back a grin. He didn't know who it was, but he liked her. Usually, women fell all over themselves for his brother. He looked back to Becket, only to see him chuckling again.

"Know her?" Jesse asked.

"That's my jolly neighbor, Sky, who has an issue with my very existence."

"Sky's here?" Clara asked, looking over at the woman. Clara smiled at her, but that smile dropped as soon as she looked back at Becket. "What she has a problem with is your security camera that films her driveway."

"Safety," Becket cut in.

"And you cut down her tree," Clara added.

"It impeded my view of the street, and I only cut what was on my side."

Clara laughed. "Liar. You forget I saw the original state of that tree, and after your little trimming fest, there was barely any tree left."

Becket's gaze returned to Sky. "Like I said...safety."

"Am I going to get a report about you?" Jesse asked, hoping like hell he wouldn't.

"Maybe. She does seem to *really* dislike me."

Clara frowned. "Strange. You're such a likeable person."

"That's what I tell her."

This time, Clara rolled her eyes.

"How's the fire department going?" Jesse asked.

Becket lifted a shoulder. "Crew's great. And everything's pretty quiet, but I can't say that too loud. Last time I did, we were flat out for a week. We've been doing mostly small callouts and training to keep up our skills."

Jesse dipped his head. The department was lucky to have his brother. Even though Becket liked to joke around, he took his position as fire chief seriously.

"Been talking to your former teammates much?" Becket asked.

Jesse nodded. "Most days we check in with one another, especially after everything that happened in Misty Peak."

Becket's eyes narrowed. He knew exactly how much the events in Misty Peak—when Jesse and his ex-teammates found themselves betrayed by one of their own—could mess with a former soldier.

"I spoke to Lock yesterday and Holden the day before. Holden's actually moving out here soon."

Clara choked on her juice. "Holden's moving here?"

"Yeah. Is that okay?"

Her eyes widened. "Of course. He's spent enough holidays with us that he's basically family."

Jesse's brows twitched. Why did she sound...off?

He was about to ask when she cut in and started talking about the shopping she was doing with their cousin Indie later today.

Jesse was looking around the diner, listening with half an ear, when his gaze caught on a woman as she stepped inside and sat at a table. His eyes narrowed.

Karen Davies.

Before he could think better of it, he rose from the booth and moved over to her table where he took a seat opposite her.

Her brows rose. "Jesse—"

"You need to leave."

"Now wait a second—"

"You broke into my house last night."

"The door was unlocked."

Like that made it okay. "You said awful things to your daughter."

"I thought she took something from me."

Thought? Past tense? His gaze lowered to a silver bracelet on her wrist. "Is that the bracelet?"

She squirmed in her seat. It was.

Jesse's jaw clicked. "You said you'd leave when you had it back. You have it back, so go."

"I'll go when I'm good and ready!"

He leaned forward and lowered his voice. "If you love her at all, you'll get out of Amber Ridge and give her the space she needs."

"You can't—"

"I *can*. Apologize to her, then go."

He didn't give her a chance to respond, just got up and returned to his booth, hoping like hell she did as he said.

CHAPTER 14

"*Y*ou slept together?"

Aspen huffed as she coated her toenail in pink polish. "Don't say it like that."

"Like what?"

Aspen eyed the phone on the coffee table. Her best friend was on speaker, but they still had to compete with the rain outside to hear each other. "Like we did more than just sleep. We didn't. He carried me to bed. I was half asleep and feeling sorry for myself, so I asked him to stay. And he did."

"Of course he did. When a beautiful woman asks a red-blooded male to sleep in her bed, he's not going to say no."

"He's been torturing me ever since." A week had passed since that morning. An entire week of torture. "Three times, I've caught him walking around shirtless, his perfect washboard abs out for the world to see. And yes, before you say it, I know this is his house, but I just feel like shouting at him to cover up his glorious body."

Callie laughed as if she was joking…she wasn't.

"Where is he tonight?" Callie asked.

Aspen's gaze went to the window. It was dark and wet.

"Working. I just hope he doesn't get home too late. The storm's expected to be bad."

"Are you okay?"

"I'm warm and dry. But unfortunately, it had already started raining when I realized I don't have food."

"Jesse wouldn't have left you at home in a storm without food or a car."

No, he wouldn't. Her gaze shifted to the note he'd left on the counter...the one about the pasta he'd said she was welcome to help herself to in the fridge. "I don't want to eat his food."

"Why not?"

"He already gives me cheap rent." Like dirt cheap. She'd actually fought him on the amount, but he'd refused to accept more. "I can't eat his food too."

"So you're just going to not eat?"

"Of course not. It's Cheap Tuesday at Burt's Pizzeria. I ordered a pepperoni." She finished her little toe and capped the bottle of nail polish.

"Wait, aren't the pizzas there supposed to be really bad?"

"*Really* bad. I'm intrigued and kind of excited to try it."

"You're such a weirdo." Callie sighed. "I miss you so much."

Aspen lifted the phone and leaned back on the couch. "I miss you too. How's the morning sickness?"

"It's awful. Lock made this curry the other night, which I usually *love*, but the second I stepped into the house, I got sick just by the smell of it. He'd spent so much time making it, but the second I reappeared, it was gone, the windows were open, and there was a takeout menu on the counter."

Aspen cringed. "I'm sorry. But on the bright side, you've got yourself a good man."

"The best." There was a small pause. "Are you doing okay with your mom there?"

"Well, I haven't heard from her in a few days, so I'm hoping she's left." It was probably wishful thinking, but she could hope.

"I'll let you know if I see her around here."

"Thank you." The line started to cut in and out just as the doorbell rang. "Oh, pizza's here. And I think I'm losing signal with the storm."

"Okay. I can't wait to hear how disgusting it is. Chat—"

The call cut out.

At least she'd gotten a good twenty-minute conversation with her best friend first.

She rose from the couch and grabbed some cash from her purse. When she opened the front door, a tall, wet, bleach-blond shaggy-haired teenager stood in front of her.

She smiled at him. "Hi."

"I have a pepperoni pizza for an Aspen."

"That's me." She handed him the cash, and he gave her the pizza.

He turned to look at something over his shoulder before turning back to Aspen. "Do you know there's a guy in his car on the street watching your house?"

Her back straightened and she looked over his shoulder. "There is?" That was kind of creepy.

"Yeah. Want me to talk to him? See who he is?"

"Oh, no, you...please don't—"

"It's fine. I don't mind." He turned and walked toward the car before she could stop him.

She called for him to come back, but her voice was drowned out by the rain.

Dammit. What if the guy was dangerous?

She watched the kid move toward the car, nerves running down her spine. If the person *was* dangerous, she had no idea what she would actually do. There was no phone service, and she didn't have a weapon. But she couldn't just walk away. The kid was only a teenager.

It was too dark to see the make or model of the car. Hell, if someone asked her the color, all she'd say is that it was dark...

maybe black or navy blue? And there was no way she could see the person inside.

Her heartbeat sped up as the kid drew closer to the vehicle.

He was only a couple feet away when the headlights turned on and the car sped away.

Water splashed the kid, and he flipped the car off before heading back to his own.

A slight chill ran over her skin as Aspen closed the door, making sure it was locked. Who was the person in the car? And were they really watching her?

No. The kid must have been confused. It was probably just someone waiting out the storm.

She moved back into the house and closed the curtains before sitting on the couch. Trying to take her mind off it, she scrolled through Netflix, picking a random movie she'd never heard of before opening the pizza box. A romantic comedy and pizza... exactly what she needed.

She took one bite of the pepperoni pizza and involuntarily made a face.

Good God, it *was* as bad as everyone said. The dough was soggy but also burnt, the tomato sauce was flavorless, and the cheese...it tasted kind of off, but also, kind of tangy.

Gross.

Burt must be *really* nice for people to keep this place in business.

She took two more bites, because maybe it would get better...

Nope. She couldn't do it. She tossed the slice back into the box.

Lightning flashed and thunder immediately boomed outside, making her jump, and the lights flickered.

Chill out, Aspen. It's just a storm.

The words had only just whispered in her head when every-thing went dark. The lights. The TV.

Looked like she wasn't watching that movie tonight.

Blindly, she reached for her phone on the coffee table and turned on the flashlight. When she could finally see, her gaze shifted to the front door. She could check the power box, but that would involve going outside into the rain in the middle of a storm.

No, thank you.

She checked the time. Eight thirty. Technically too early for bed. Well, actually, there was no technically about it. It *was* far too early…for her, anyway. Maybe she could do some writing before she slept. She'd been on a roll lately, which was good because, boy, did she have some catching up to do.

Pointing the flashlight in front of her, she put the pizza in the fridge and went to her room.

She opened her laptop and pressed the power key. Then her fingers started moving. Sometimes it was like this. She'd often thought of it as magic. Her mind just took over and a story moved from her head to paper, a bit like a movie.

Sometimes she wondered where the story ideas came from. Sometimes she wondered if it was from developing a really good imagination as a kid, kind of like a form of escapism from a mother who'd been mentally unwell.

But other times she wondered if it was just the romantic in her trying to create a happy ever after for everyone.

She got about an hour of work in before the battery died.

Great.

Maybe this was the universe telling her she needed an early night tonight.

She changed into her pajamas and slid into bed. Closing her eyes, she tried to sleep, but the sound of the rain pounding against the windows was loud.

She grabbed a pillow and pressed it over her head.

Nope. That didn't help.

She was just taking it off her face when her eyes caught on the window. She hadn't closed the curtains, and right there, on the other side of the glass, was the outline of a person.

* * *

"You still pissed at me?"

Jesse shot a glance at Luke before turning back to the road. "No."

"Why don't I believe you?"

"Because you still feel like shit about what you did."

"Hm. Nope. That's not it. I think it's the scowl on your face."

He turned right, the rain making it hard to see the road in front of the car. "I'm scowling because I don't like Aspen being home by herself in this storm." And it was just getting worse by the minute. At least he could go home after this callout.

"Ah, I see."

Jesse frowned. "What do you see?"

"You want to be cuddling your cute roommate on the couch while listening to the rain outside. Romantic."

"Don't call her cute." It sounded wrong coming from him.

"Sexy?"

"I'm not talking about Aspen. Are you back to dating Margot?" The two had been hanging out a lot together around the station.

He lifted a shoulder. "On and off."

"What does that mean?"

"It means we're not exclusive. We see each other when we want to see each other."

"So you're sleeping with other people too?"

"When we feel like it."

Jesus. They worked together. It was never going to end well.

"Hey. She's just as against the idea of an exclusive relationship as I am." He looked at the GPS. "So this is an Airbnb?"

"Yeah, the owner of the house is away right now, but he has

external cameras. They're on his listing, so anyone who stays there already knows about them. But apparently the person there right now covered the cameras. When he contacted them, asking for the cameras to be uncovered, they did, but then the Wi-Fi went out and the cameras went offline."

"Could be the storm?"

Jesse shook his head. "Happened before the storm."

"What are they trying to hide?"

"My thoughts exactly."

He pulled up in front of the log cabin. The curtains were drawn, but faint light came from the windows. Someone was home.

Jesse climbed out and jogged through the rain toward the door, Luke close behind him. He lifted his fist and knocked. Immediately, a noise sounded from inside. Footsteps against wooden floorboards...but not *toward* the door.

A few seconds passed. When no one answered, Jesse knocked again before calling, "This is Sheriff Hayes and Deputy Pine. We know someone's inside. We need you to answer the door. If you don't, *we will* be entering the premises. We have permission from the owner."

It was only technically true. George, the owner, hadn't told them to enter, but he'd wanted Jesse to do everything he could to get the cameras back up and running.

Another few seconds passed. Jesse almost lost hope of the person inside coming out, but then footsteps sounded again and the door swung open.

Jesse frowned. "Karen?"

Aspen's mother put a fist on her hip. "What do you want?"

"What are you still doing here in Amber Ridge?"

"Unless there's a law that says I have to get out of town, I'd say that's none of your business."

Luke's gaze shifted between them. "You two know each other?"

"This is Aspen's mother," Jesse said between gritted teeth.

Karen lifted a brow. "You never answered my question. What do you want? This Airbnb is paid for. I've done nothing wrong."

"You covered the cameras—"

"Then *uncovered* them," Karen cut in.

"Did you then tamper with the Wi-Fi?"

The flare of her eyes gave Jesse his answer, contradicting the shake of her head. "No. I didn't."

"We need to take a look at the Wi-Fi router inside the house."

"No. I'm renting this place, and I don't give you permission to come onto the property."

"Actually, by tampering with the Wi-Fi and effectively turning off the external cameras, you're breaking the terms and conditions that you agreed to when renting this cabin, so unless you let us in to look at the router, we'll need you to leave immediately."

Her eyes narrowed. "*Fine.* But checking the Wi-Fi is *all* I give you permission to do. You check it and you leave." She turned and walked toward the kitchen counter, leaving the door open.

"Is there something you don't want us to see?" Jesse asked as he followed her.

"No."

Why did that answer come unnaturally quick?

Karen stopped beside a shelf in the kitchen where the Wi-Fi box sat.

Luke picked it up, and they both saw the damaged cord at the same time.

"Did you do this?" Luke asked.

"No. Maybe it was a rat. I've seen them scurrying around here. I could probably get a partial refund because of this."

Jesse almost laughed. "Looks like scissors."

"Well, if someone cut it, it wasn't me." She raised a brow, challenging him to argue with her.

Jesus, the woman didn't make this easy. "I'm going to send Claudia out here, one of my deputies, to fix this router." It wasn't in their job description, but seeing as this involved Aspen's mother, he was making it their job. "Once the Wi-Fi is up and running again, I don't want any more problems with the external cameras. Do you understand?"

Karen's lips pressed together. "Are you trying to insinuate something, *Sheriff Hayes*?"

She knew exactly what he was insinuating, and she also knew it was true. Jesse just didn't know what it was that she didn't want anyone else to see.

Luke cleared his throat. "We just need your confirmation that there won't be any more problems, ma'am."

Her gaze shifted to Luke, but there was an air of defiance in her expression. "There won't be any more problems of *my* doing."

Interesting choice of words. "You got your return ticket booked for Misty Peak?"

Karen rounded the counter and moved to the door, where she tugged it open. "Have a good evening, gentlemen."

Jesse's jaw clicked, and he headed outside.

Once in the car, Luke shot a look at him. "That was a bit frosty. Not in good relations with the in-law?"

"Call Claudia. Get her out here immediately. I want the Wi-Fi back up and running as soon as possible."

Luke pulled out his phone.

Jesse drove faster than he should have back to the station. He wanted to get to Aspen, and he wanted to get to her *fast*. The storm was getting worse, and something in his gut told him he needed to be with her.

When he reached the station, he didn't get out. "Do me a favor and write up the paperwork on this one for me. I need to get to Aspen."

Luke frowned but dipped his head. "Sure thing."

The second Luke was out, Jesse drove to his house, glad he didn't live too far. He tried calling her on the way, but it went straight to voicemail.

He parked in the drive and jogged through the rain to the door. The lights were out down the entire street. The power must have gone out. He checked his phone.

No signal. Dammit, she'd been home alone with no power and no signal. That wasn't fucking safe.

He'd just opened the door when a scream pierced the air.

Aspen's scream.

CHAPTER 15

*T*he scream had barely left Aspen's lips when her bedroom door flew open and a very big, very angry Jesse stepped in, gun and flashlight in hand.

Her heart jumped into her throat. "Jesse!"

He scanned the room as if searching for a threat before closing the distance between them and sitting on the edge of the bed. He cupped her cheek. "Are you okay?"

Her gaze flew back to the window.

Gone. They were gone. Or at least, they weren't at the window anymore. "I saw someone out there. Only their outline, but they were there, I swear."

His eyes narrowed on the window. When he got up, she almost grabbed him to pull him back down. Keep him in what felt like the relative safety of her bed. But it wasn't really safe if someone was watching her, was it?

He didn't get too close to the glass, but his pistol remained raised, making the fine hairs on her arms stand on edge.

"I'm going to check outside." He shut the curtains and turned toward the door. "Don't follow me."

She scrambled off the bed, catching his arm in the hall. "I don't want you to go out there."

"I have to." There was no emotion on his face. None. It was like she was looking at a stranger. There was nothing about this version of Jesse that felt familiar.

He started to turn, but she yanked him back. "Jesse...we don't know who's out there. They might have a weapon."

"So do I."

"But—"

"Hey," he cut her off, a sliver of emotion slipping into his features for the first time. "Remember...trust me."

She nodded even though it was the last thing she wanted to do, but what choice did she have?

"Lock the door after me." He kissed her forehead, his lips lingering for a second before he headed toward the back door off the kitchen. When he opened it, wind rushed inside the house, then he was gone. She clicked the lock and stepped back, wrapping her arms around her waist, digging her nails into her skin.

The house was dark. Almost pitch black. The logical thing to do was get her phone for some light. She didn't. She couldn't move. She needed confirmation that Jesse was safe.

Minutes ticked by, and those minutes felt like hours. God, how long did it take to check a yard? Was he okay? It would be so easy for someone to hide behind a tree or the side of a house and shoot.

But Jesse was smart. Trained. No one would get the jump on him.

A key sounded in the door and it opened, air once again whooshing inside as Jesse stepped in. He was soaking wet, his uniform sticking to his skin, water dripping down his face.

She didn't care. She stepped forward and set her hands on his chest. "Are you okay?"

"I didn't find anyone. They must have run while I was coming in."

She swallowed. "I don't understand. Who would stand outside my window in the middle of a storm? That's crazy."

Something flashed over Jesse's face. He opened his mouth, but Aspen got in first.

She gasped. "Oh my God, the pizza delivery kid."

"Pete? You think it was him?"

"No. He saw someone sitting in their car on the street. He even thought they were watching the house. He went over to talk to them, but they drove off before he could reach them."

Jesse's jaw visibly clenched. "I'll talk to Pete tomorrow."

Aspen's gaze lowered to his shirt. "You're soaked."

An entire five seconds of silence passed before she realized she was still touching his chest. Not just touching—exploring. Moving her hands over his hard ridges, feeling every muscle beneath her fingertips.

She looked up to see his eyes had become a darker shade of brown. And the way he was looking at her...

She took a hurried step back. "I'll get you a towel."

She spun and moved to the linen closet, breathing through the tingle in her lower belly. She shouldn't be thinking about anything but the stranger in the window right now. That should be taking up her entire focus.

Movement sounded behind her, near his room, but she didn't turn. She took out a large navy towel. When she reached his bedroom, she swallowed hard.

He'd set his flashlight pointing up to cast a dim glow over the room.

His shirt was already off, and his chest glistened with drops of water. For the second time that night, her fingers itched to touch him. Run her hands over his now bare skin.

She internally shook her head.

Stop it, Aspen.

Her gaze remained focused on his face, just his face, as she crossed the space between them.

She stepped forward and handed him the towel, their hands grazing as he took it.

"I didn't like you going out there tonight," she whispered.

"I know how to take care of myself."

She knew that. Out of everyone in her life, this man was one of the deadliest. That didn't change how not okay she was with him going outside when some weirdo was lurking around.

He touched her chin with his thumb and tilted her face up, his gaze boring into hers. "You don't need to worry about me."

"You worry about me."

"That's different."

His breath brushed her skin, causing little whispers of awareness to shoot down to her lower belly. She swallowed, studying his intense gaze. The way his damp hair clung to his forehead.

She reached up and grazed a lock from his face. "It isn't. I want you to be safe, just like you want me to be safe."

He gripped her waist, tugging her closer so her thighs touched his damp pants. "I like that you care."

Without her permission, her focus lowered to his lips. They were full lips...and God, they looked kissable.

"If you keep looking at me like that, I can't be held responsible for what happens next," he whispered.

Her gaze flew back to his, her mind a jumbled mess of possibilities. "It would be stupid of me to kiss you right now, wouldn't it? Tell me it would be stupid."

"I can think of many words to describe what a kiss between you and me would be, but stupid isn't one of them. I could lie, but do you really want me to do that?"

"I don't know what I want."

He lowered his head, his lips brushing her cheek as he whispered, "Liar."

He lifted his head, and suddenly his lips were right there, a mere fraction from hers.

She couldn't stop herself—she lifted to her toes and kissed him.

* * *

JESSE'S BLOOD roared between his ears, deafening the storm outside. Aspen's lips were on his, and they were just as soft as he knew they would be.

He swiped his mouth across hers, and a sweet moan slipped from her throat into the air, making every territorial part of him scream *mine*.

He turned them and leaned her against the wall, letting her soft curves press into his hard edges. But it wasn't enough. He lifted her and she gasped, her legs wrapping around his waist, and the second her lips separated, he slid his tongue inside, curving it around hers.

Jesus, she tasted good. So good he felt like he could drown in her kiss.

He massaged his tongue against hers as he slipped a hand beneath the material of her shirt. Slowly, he glided his palm up her waist, the smoothness of her skin seeping into him. When he reached her bare breast, he cupped her, soaking up the soft moans that cut through the air.

She was his addiction. His drug. And he had no fucking control over his need for her.

As he held the silky weight of her breast in his palm, he rolled her nipple with his thumb and forefinger.

She moaned, and the sound shot straight to his cock.

"Perfect," he growled softly. "Your breasts are perfect."

She tugged at his hair, arching her back and pressing into him as he thrummed her tight nipple back and forth.

More earth-shattering groans. So. Fucking. Perfect.

She ground her hips against him, making his cock so hard it was almost painful.

"Jesse...yes."

Hearing his name as a moan on her lips was like fire in his veins.

He grazed his hand back down her side, this time slipping his fingers into the waistband of her pajama shorts. He swiped her clit, and she cried out as her entire body trembled. He stroked her again before pressing his thumb to her clit and rolling it in a circular motion.

She writhed and groaned, digging her nails into his shoulders, almost breaking skin.

Every sound she made did something to him. Changed him. And fuck if he ever wanted to change back.

He touched two fingers to her entrance. Heard her breath catch. Then he slid inside her, filling her.

He pumped his fingers in and out, lowering his head and taking her nipple between his lips.

He wanted her on fire. He wanted her to need him with the same intensity that he needed her.

He sucked, and suddenly, her body tensed. Her nails cut into him as she screamed and broke, her walls throbbing against his fingers.

He kept pumping his fingers into her until her shudders slowed and her eyes fluttered open.

God, she was beautiful.

He straightened her clothes and lowered her to the floor. The second she was on her feet, she reached for him, but he gently grabbed her wrist.

"Not tonight." He wanted her—fuck, he wanted her. But he needed her to be all in first, not recovering from a pervert at her window. "That was just for you."

Her brows flickered. "You don't want me to touch you?"

"Not tonight."

Hurt cut across her features. And maybe some embarrassment.

Shit. "Aspen—"

He reached for her, but she pulled away.

"I'm sorry, I—" She pushed loose strands of hair from her face. "I should go."

"Wait, we need to talk—"

"No." She sidestepped his second attempt to touch her. "Maybe in the morning." Then she turned, hurrying out of the room and down the hall. The sound of her door closing made a resounding thump.

Jesus, he couldn't have handled that worse if he'd tried.

He wanted to go after her. Explain to her just how fucking much he wanted her but why he also wanted to go slow. He *needed* slow.

But then his phone rang.

He pulled it out. He had a signal again. Not much, but a couple bars were better than nothing. It was the station. "Jesse speaking."

"Jesse. It's Claudia."

"Did you make it to the house?" He felt like shit for asking her to go out there in this weather, but this was important to him because it involved Aspen.

"The woman gave me hell, but I got in. Unfortunately, I need to order a new cable. It will take a few days to come in."

Of course it would. "Okay. Did you let George, the owner, know?"

"I did. He said he'd prefer not to kick her out because he hasn't had many bookings on the property and is losing money."

Yeah, he'd gotten that feeling earlier. "Thanks for going out there, especially in the storm."

"No problem. Also, my friend is still looking into Dylan Bollard. I can tell you that he hasn't used his bank cards in days."

Jesse frowned. "You're kidding?"

"Nope. Could be a coincidence. Or he could be trying to hide his movement. I did find one thing."

"What?"

"I called his workplace. His employer spoke to me. Told me that as of a week ago, he took leave from work."

Jesse's muscles tensed, his gaze moving to the window. Leave from work and potentially concealing his location...it left a bad fucking taste in his mouth. "Keep looking into it."

"Will do."

Jesse hung up. He didn't like this. Any of it.

CHAPTER 16

*J*esse pulled up in front of Burt's Pizzeria. Before getting out of the car, he checked his phone. Still nothing from Aspen. He'd sent her a text a few hours ago and she hadn't replied.

"Why do you keep checking that thing?"

He glanced over at Luke in the passenger seat. "I'm not Aspen's favorite person right now."

That was a damn understatement. She'd come out to breakfast this morning but had barely said two words to him. When he'd tried to touch her hip, she'd slipped away from him and moved to the other side of the island.

"Uh-oh, what did you do?"

Jesse scrubbed a hand over his face. He'd either embarrassed her or made her feel unwanted. Maybe both. "I screwed up. Come on, let's go." He climbed out of the car before Luke could ask any more questions.

It didn't take long for Luke to catch up to him. "Fine. But at least tell me if she ate the pizza last night."

"She ordered pepperoni."

Luke cringed, because yeah, pepperoni was the worst on the

menu, and that was saying something. "Rookie error. I don't know what it is about his pepperoni that makes it taste so..."

"Fishy." Add that to the soggy dough and smelly cheese...it was all-around bad.

"Luckily, we like Burt," Luke muttered as they stepped inside the pizzeria.

Burt looked up from behind the counter, a huge-ass smile spreading across his face. "Jesse! Luke! My favorite boys."

Burt was a short, round, balding man who had the biggest smile you'd ever seen. He also had a big voice and an even bigger laugh. He circled the counter and pulled Luke, then Jesse, into a hug.

"Please tell me you're here for pleasure, not business," Burt said, stepping back. "I can have a Margherita pizza in the oven in minutes. Pair it with some garlic bread and a glass of wine? On the house for friends, of course."

Luke patted his stomach. "I just ate."

Burt threw up his arms. "Hey, there's always room for pizza. Come on."

The older man started to turn, but Jesse touched his arm. "Burt, we need to speak to Pete. Is he here?"

The smile dropped from Burt's face. "What's my nephew done now? Was he speeding through town again? Do I need to—"

Jesse shook his head. "He didn't do anything wrong. We just need to ask him about something. He could really help us."

"Oh. Well, if Pete can help with an investigation, he certainly will. He should be back any minute. Actually, there he is."

Jesse followed Burt's gaze outside to see Pete pulling up in his old beat-up Kia. Jesse gripped Burt's shoulder. "Thanks."

"Rain check on the pizza," Luke added as they stepped outside.

"Anytime," Burt called. "Don't be strangers."

Pete looked up as he climbed out of his car, immediately rolling his eyes. "If this is about that cranky old bag Mrs. Allen,

I'm the one who should be pressing charges. She's hit me with that cane so many times, I probably have brain damage. It's not my fault she crosses the road at the pace of a snail."

"This isn't about Mrs. Allen," Jesse said as they stopped in front of him.

"It isn't?" Pete shifted his gaze from Jesse to Luke and back. "Is it about old man Jack? Because I didn't almost hit him. I gave him a wide berth around that corner."

Jesus, the kid should not be a delivery driver. "It's about the delivery you made to my house last night. A woman by the name of Aspen took it."

"Oh. I didn't do anything to her."

"Did you approach a car after you delivered the pizza?" Luke asked.

"Yeah. Some jerk in a Beamer."

"They were driving a BMW?" Jesse asked.

"A black one. He looked like he was watching the house, so I went over to ask him what he was doing, but he didn't even roll down his window. Just sped off the second I got close. Almost ran over my damn foot."

Damn, the kid probably didn't have much information then. "Did you see what he looked like?"

"The windows were tinted, but it was definitely a dude. I saw short, dark hair and he had broad shoulders. Looked thin. Maybe had a goatee."

Jesse's chest tightened. Dylan fit that description, but it wasn't enough to identify him. Was it possible the asshole was here in Amber Ridge? Was it even possible he'd been the person in Aspen's bedroom window last night?

Fuck. The idea made him want to drop everything and find her. Not let her out of his sight.

"Anything else you can tell us?" Luke asked.

Pete shoved his shaggy hair off his forehead. "Nah. Don't think so. Why? Is he in trouble? Was the Beamer stolen?"

Jesse patted the kid's shoulder. "Thanks for your help. Call us if you remember anything else."

"Come on," Pete called as they headed back to the car. "Just tell me one thing...is he gonna get put in the slammer?"

Luke shook his head once he was in the passenger seat. "That kid's actually kind of funny. Shame he's such a shit driver."

Jesse didn't respond. His mind was somewhere else. On the pit in his gut. The tightness of his chest.

"You okay, boss?"

His frown deepened. "It could be Dylan. If her mother told him where Aspen's living, he could be here. It's possible he was watching the house and Pete temporarily scared him. Then he came back. Watched her through her bedroom window."

The idea made him want to be sick.

Luke frowned. "That's pretty extreme behavior. You really think he'd do that to an ex?"

Jesse's mind went back to the way Dylan had looked at Aspen in Misty Peak. Like she was a possession. Like he *owned* her. Then he recalled what Claudia had shared about Dylan's ex-fiancée.

"Yes, I *do* think he'd do that." He pulled out his phone. He needed to call her. Hear her voice. Anything to reassure him that she was okay.

It rang. Then it rang some more. It was on the fourth ring that he realized she wasn't going to answer.

He hung up and pulled the car out of the parking lot.

"Uh, this isn't the way back to the station," Luke said after a few turns.

"I need to check on her." He needed eyes on her right the hell now.

* * *

ASPEN SAW Jesse's name flash over the screen of her phone. She didn't answer it.

She was overreacting. She *knew* she was overreacting, but she couldn't seem to stop.

She'd fallen to pieces in his arms. A million pieces, and he'd watched. Held her as she'd shattered.

But when she'd tried to touch *him*, he'd pushed her away.

She cringed and shoved her phone into her back pocket before moving down the aisle of the grocery store. Jesse had told her not to leave the house after the face-in-the-window incident last night. And she hadn't...all day. But every hour that passed made the silence feel more...eerie. And every time she passed Jesse's room, that hot embarrassment washed over her again like a blaze of fire until she had to get out.

Being a late Saturday afternoon, the store was busier than she would have thought. She dropped a couple of bags of noodles into her basket. She'd been living off the stuff lately. Next, she detoured for a loaf of bread, then found some tuna.

She was halfway down another aisle when a glimpse of a man at the end made her gasp and stumble back. She bumped into a cart behind her, and the cans of tuna fell from her hand.

She quickly picked them up and mumbled an apology to the person behind her, but when she looked back to the end of the aisle, the man was gone.

Dylan.

Had she really seen him? It was just a quick side view, but his profile and the way he moved were so familiar. And that sweater...gray with a picture of an eagle in the middle...he'd had one exactly the same.

She shook her head. It couldn't have been him. She wasn't in Misty Peak anymore. She was on the other side of the country. She was safe.

So why were her hands shaking? Because her mother had her address and could have passed it on to Dylan?

She shot forward, weaving through the crowd, sidestepping

carts and slipping between baskets. She had to know if it was him. She needed confirmation that he *wasn't* here.

When she reached the end of the aisle, she checked left and right. Where had he gone? She glanced down the first aisle. Several people took up space, none of them wearing a gray sweater. She shifted to the next. This one was almost empty, and again, he wasn't there.

The third aisle was the busiest, with people and carts blocking every inch of space.

And that's where she saw the back of the gray sweater.

Her pulse raced, her skin cool and sensitive. She shot forward, shuffling through people. She nudged a woman's shoulder and muttered an apology, her gaze never leaving the man.

It might not be him. Other people could have the same sweater.

Someone who stood at the same height though? Someone with the same broad shoulders who moved in a similar way to Dylan?

Her feet moved faster. The guy exited the aisle and turned left.

Desperation had her speeding up. She couldn't lose him. She needed to know it wasn't him.

She jogged forward and had just stepped out of the aisle when she collided with a big chest. Her basket dropped, falling to its side, cans of tuna rolling out.

"Aspen."

Her gaze flew up to see a pair of brown eyes. Eyes slightly darker than Jesse's, but also very similar.

"Becket."

A frown etched his brow. "Are you okay?"

"I..." Her gaze shifted behind him. People were everywhere, but none wearing the sweater.

God, what was she doing? Chasing down a guy because he

wore a sweater that was similar to Dylan's? Dylan was in Misty Peak.

Heat crawled up her neck, and she shook her head. "Nothing. I was just...in a rush." Yeah, in a rush to approach a stranger and make an idiot of herself.

He held her gaze for a second longer, looking down at the basket. "Let me help you pick this stuff up."

"Oh no, you don't have to do that."

But he was already on the floor. She lowered with him.

He lifted cans of tuna and set them in the basket. "Is my brother not feeding you? You're eating two-dollar tuna and noodles?"

"It's not his responsibility to feed me."

One side of Becket's mouth lifted. "I think he might disagree."

"There are a few things we disagree on." They both rose. "Well, thank you for helping me, and sorry about running into your chest."

"Are you walking home?"

"I am. No car means a lot of walking. But I don't mind. Sunshine and exercise are good for me."

"It's not too sunny out there anymore." Becket checked his watch. "In fact, it will be dark soon. I'll drive you back."

"Oh...you don't have to."

"I know. I want to."

"You came here to shop." She looked at his empty hands. "You don't have anything yet."

"They didn't have what I needed."

Why didn't she believe him?

She wanted to say no, because honestly, why would he want to walk her home? Had Jesse told him about the face in the window? Was he just trying to help Jesse by protecting his housemate?

But if it was getting dark outside, she didn't really want to walk by herself anyway. "Okay. Um, thanks."

They headed to the counter, and while she paid, Becket took his phone out and began typing something.

The second she lifted her bag, Becket slid it out of her fingers. "I've got it."

"Driving me home *and* carrying my bag. You're quite a gentleman."

He chuckled as they stepped outside. "My mother raised me right. Some lucky lady should snap me up."

They stopped at a truck, and he held the passenger-side door open for her. She climbed in and he got behind the wheel.

"You're not dating anyone?" she asked as he reversed out of the parking space.

"No. My schedule at the fire station's always changing, so it's hard to date." His phone beeped, but he didn't touch it.

"Can I ask you something?" she asked quietly.

He looked down at her. "Shoot."

"Jesse's a good guy, isn't he? I mean, he *seems* like one, and I think he is, but—"

"Aspen." Becket stopped at a light, the small hint of a smile slipping from his face. "Jesse's my brother, so I would never in a million years say this to his face...but he's the best man I know. Ten times the man *I* am. If there's one person in this world you're safe with, it's him."

Her heart gave a little jump. "I shouldn't have to ask, should I? It's just..."

"You've been hurt."

She frowned at him. How did he know? Was it written all over her face?

"Trust me when I tell you, I've met some of the scum of the earth." Becket's gaze moved back to the street in front of him, as if he was searching for that scum. Either that, or remembering it. He glanced back at her. "Jesse's one of the good guys. But it's okay to take your time to trust in that. Make him work for it."

The corners of her mouth lifted. "Thank you."

The light turned green and he started driving again. They spent the short drive talking. Aspen asked Becket about his job, and in return, he asked about hers. He was easy to talk to. But she didn't miss the way his gaze continually scanned the streets. His military background was definitely evident.

They reached the house just as Jesse pulled up in the drive.

"You were texting him, weren't you?" she asked, not surprised.

The corner of Becket's mouth twitched. "He's my brother."

CHAPTER 17

*S*he'd walked to the grocery store, in the evening, by herself, the day after she'd seen a face in her bedroom window.

Jesus.

"Better calm down, Jess," Luke said quietly. "We're only a street away."

He couldn't calm down. Someone had been *watching* her last night, and she'd gone out by herself after he'd asked her not to. How easy would it have been for the perp to grab her?

Too easy.

He pulled onto his street, immediately spotting Aspen and his brother parked at the curb. The second he pulled into his drive, he was up and out, marching toward her.

"Are you okay?" he asked, before he'd even stopped walking.

She frowned as she stepped onto the front yard. "Of course. Why wouldn't I be?"

"I told you to stay home."

Her back straightened, and he swore his brother cringed.

"*Told me?*" Aspen asked.

Her low voice probably should have been a warning. It was a warning he didn't take.

He inched closer. "Someone stood in a storm and watched you through your bedroom window last night. Probably the same asshole Pete saw watching the house. Fuck, he could have been watching you when you left the house today, while you were alone and unarmed."

Becket cleared his throat. "I'm going to put these groceries in the house." His brother leaned in as he passed him. "Ease up, buddy."

Jesse fisted his hands. He *knew* he needed to ease up. And by the glare Aspen was throwing his way, he wasn't doing himself any favors getting back into her good graces.

Aspen stepped forward. "I *know* someone was looking through my window last night. I also know there was a car parked across the street. I was there both times. It's why I had to get out of the house. I was here all day, alone, and I was going insane. It was my decision, which, shocker, I am actually allowed to make. You don't tell me what I can and can't do."

He lowered his head and his voice. "I'm the town sheriff, and I'm trying to keep you safe."

Her eyes narrowed.

Shit. Wrong thing to say.

"Well, *Sheriff*, if we're done here, I'm going inside."

She went to move past him, but he snagged her wrist. "Aspen. Look, I'm sorry. I was worried." He looked at his watch. "I've got two hours left of my shift, and I want you to come to the station with me."

"Why?"

"Because I want to have eyes on you." He *needed* to have eyes on her. He wouldn't be able to think straight with her here and him at the station.

Her brows flickered. "Because of last night?"

"Yes."

By the look in her eyes, she knew he wasn't telling her the whole truth, but on the lawn of his house, with his brother and Luke within listening distance, wasn't the time or place.

"I'll lock the doors," she pushed. "I'll be fine."

"It's not enough." Her mouth opened like she was going to argue with him more, but he closed the last bit of distance and touched her hip. "Please? You can bring your laptop. I'll set you up in a quiet room, and there's tea and coffee."

She was going to say no. He could see it in her eyes. In the way she was inching back and putting distance between them.

But then her gaze shifted to the street, and something flickered in her eyes. Maybe a small bit of fear? Apprehension?

"Okay," she finally said. "I'll work at the station."

Thank God.

She went inside and grabbed her laptop, and Jesse thanked his brother before they climbed into the car. Aspen didn't speak much on the way. In fact, Luke seemed like the only one filling the silence. He didn't need much in the way of response. It was like the man could maintain an entire conversation all on his own.

When they reached the station, he placed a hand on the small of Aspen's back as the three of them headed inside.

Bea looked up and smiled. "Hey."

"Hi, Bea. This is Aspen. She'll be working in one of the empty offices until the end of my shift."

"Oh, sure. Is everything okay?"

"Everything's fine," Luke said, straightening when Margot appeared down the hall.

Jesse shook his head, never sure what to make of those two.

"Come on," he said, as he led Aspen around the desk to an unoccupied room off a hall. He flicked on the light.

Aspen frowned. "There's no window in here."

"Sorry about that. I finish in less than two hours though."

She nodded slowly. "So, what exactly did your brother text you?"

"That you ran into him at the grocery store. And that you looked scared."

"Tattletale. And you told him to stay with me until I got to you."

"Actually, he offered to drive you home, *then* I texted him, telling him not to leave your side."

"Humph."

He inched closer. "What scared you?"

Her eyes widened before she blinked. "Nothing."

He swallowed the disappointment. Was she not telling him because she was angry at him? Or because she still didn't trust him? "I'm sorry I got angry about you walking to the grocery store."

"You said that already."

"I'm saying it again. And I'm sorry I made you feel like I didn't want you last night."

Her eyes flared. "You didn't—"

"I did." He stepped closer. "And I *do* want you."

Her chest rose, her lips parting to form an O.

He lowered his mouth to her ear. "And when the time's right, I *will* have you."

The air that drew into her chest was sharp.

He kissed her on the cheek, letting his lips linger. "Text if you need anything."

When he got back to the front desk, it was to see Luke talking to Bea.

Luke gave him a chin lift. "Hey. Aspen settle in okay?"

"As settled as she can be in that small room. Are you okay doing any callouts for the next couple hours so I can stay in the office near Aspen?"

"Sure. I'll take Margot."

"Thanks." He went into his office. Now he just needed to keep his mind off Aspen and on his job.

Yeah, easier said than done.

He lifted his phone and texted his brother.

Jesse: Thanks again for driving her home.

Becket: Is she okay?

Jesse: Seems to be. You said she looked scared at the grocery store?

Becket: Not scared...terrified.

Jesse's chest tightened. He leaned back in his seat, gaze on the door. So what had scared her? And why wouldn't she tell him?

* * *

SHE COULDN'T WORK HERE. Sure, there were some people who could write anywhere, anytime. They were unicorns who just got the job done, and she wasn't one of them. She needed light and movement. She at least needed a window.

Were the walls closing in on her? Because they felt like they were closing in on her.

And why was it so quiet? Weren't sheriff's offices supposed to be loud? The wrongly accused were supposed to yell and argue and threaten to fight the deputies for their freedom. Or was that only in movies?

Obviously, there weren't enough bad guys in Amber Ridge.

She lifted her phone and texted her best friend.

Aspen: I'm dying.

Callie: You are not.

Aspen: Okay, maybe not dying, but definitely not thriving.

Callie: What's wrong?

Aspen: I'm working in a small dark room that kind of feels like it's getting smaller by the minute...Jesse put me here.

Callie: What room and why did he put you there?

Aspen: He didn't want me to be at the house by myself after what happened yesterday. He even got angry at me for going to the grocery store.

Callie: Good.

Good? Good! Whose side was she on?

She hit her friend's number, and Callie picked up on the first ring.

"I'm on the side that keeps you safe," Callie said before Aspen could get a word in.

"Are you a mind reader?"

"No, I just know you too well."

"Hm."

"Aspen, he's trying to protect you."

She knew that...so why was she fighting him?

"We kissed." The second the words were out, she scrunched her eyes.

They didn't just kiss, but she could barely wrap her head around what had happened *after* the kiss.

Callie did a half gasp, half scream. "Finally!"

"Finally?"

"Come on. Jesse is kind and smart and sexy, and you're *living* with him. I thought you would have hooked up ages ago." Her voice softened. "And I can't help but think that the old Aspen would have."

The old Aspen...the pre-Dylan Aspen.

She grazed her fingertips over the keys of her laptop. "I just...I don't know how I'm supposed to trust my judgment after Dylan."

"Oh, honey. Will you ever tell me exactly what he did to you?"

She swallowed, the little bomb of truth on the tip of her tongue. She should have told her best friend long ago. Usually, they told each other everything. But the shame that burrowed deep inside her for staying with him after what he'd done *still* drowned her.

But it was time...past time.

She opened her mouth to finally tell Callie, but the door opened and Bea stepped in.

"Sorry, Cal, I have to go. Someone's here. Chat soon."

Callie sighed. "Talk soon, honey."

The woman in front of her cringed. "Sorry, I didn't realize you were on the phone."

"You're fine." Aspen set her cell on the desk. "Is everything okay?"

She placed a mug down. "I thought you might like a coffee."

"Oh, I would *love* a coffee!" She lifted the mug and sipped, barely stopping herself from choking.

Oh, Jesus. Not good. Really not good. Completely sugarless and with a bitter aftertaste. Did people in this town take lessons on how to make bad coffee?

She forced a smile at the woman. "Thank you."

"You're welcome. Do you need anything else? Something to eat? Pen and paper?"

Aspen was about to respond, but then Luke passed the room, and Bea's gaze shot straight to him. Was there desire in the other woman's eyes?

A small smile touched Aspen's lips, the romance author in her definitely catching a little spark. "You like him?"

Bea's eyes widened as she looked back at Aspen. "Luke? No. We're friends."

Maybe. Or maybe not.

Actually, that would make a good story. A workplace romance about a receptionist and a deputy. That was kind of sexy.

"What about you and Jesse?" Bea asked, dragging Aspen out of her head.

"Me and Jesse?"

"You're dating, right?"

"No." Well, that came out faster than intended. "We're not dating. We're friends...and roommates."

Although, what they'd done last night hadn't been very *friendly*.

Bea nodded, an odd smile on her face. She didn't believe her. Well, she probably wouldn't have believed her either.

Aspen cleared her throat. "Well, thank you again for the coffee."

Bea dipped her head. "You're welcome. Shout out if you need anything else."

"I will."

Bea left the room, and Aspen sipped the warm drink again.

Argh. Mistake. And definitely not better on the second sip. But God, she needed caffeine.

Maybe sugar would fix this inability to write. A boost of energy often helped.

She rose from the desk and opened the door, only to stop. She had no idea where the kitchen was. She started down the hall, passing offices and what looked like a storage room. When she turned the corner, she saw a glimpse of a fridge just inside a room down the hall on the right.

There you are.

She was nearing the room when Luke's voice sounded from inside.

"...and Karen Davies was there."

Aspen stopped. He was talking about her mother? Why? And *where* had her mom been?

"Who's Karen Davies?" Bea asked.

"Aspen's mother. She was pretty hostile, so I pestered Jesse on the way back to the station about her background, and apparently she's crazy."

Aspen's muscles tightened.

"Crazy how?" Bea asked.

"One minute she's completely normal and friendly, and the next, she'll start threatening to kill you."

Aspen stepped back, hurt slipping through her. It wasn't a

secret that her mother didn't have the best mental health. But it still hurt that Jesse was sharing the information, and now Luke was gossiping about it at the station.

Someone blew out a breath before Bea spoke. "Wow. Mental illness can be hereditary, right? Do you think Aspen has something going on?"

"Who knows, maybe. I'm pretty sure he went as far as to refer to Karen as insane."

Aspen spun and headed back to the office, tears stinging her eyes. She hated that she was letting people she didn't know upset her. She shouldn't be. But, God, it just threw her straight back to when she was a kid at school and people would say the exact same things, sometimes to her face. No one had ever wanted to *help* her or her mother, they'd just wanted to gossip about them like they were entertainment.

She stepped back into the small room and almost walked straight into Jesse's broad chest.

He gripped her upper arms to steady her, his brows tugging together. "Hey. What's wrong?"

"I'm going home now." She wanted to be angry, but damn those tears building in her eyes.

If possible, his frown deepened. "You're upset. What happened?"

"Nothing."

"*Something* happened." He stepped closer. "Tell me."

Suddenly, the combination of her mother and Dylan and work and the gossip all hit her like a ton of bricks, and she just felt tired. *Really* tired. "I'd just like to go home, Jesse."

He held her gaze for another beat, almost searching...as if trying to figure her out just by looking at her.

In the end, he just nodded. "Okay, let's go."

CHAPTER 18

*a*spen leaned her head back against the car seat. She was ready for bed. Past ready. But even with her eyes closed, she felt Jesse's gaze on her. He'd had his eyes on her since they'd left the station.

When he pulled into his driveway, she unfastened her seat belt and climbed out. Neither said anything as they moved to the door, or when Jesse unlocked and opened it. She made it halfway down the hall before he spoke.

"Aspen. Tell me what upset you. You were fine when I left that room."

She nibbled her bottom lip before turning, forcing herself to meet his gaze. "Did you get a callout involving my mother?"

His brows flickered. "Yes."

"Why didn't you tell me?"

"It was the night you saw someone in your window. We were dealing with other stuff, and after that, I just got distracted. I'm sorry. I wasn't trying to hide it."

"And did you then tell Luke that my mother's insane?"

His frown deepened.

"Because I know she needs help," Aspen rushed to add. "I've

139

shared plenty with you about her mental health, but you calling her insane to your friend—"

He was in front of her within a second. "I didn't use the word 'insane.' I told him that she's *unstable*. That one second she's fine, and the next—"

"She's sending me death threats."

"He was the deputy with me on the case that day. I had to give him a bit of background information."

She nodded. It made sense. But there was still a part of her that felt like she'd trusted him with one of the hardest parts of her life, and that information had not only been shared but then used as water-cooler gossip.

Jesse touched her hip. "What exactly did he say to you?"

"Nothing. But he was more than willing to share with Bea in the kitchen."

"I'm going to kill him," he growled.

She shook her head, scrubbing her hands over her face. "It's not just that. It just hit me tonight how tired I am. I'm tired of my mother and Dylan and the problems I'm having writing, when writing used to come so easily. And I'm tired of thinking about you and last night and what we almost did."

"I told you...I wanted to. You have no idea how much I wanted to. Because I want *you*."

"I was there and willing. You turned me away."

"Because one night with you would never be enough, Aspen. So I need to know that you're in this. I'm terrified of pushing too hard and scaring you away."

Her heart took off at a faster pace, an intoxicating mix of heat and awareness dancing over her skin.

He tugged her against him, his hands big and warm on her hips. "I'm sorry if I made you think you weren't wanted. That couldn't be further from the truth."

She should step away. Being close to him was dangerous.

Hearing him say those words was dangerous. But she couldn't. She closed her eyes, and the words repeated in her head, sinking deeper inside her. And his scent, that sexy sandalwood...it surrounded her.

"Why?" she whispered.

"Why what?"

"Why do you want me?" She forced her gaze up to meet his again. "I'm not brave or smart or strong. I don't have money or a good family to share. I don't even have my life together."

That familiar frown returned to his face, and one of the hands on her hip slid up her side, only stopping to cup her cheek. "You were brave enough to leave everything you knew in Tennessee, including your best friend, and move across the country to look for a fresh start. You were smart enough to leave a relationship you knew was toxic. And after your mother broke in, you were strong enough to send her away." He tilted his head. "And I don't care about the other stuff. Even if you had them, they would be the least interesting things about you. I like you because I am *addicted* to everything about you. I'm addicted to your smile. Your laugh. I'm addicted to seeing you first thing in the morning and before I go to bed at night."

Turn around, Aspen. Walk away before you do something you can't take back.

But she didn't. She couldn't. She slipped her hands up his chest, letting the heat of his skin beneath his shirt warm her. Allowing the strong rhythm of his heart to beat into her.

"Tell me I won't regret this," she whispered, almost pleading as she looked up into his eyes. "Tell me this won't hurt me."

"You won't regret this. And I would *never* hurt you."

She couldn't stop herself. She lifted to her toes and kissed him.

He growled as he lifted her into his arms, pulling her entire body flush against his. The kiss was wild and desperate and everything her body craved. *He* was everything she craved.

She kissed him hard before parting her lips to let him in. He delved inside her mouth, and she tasted him. Drowned in him.

He turned them and headed toward the bedroom. When her back touched the mattress, she threaded her fingers through his hair, as if needing something to hold onto. Needed to keep him exactly where he was.

She arched, pressing her body to his. His warmth and strength were everywhere.

His fingers slipped beneath her top and pushed the thin material up. She lifted her arms, and the second it was over her head, she reached for his shirt, needing to feel his skin against hers. Then she slid her fingers down his body. Against the hard ridges of his chest. Perfect. Everything about him was perfect.

His hands slid behind her and unclasped her bra. It loosened and he swooped, taking one pebbled nipple between his lips.

Fire burned through her limbs.

Oh, God.

She cried out, her fingers digging into his flesh. He rolled her nipple with his tongue, then sucked, making her core throb. When his teeth grazed her sensitive bud, she jolted.

What was he doing to her?

With a desperation she didn't even recognize, she guided his head back to her so she could kiss him. Sink her tongue inside his mouth and taste him again. Her fingers shook as she reached for the button of his pants. The second it was undone, she reached inside and wrapped her fingers around his cock.

The growl that released from his throat was almost primal. And it drove her to start exploring. To slide her palm up and down his length. To stroke him from base to tip.

He hung his head, dropping his temple to her neck, his shuddering breaths whispering over her skin as the muscles in his arms bunched.

Touching such a powerful man, having such an obvious effect, made her feel powerful, and need churned inside her.

She hadn't had nearly enough time to explore him when he grabbed her wrist, stilling her.

"Jesse—"

He cut off her words with another earth-shattering kiss. His fingers went to her jeans and panties, pushing both down. Then she was completely naked beneath him, his cock between her thighs, making her heart beat faster.

But he didn't kiss her again. Instead, he looked so intensely into her eyes that she could barely breathe. He looked at her like he could see every emotion she tried to hide. Hear every unsaid word. Like he could read every detail about her.

"Tell me you want this," he said, warm breath whispering over her skin. "Tell me you want *me*."

She'd tried so hard to convince herself she didn't, for so long. But now? "I do, Jesse. I want you. I don't know how to *not* want you."

His temple touched hers, and his eyes closed like her words pained him. Then he reached out and pulled a small foil from the bedside drawer. He tore it open with his teeth and slid the condom over himself. When he returned to her, her breathing was shallow. He was right at her entrance. And it made the throb in her lower belly intensify.

There was fear, but no doubt.

"Thank you," he whispered.

"For what?"

"Coming into my life and making everything better." Then he slid inside her, and she groaned as he stretched her. Filled her. Made her his.

* * *

JESSE COULDN'T BREATHE. He dropped his head as her walls hugged his cock.

Fuck, she was tight. Every part of him urged him to move. To

143

lift his hips and thrust back inside her. Instead, he lowered his head and kissed her. This kiss was slower. A gentle sweep of his lips against hers, then a slow swipe of his tongue inside her mouth.

He would never tire of kissing this woman. Not if he lived a hundred years and they shared a million moments just like this one.

"Mm." Her moan had barely slipped into the air when she wrapped a leg around his waist and tugged him deeper.

He growled, his cock turning to stone.

"Move," she whispered, nibbling his bottom lip.

He lifted his hips and thrust back down. The air whooshed from her chest, brushing over his face, making his skin burn.

He lifted and thrust again, his mouth falling to her neck and sucking. Even her skin tasted sweet. And it made him want to devour her. Spend hours tasting every inch of her.

He continued to move, to lift in and out of her. When he found her breast again, he swiped her nipple back and forth with the pad of his thumb before rolling it in a circle. He was rewarded by more sweet fucking moans.

Her nails scratched down, then back up his arms before she grasped his shoulders, like she needed him as her anchor as much as he needed her to be his.

Everything about Aspen was fucking magic. From the sounds she made that shot straight into his chest to the way she gave herself to him so freely.

She was everything he hadn't realized he'd been waiting for. Everything he hadn't realized he needed. And he did need her. All of her, all the time.

She started lifting her hips, meeting him thrust for thrust.

Shit, he was close, but he needed to feel her break apart first.

He moved his hand from her breast to her clit and stroked.

The cry that spilled from her lips gutted him. He swiped again, this time applying a bit more pressure as he circled her clit with his thumb. He lowered his head and took a nipple between his lips again and sucked hard.

Her body arched off the sheets. Then she screamed as her muscles tensed, her fingers grabbing and pulling at his hair as she splintered. He released her nipple and lifted his head, his eyes going to her face as he continued to thrust. Watching as she fell apart.

Fucking gorgeous. All of her.

He quickened his pace, taking her deeper, his thumb never stilling over her clit, wanting to drag out her orgasm as long as he could.

She yanked him close, sinking her teeth into his shoulder. The bite of pain sent him over the edge. He fucking shattered, growling as her walls throbbed around him.

He kept thrusting, not stopping until he had nothing left. Until every ounce of strength and energy were gone and it was just the sounds of their heaving breaths in the room.

He dropped beside her and tugged her against him.

What the hell had just happened? He'd known being with Aspen would be good. But that wasn't just good. It went deeper than that. It was a feeling of rightness that he'd never experienced in his life. A connection that touched parts of him that had never been touched.

He kissed her forehead. It was all he could do because he didn't have words. Hell, he wasn't even sure if there *were* words after what they'd just shared.

Like she was the same, she also remained silent, sinking deeper into his side.

He closed his eyes and let the moment slip over him. Tonight had changed things, and there was no going back.

CHAPTER 19

A thumb swiped Aspen's hip. It was warm and gentle and made her skin tingle. Her eyes remained closed as soft thuds beat against her ear.

A heartbeat.

Jesse's heartbeat.

Her eyes popped open to see a large bare chest beneath her cheek. Her arm was slung over a hard stomach, and even though her legs were beneath the sheets, she could feel Jesse's tangled with hers.

She'd had sex with Jesse last night. She'd had *freaking sex* with Jesse last night.

She scrunched her eyes closed, and moments from the previous night flashed back in her head. His lips on hers. His hands everywhere.

But it hadn't felt like just sex. It'd felt like more than that. Deeper.

Old fear gripped her heart, squeezing, almost cutting off the air from her lungs.

No. She couldn't let fear control her forever. That meant Dylan won. Yes, she'd gotten into a bad relationship. Yes, the man she'd been dating had turned out to be someone completely different.

Jesse wasn't like that.

But what if she hadn't seen every part of him?

"Aspen?"

Her head shot up, eyes wide as they collided with Jesse's.

"Jesse...hi."

His thumb rubbed her hip again, causing a shudder to roll down her spine. "I can almost hear you thinking."

"You can't hear someone think."

"Maybe not. But by the tensing of your muscles and the fisting of your hand, I know something's going on in your head. Want to share?"

No. That was the last thing she wanted to do. Like smack dab right at the bottom. Plus, her head was such a mess, she didn't even know how to articulate her thoughts.

"It's nothing. I just...I overthink things. Hazard of being an author." Hazard of being Aspen.

Concern flickered over his features. "What are you over-thinking?"

Us. The word stuck to the tip of her tongue like glue.

When she took too long to answer, he rolled them so he hovered over her. "If it's us..."

Bingo.

"...I might have some work to do." He lowered his head, and she gasped when his lips touched her neck. But the gasp quickly turned into a moan as he grazed little kisses across her skin.

Holy hell, how did he always know exactly how to touch her to make thinking so hard?

His hand smoothed down the side of her body, and when he lifted his head, she immediately wanted to tug him back down to her. Demand he kiss all the parts of her body he'd missed.

His intense, dark gaze collided with hers. "I'm sorry again about Luke."

The reminder of Luke and his conversation with Bea about her mother crashed her back to reality, making her heated skin suddenly feel a bit cooler.

"What was the callout?" she asked. The question was one she probably should have asked last night, but her head had been a mess.

"She blocked the external cameras at the Airbnb where she's staying. The owner asked her to uncover them, but it looks like she then messed with the Wi-Fi router. The owner asked us to drop in and get it back up and running."

Aspen frowned. "Why would she do that?"

"I asked her, but…"

"She wouldn't tell you. Sounds like my mother. She'd probably just concoct some story about being watched. It wouldn't be the first time." She shook her head. "I hope she leaves soon." But when had Karen Davies ever done what Aspen wanted?

"I've asked the owner to let me know when she checks out." His hand grazed back up her side. "You didn't eat last night. I need to feed you."

"Food sounds good." As if her stomach heard, it gave a huge, everyone-in-the-neighborhood-probably-heard growl.

Oh, God.

Jesse laughed while Aspen covered her face with her hands. "I'm so embarrassed."

"Don't be. It's a reminder that I'm not feeding you enough." He kissed her neck again, and she groaned.

But when she lowered her hands, Jesse's smile had dropped.

A bad feeling churned in her belly. "What?"

"I know you don't like working at the station, but if you don't, I'd like you to stay here, with the doors locked, while I'm at work."

"Because of the person in my window the other night?"

There was a pause, and that pit in her belly deepened.

"Because Dylan might be in town."

A chill swept over Aspen's skin, and suddenly Jesse's weight went from comforting to almost claustrophobic.

She pushed at his shoulders, and he drew back, but his gaze never left her face.

"What do you mean, Dylan might be in town?" she asked, the words sounding wrong on her lips. She sat up, pulling the sheet with her.

Dylan *couldn't* be here. Amber Ridge was supposed to be her retreat. Her safe place. There was supposed to be half of an entire freaking country between them.

Jesse's gaze shifted between her eyes. "We're not certain. But he hasn't used his bank cards for days, and he's taken leave from work."

Her heart started to pound; giant, loud thumps that beat into her ears, drowning out the world around her.

"Aspen—" He reached out a hand, maybe to cup her cheek, but he moved so fast that she flinched.

Her heart stopped, embarrassment heating her cheeks.

Anger transformed his expression, but somehow, she knew that anger wasn't aimed toward her. "Aspen...I need you to tell me something."

That statement made her want to run.

"Did he physically hurt you?"

She didn't move...not a muscle. People had asked her what had happened—Callie in particular—but she hadn't told a single soul. Because the words hurt...they physically hurt. And saying them out loud, telling another soul that someone had assaulted her, *hit* her, and she'd stayed...it made her feel physically ill.

But really, Jesse didn't need her to confirm or deny anything. He already knew. He was the one who'd told her about Dylan putting his fiancée in a coma. He was the one who'd suspected it was Dylan who'd beaten her so badly.

He knew she'd been abused too. He was just waiting for Aspen to admit it.

So why couldn't she? Why was it so hard to put those words out into the world?

"I need to shower." She climbed off the bed, but not before seeing the disappointment on Jesse's face.

She was running from this, and it made her feel weak all over again, but she couldn't muster the strength to be stronger. She grabbed the first shirt she could find. Jesse's shirt. And the second it covered her body, his scent surrounded her.

Out. She had to get out. Away from Jesse and his questions and the way they sucked her back in time and made her feel vulnerable and pathetic all over again.

"Aspen."

She stopped halfway to the door, her eyes closing.

"Please." He was closer now. Then his hands touched her waist. "Trust me with the truth, even if that truth is the worst thing that's ever happened to you. You don't need to be afraid with me."

Afraid...she *was* afraid. And she didn't know how to chase that fear away. The words she needed to speak felt impossible. Would he look at her differently if he knew? Of course he would. How could he not? She looked at herself differently.

"I will. I just... Not right now. Please."

His mouth lowered to her neck, and he pressed one light kiss there. "I'll wait for you."

Inside her bedroom, she closed her door and rested her head against the wood, wishing she was stronger. Wishing she could be the person she was before Dylan had changed everything.

* * *

JESSE SLAMMED the car door and moved into the station. He was in a bad fucking mood.

Last night had been everything he'd known it would be.

Aspen had finally trusted him with her body, and it felt so damn right. *They'd* felt so damn right.

He'd thought that was it. That she was finally his and they could move forward together. That she might let him in on an emotional level too. Trust him with her past.

But she wasn't ready.

He stepped into the station, and Bea and Margot glanced up from behind the desk.

Bea smiled. "Good morning."

"Hey, Sheriff." Margot grinned.

He dipped his head at the women. "Morning. Did I miss much last night?"

Bea shook her head. "Nope."

"I actually have it on good authority that the deputies were bored out of their minds," Margot added.

Good. It would make for an easy morning. "Thanks."

Margot cocked her head. "Are you okay?"

Not even close. "Just gearing up for the day."

In his office, he logged in to his computer and was checking his emails when Luke stepped in. He held up a laptop. "Your girlfriend left this here last night."

Shit. She was going to need that.

"I'll text her." He lifted his phone.

Jesse: Hey. I've got your laptop at the station. Want me to drop it off?

Luke dropped into the seat opposite the desk. "Everything okay? You've got that 'I need to kill someone' look on your face."

The three dots popped up on his phone, then disappeared. He blew out a breath and set his cell on his desk. "Were you telling Bea the stuff I told you about Karen Davies last night?"

Luke's eyes widened, his mouth opening and closing before he answered the question. "Uh...yeah. Sorry. Bea and I are friends, and we were just talking—"

"I told you that stuff because it was work related, not so you could gossip about it to our receptionist."

"I know. I'm sorry, man. It won't happen again." He frowned. "How did you even know? Did Bea—"

"Aspen heard."

Luke cringed. "Jesus. I'm an asshole. I don't know what I was thinking." He scrubbed a hand over his face. "I'll apologize to her next time I see her. Was she angry?"

"Yes, but more angry at me than you."

His phone beeped, and he picked it up to see Aspen's response.

Aspen: I don't need to work today. You can just bring it home tonight.

Great. She was so desperate to avoid him that she was willing to do nothing all day.

Luke leaned forward. "Are you in the doghouse now?"

"Yeah, but that's not all your doing." The image of her running out of the bedroom made a vein throb in his temple. If he dropped off the laptop, he wouldn't be able to leave. Hell, he'd stay and kiss the woman until he knew she was happy, then he'd probably never make it back to work. "Are you able to drop the laptop off at my place for me?"

Luke's brows lifted. "Me?"

"Yeah. I'm a bit snowed under this morning." He glanced at his almost empty inbox. A fucking lie if ever he told one.

"Yeah, I can take it to her. It'll give me a chance to apologize." Luke rose. "I really am sorry, Jesse. It was unprofessional of me to talk to Bea about Karen. It won't happen again."

"I know it won't."

Luke nodded before stepping out of the office.

The second Luke was gone, Jesse lifted his phone.

Jesse: I want you to have your laptop. Luke's dropping it off. I hope that's okay.

Aspen: Thank you, I appreciate it.

He dropped his phone to the desk when what he really wanted to do was throw the thing across the room. He was frustrated. Hell, frustrated didn't even do justice to what he was feeling.

He turned to his computer and tried to concentrate. He replied to a few emails. Signed off on a few reports. And he made so many mistakes, it was obvious he should have just stayed in bed.

He leaned back in the chair, running his fingers through his hair as he recalled waking up to Aspen's warm body. The feel of her soft skin against him. Her hair splayed on his skin.

The woman was in his fucking blood.

A tap on the door had him straightening. "Come in."

Claudia stepped into his office. "Hey, Jesse. I have something for you, but you're not gonna like it."

Of course he wouldn't. "Tell me."

"You know how my friend's been keeping an eye on Bollard's bank cards as a way of tracking him?"

His muscles tensed. "Yeah."

"He used one of them yesterday."

He almost didn't want to ask. "Where?"

"Bozeman."

Blood roared between Jesse's ears, so loud it deafened the world around him. Bozeman was less than an hour east of Amber Ridge.

That basically confirmed it. Dylan was here, in Amber Ridge...and he was here for Aspen.

CHAPTER 20

*A*spen sipped her coffee as she sat on the bed and looked out the window into the backyard. She was distracted.

Jesse was on her mind. He'd been on her mind all morning.

Why was it so hard to be honest with him? To tell him that her ex-boyfriend had hit her and she'd stayed? She *wanted* to be stronger than this, but there was this stupid block, and because of it, she was disappointing everyone.

Well, it was time to start breaking that block, one person at a time.

She took two deep breaths before lifting her phone. It rang three times before Callie picked up.

"Hey. Good timing, I just finished teaching a class. It was a good one. Everyone was sweating up a storm. You would have hated it."

Aspen swallowed. "Do you have a second to chat?"

"Of course. I always have time for you. Is everything okay?"

Her eyes closed and her nose wrinkled. "I'm ready to tell you." Well, not completely ready. She wasn't sure she'd ever be *that* ready.

There was a small pause before Callie spoke. "You can tell me anything, Aspen."

"Dylan hurt me." Her nose wrinkled. It was the first time she'd said those words out loud...but surprisingly, they didn't hurt as much as she'd thought they would. Maybe they even lifted a small weight off her chest.

Callie's voice got low. "Hurt you how?"

"He hit me." When Callie kept quiet, Aspen kept going. She had to get it out before she froze or got scared or ran from this conversation. "Then he said sorry. He gave me flowers and begged me to take him back...and I did."

Okay, that part hurt.

"Oh, Aspen."

"The next time, he pushed me into a bookshelf. There were a couple of times when he grabbed my arm so tightly, he bruised me. And the last time, he hit me so hard I fell onto the coffee table and it broke. I had to kick him in the balls to get away."

She absently ran her fingers over her palm, almost able to feel the glass cutting into her all over again.

Callie's breathing was a little heavier, and when she spoke next, she sounded like she was crying. "Why wouldn't you tell me?"

"Because I was embarrassed."

"But—"

"I know you're going to tell me that I shouldn't have been. That it was *him* who did the wrong thing, not me. But the abuse actually started before it became physical. I should have left so much earlier, but he made me feel like...like I needed him. He'd yell at me. Try to control my movements. And when he hurt me, he made me feel like it was *my* fault. Then he was so nice after, and I just turned into this pathetic woman who accepted his excuses."

"Aspen, you *never* have to feel embarrassed with me. You never have to feel ashamed or like you did anything wrong.

You're my best friend, and someone hurt you. I needed to know that."

"I know." And she really did. If situations were reversed, she'd be unbelievably hurt that her best friend hadn't shared this. But her head had been a jumbled mess since Dylan. There wasn't a single fragment of her life that he hadn't touched or affected.

"Even though I never saw the bruises, I think a part of me knew it was something like that," Callie said quietly. "But I was hoping I was wrong."

"I covered the bruises with makeup. I wore long sleeves. And I smiled and used humor to cover the pain."

A sniff sounded over the line. "But you're out now. You're safe."

So she'd thought. Dylan was starting to feel like the nightmare she couldn't wake up from. "Dylan might be in Amber Ridge."

"That son of a bitch! Lock and I will be on the next flight over there—"

"*No.*" The word was out so quickly, Callie hadn't even finished the sentence. "You're pregnant. I don't want you anywhere near Dylan. You're staying in Misty Peak, where you're safe. I have Jesse looking after me, and he's just as capable of protecting me as Lock would be."

"But—"

"No buts. You need to promise me you're not coming, Callie. Please, for me."

Callie's voice softened. "Fine. I'm not coming *yet*. But I hate that I'm not there. And I hate that you didn't tell me. But I also get it. You went through a trauma and you needed time to process it. I'm glad you were strong enough to end things with him."

Strong…it was a word she hadn't associated with herself since Dylan.

"I'm going to tell Jesse." Even if it felt like the hardest mountain to climb.

"That's good. Let him in, A."

She blinked back tears. "I miss you."

"Oh, Aspen, I miss you so much."

The doorbell rang. That would be Luke with her laptop. "I need to go, but thank you for listening to me. I'm sorry it took me so long to tell you."

"You never have to apologize to me, Aspen. I'll always be here for you, no matter what."

"I love you."

"I love you too."

Aspen hung up, immediately wishing she hadn't. God, she wished she had her best friend by her side. But she hadn't been lying...she didn't want Callie anywhere near Amber Ridge if Dylan was here.

Dropping the phone to her mattress, she rose and walked to the front door, where she looked through the peephole. Luke's back was toward her, and he wasn't in uniform, but her laptop hung from his hand.

She flicked the lock on the door and opened it. "Hey. Thanks for—"

He turned—and terror hit her in the belly, knocking the air right out of her. "Dylan..."

"Hi, Aspen."

She tried to shove the door closed but he slammed his palm on the wood, pushing against her.

"Really?" he said in an almost humorous tone. "I don't even get a hello?"

He was too strong. He forced his way inside and she jumped back, fear making her head swirl.

"Get out."

He lifted a brow as he tossed her laptop onto the side table. "Out? I just got here."

"You're not welcome. You shouldn't even be in Amber Ridge."

"I can be wherever the hell I want." He stepped toward her.

"And if you hadn't run like a fucking rat, I wouldn't have needed to come."

"I wouldn't have had to leave if you'd left me alone."

He laughed, but this time, there was no humor in the sound.

His gaze caught on a photo on the wall. One of Jesse and his siblings. "And do you know what makes me even angrier? That you're living with *him*. Have you had sex with him?" He didn't wait for her to respond. "Of course you have, because you're a fucking whore."

As he continued to move forward, she stepped back, getting closer and closer to her room, where there was a lock on the door and her phone on the bed.

"What I do with my life is none of your business," she said firmly. "We broke up."

Fury darkened his eyes to black. "*You* broke up with *me*. You never stopped being mine."

He lunged, and she turned and sprinted down the hall.

The second she was in her bedroom, she slammed the door and flipped the lock. A loud thud of a body hitting wood sounded, making her jump.

"Open the door, Aspen, *now*."

She stumbled back, her heart catapulting into her throat. Her gaze rapidly shot around the room. Phone. She needed her phone. She sprinted to her unmade bed and ran her fingers over the sheets.

Shit. Where was it?

Another bang, what she assumed was a shoulder slamming into the door, caused her to flinch.

Come on, come on! It's here somewhere.

Finally, she felt the edge of the cell.

Thank God.

Another slam of a shoulder on the door. The wood creaked, the lock groaning at the weight of his body. He was going to get through. She knew that with every fiber of her being, and the thought was terrifying.

The tremble in her fingers made it hard to unlock her phone. Twice she keyed in the wrong numbers. And when she finally had it open, it took her far too long to find his name.

Finally, she hit Call, and it rang.

Another slam against the wood. Another groan of the lock.

One ring, and he answered. "Aspen—"

"I need help!"

Jesse's voice changed. Became harder...alarmed. "What's wrong?"

"Dylan's here."

Movement sounded over the line. "What do you mean, he's there?"

Another bang. She didn't have long. She searched the room for a weapon. There had to be something. "He's inside the house! I've locked myself in the bedroom but—" The next bang made her entire body flinch. "He's going to break in."

"Luke will be there soon—"

"No. Dylan had my laptop, Jesse! He must have done something to Luke." Her gaze landed on a bottle of perfume sitting on the dresser. She sprinted across the room and snatched it up.

"Aspen, I'm coming."

He wouldn't get there in time.

The door slammed open and the phone dropped from her fingers. She turned, the perfume hidden behind her back.

"Making me angry isn't fucking smart, Aspen." He inched forward, suddenly looking ten times taller than the last time she'd seen him. "After you broke up with me, I tried to give you a chance to make things right. You chose not to. Then you left. Made me search for you. *Big* mistake."

Her back hit the dresser. A couple more steps and he'd be within touching distance.

"You *hurt me*, Dylan. You broke us! How was I supposed to stay?"

"I did those things because you made me *angry*. You pushed me to do all that, just like you pushed me to search for you."

He was serious. He really blamed *her* for his actions.

He moved so quickly, she didn't have time to run. He wrapped his fingers around her neck and squeezed, lifting her up until only her toes touched the floor. "You don't *fucking* leave me. *I* say when we're done."

Air... She needed...air.

She swung her arm around and sprayed the perfume into his eyes.

He howled and dropped her, her body hitting the floor hard. She gasped for air, grabbing at her throat. She wanted to stay exactly where she was. Breathe. Recover. But she forced herself to get up and run. She got three steps in before Dylan's large body landed on top of hers. Her head hit the floorboards hard, and black dots danced in her vision.

He flipped her over. His eyes were half closed, red and watery, as he blinked rapidly. "You're going to pay for that, whore!"

He swung his arm back, but she moved her head just in time. His fist hit the floor, and she swung a knee up between his legs. He cried out, and she rolled away.

She was just pushing to her feet when a gunshot rang through the room.

She screamed and looked up to see Luke in the doorway. Blood trickled down the side of his head, and he swayed on his feet. Her gaze shifted to the gun in his hand, then back to Dylan.

"Hands up," Luke shouted, his words almost slurred.

God, he looked a step away from passing out.

"Backup is on the way," he shouted, but his eyes were half closed.

She turned back to see Dylan pushing to his feet. He was only up for a second when Luke swayed again, this time the hand with the gun lowering slightly as he grabbed the doorframe to steady himself.

Dylan took off, sprinting forward and shoving Luke to the floor as he ran.

* * *

JESSE SPED TOWARD HIS HOUSE. The drive was short, but right now it felt too fucking long.

Dylan had gotten in. Dylan was in his house *with* Aspen, and Jesse wasn't there to protect her.

He took a hard right and his gaze went to the rearview mirror. A few deputies trailed behind, but dammit, he needed someone there right fucking now.

His muscles tightened when he looked at his phone. He hadn't disconnected the call. There'd been a gunshot and Luke's voice. But after loud footsteps, there'd been almost nothing.

Had someone been shot? Who?

He took a sharp left onto his street and slammed his foot onto the brake outside his house. The second he was out of the car, he was running, sprinting up the walk and into the open doorway.

Inside, he did a quick scan of the living room and kitchen, weapon raised, before racing down the hallway to Aspen's room. He stopped at the sight of Luke sitting on the floor, head in his hands, and Aspen kneeling beside him.

Her eyes met his and the air rushed from his chest. She'd only just risen to her feet when he tugged her into his arms. "Thank God you're okay."

"Luke saved me."

Luke coughed from the floor. "No. I'm the reason the asshole got in." He pushed to his feet but immediately reached for the wall.

"Hey." Jesse grabbed his arm. "You're bleeding." It was dripping from his head.

"I'd barely stepped out of my car when he hit me from behind."

"I think he has a concussion," Aspen said quietly. "I've called an ambulance."

Footsteps sounded from the other room, and a second later, Claudia, Margot and two other deputies stepped inside.

Margot gasped and ran straight to Luke. "Oh my God, are you okay?"

While the deputies took care of Luke, Jesse steered Aspen toward the bed. She perched on the edge, and he knelt in front of her, his gaze immediately going to the red finger marks on her neck. Anger gripped him, damn near sucking the air right from his chest.

"He put his hands on you." It wasn't a question. Fuck, he needed to get control of himself. "Tell me what happened."

"I thought it was Luke. His back was toward me, and I didn't look at him properly, only saw the laptop in his hand, so I opened the door. I couldn't shut it in time, and Dylan pushed his way in. Then he was calling me a whore. Telling me I shouldn't have left." She drew in a ragged breath. "I ran in here and locked the door to call you, but he broke the lock. I fought him. Then Luke shot at the corner."

Probably because he knew his faculties were compromised and didn't want to risk hitting Aspen.

"Then Luke almost passed out and Dylan ran," Aspen continued. "I'm sorry."

Why the hell was *she* sorry? Jesse tugged her back into his arms. "*I'm* sorry. I should have brought your laptop myself. You should have been safe in my home."

If he'd been the one to bring the laptop, that fucker would be a dead man right now. Next time he showed his face, he would be.

CHAPTER 21

*A*spen watched Jesse move around the kitchen from her position on the living room couch. She'd tried to eat the Thai food he'd ordered, but she couldn't seem to stomach anything at the moment.

Memories of Dylan's fingers around her throat had her belly in knots.

He was here...in Amber Ridge...and today, he'd attacked her. It didn't seem real.

He'd been angry before, but today was different. Today he'd almost looked like he could kill her.

A shudder rocked her spine.

Jesse crossed the space between them and handed her a mug. "Hot cocoa."

"Thank you."

While she gave him a small smile, his frown had been firmly in place all afternoon.

He lowered to the couch, and she leaned forward and touched his hand. "Jesse. I'm okay. And Luke's only got a concussion."

Granted, it was a bad concussion, and he'd need some time off work, but he'd be okay.

"I should have been here," he said for what had to be the tenth time that afternoon. "I asked Luke to come because I'm a greedy bastard, and I thought I wouldn't be able to leave you. But if I'd come, Dylan would never have gotten the jump on me. He'd be in a fucking cell right now."

She tilted her head. "Dylan's a terrible person, but he's not an idiot. He knows your background in special operations. He never would have tried on you what he did to Luke. He saw Luke as an opportunity." She softened her voice. "This is Dylan's fault...but you know that. Why are you trying to blame yourself?"

"Because I need to blame *someone*."

"Blame him."

"He's not here." That familiar anger edged his voice.

She lowered her gaze to the steam coming off the cocoa. "Blame me, then. I'm the one who dated the psychopath."

"I would *never* blame you."

"You should."

"Aspen, it isn't your fault that your ex is a psychotic asshole." He said it slowly, like that would somehow convince her.

It didn't. A part of her would always blame herself for not seeing his true colors earlier...and then for not leaving earlier.

It was time to tell Jesse. Past time.

She took a deep breath before looking up. "It was six months into our relationship when I started to notice something was off. He got really possessive. Started wanting to know where I was going every day and how long I'd be gone. I should have gotten out then, the red flags were there. But I didn't."

Jesse didn't say anything, just watched her, waiting for the rest.

"Two months after that, he hit me."

The veins in Jesse's neck popped, rage blazing in his eyes, darkening them to almost black. But still he remained silent, like he knew she needed his silence to continue.

"I remember that first time so well. I wanted to go to the bar with friends, but he wanted me to stay home with him. We fought, and he hit me. You'd think that would be where our story ended...but it's not."

Tears burned her eyes at the admission. Tears of regret. Embarrassment. And shame...so much shame.

She looked down, not wanting him to see. "I was too ashamed to go to Callie, so I called my mother, but she was in one of her moods. I never even had a chance to tell her what happened before she started yelling at me. I hung up. Dylan found me in this spot where I used to write, in the park." She shook her head. "One apology, some flowers, and a promise that it would never happen again...and pathetic, desperate-for-love me took him back. What does that say about me?"

"It says you were confused about what love was because you hadn't been loved properly by others."

Her eyes flashed up to see the anger still there. But also something else. Empathy mixed with sadness, maybe.

Then the rage returned. "But don't ask me what that says about *him*."

She blinked back the tears.

"What happened next?" he asked.

Her gaze returned to the steam. "Three weeks later, he shoved me against a bookshelf. I can't even remember what we were arguing about that time. A month after that, we had this huge fight about me not wanting to move in with him. He grabbed my arm so tightly I thought he was going to break something."

A muscle in Jesse's jaw clenched.

"He looked like he was going to hit me, but I talked him down, told him I'd move in and he left for work. The second he drove away, I packed my things. But he came back." Her pulse picked up, and it was only Jesse's gentle touch on her thigh that gave her the strength to keep going. "He saw what I was doing and hit me.

I fell onto the glass coffee table and it shattered. He lunged for me, but I kicked him and ran."

The muscles in Jesse's arms were bunching, small veins popping out.

She shook her head. "It took three times—*three assaults*—for me to finally get out. And I never told law enforcement. I'll never forgive myself for that."

"Aspen, listen to me."

She didn't want to. The shame was bearing down on her like a weight, pressing on her chest, urging her focus to rest anywhere but on him.

He leaned forward and tilted her chin up. Then his eyes beamed into hers. "Everything that asshole did…every time he touched you in a way he shouldn't have, scared you, or said something that made you feel less than…that was on him. All of it."

A tear trickled down her cheek. "But I could have left earlier."

"It's not that simple."

It was true. In the moment, it had felt confusing and hard and messy. "I've been so embarrassed. That night in Misty Peak, when he dragged me out of the bar and you guys came out and saved me…you asked me if I wanted to press charges. I said no because I was so scared people would find out what he'd done to me. I was scared people would realize that I'd stayed with him after he'd hit me and figure out that I'm not brave or strong."

He slipped the mug from her fingers and set it on the coffee table. Then he took her hands. "Aspen, remember what I told you? You *are* strong. You had to be to leave him. And you had to be brave to leave the town you grew up in to get away from him. Don't ever let anyone convince you otherwise."

She wanted to believe him.

"And you are worthy of a love so much better than whatever the hell that asshole gave you. You are worthy of safe love. A love that protects you. Do you understand?"

Worthy…it was something she hadn't associated with herself for a while. "I haven't believed that for a long time."

"Then it's my job to make you believe it."

He nudged her close, and she dug her head into his chest.

"Thank you," she breathed.

She wasn't sure what she was thanking him for. His words. His presence. His protection. Maybe everything. Since the day they'd met, he'd been there for her without asking for anything in return.

His arms wrapped around her, cocooning her in his strength and warmth. "I'd do anything for you, Aspen. You know that, right?"

"I'm starting to." She closed her eyes, letting all that was Jesse soothe her. She'd made really shitty decisions with Dylan. But the decision to get to know Jesse almost felt like her redemption.

* * *

MINUTES TICKED BY, but Jesse couldn't move. He wanted to remain exactly where he was, Aspen in his arms, for as long as he could.

It didn't take long for her breathing to even out. For her chest to rise and fall in a steady rhythm. She was falling asleep. Good. He'd been worried that she wouldn't be able to sleep after everything today had brought.

That familiar fury crawled around his chest, threatening to punch right out of him. But he kept it inside…barely.

Gently, he scooped his arms behind her knees and back and lifted her as he stood.

She drew in a long breath before looking up at him, eyes half hooded. "Not my room," she whispered. "I don't want to be in there."

His chest tightened. Of course she didn't want to be in the

room where that scumbag had attacked her. He wouldn't be surprised if she stopped feeling safe anywhere in his house.

He forced the rage off his face and changed direction. He stepped into his room and placed her on the bed. She snuggled into the pillow as he pulled up the sheets.

"Don't be gone long," she said quietly.

He grazed a lock of hair from her face, for the millionth time getting lost in just how beautiful she was. "Never."

The second her eyes closed, his gaze lowered to her neck. To the red bruising in the form of fingerprints.

And this time, he didn't hide anything. He let the anger carve itself into his face, thickening the muscles in his neck and fisting his hands. Every part of him wished Dylan was in the room with him right now so he could show him exactly what happened when he messed with the wrong person.

He turned and headed out of the bedroom to check all the locks on the doors and windows. He'd hear if someone breached his house, and he could go from dead asleep to awake and alert in a matter of seconds. But a lock would slow the intruder down.

He'd just checked the last room when his phone buzzed with a text from his brother.

Becket: Thanks for the photo. I'll keep an eye out for the fucker.

He'd sent a photo of Dylan to his brother because he needed all the backup he could get.

Jesse: Thanks. I appreciate it.

Next, he called Holden, and his best friend answered on the first ring.

"Hey, Jesse. It's late. Everything okay?"

"I need you here sooner." His friend had said he'd be moving in a month or two, but Jesse needed the backup of his former Ghost Ops team member *now*.

"What's wrong?"

"You know how I told you Aspen's living with me because of an ex from her hometown?"

"Yeah?" There was a dangerous edge to his voice.

"Well, that ex is here, in Amber Ridge. And tonight, he attacked one of my deputies, then Aspen."

Holden cursed. "Are they both okay?"

"Luke has a concussion and Aspen has bruising on her neck... and he got away."

"I'll tie up some loose ends here and be there within the week."

Jesse closed his eyes, relief punching him in the gut. "Thank you."

"Watch your back until I get there."

"Always."

He hung up and went into the bathroom. He needed to wash this damn day away. But even when he got under the shower spray, his mind didn't stop, repeating what had happened today over and over again like a damn movie reel. Only this was real fucking life.

He hadn't known Aspen for long, but his heart didn't seem to care. He *needed* her. He needed her safe and close and protected. He couldn't lose her when they'd barely begun.

Ten minutes later, he turned off the shower and returned to the bedroom. The second he stepped inside, his gaze went to her. Tracing the features of her face. Taking in every rise and fall of her chest.

He pulled on some briefs and slid beneath the sheets. Even though he'd done it as silently as he could, she immediately rolled over and rested her cheek on his chest...like she felt his presence as heavily as he felt hers.

He wrapped an arm around her and tugged her closer, and she breathed out a sigh.

Even with Aspen in his arms, he still struggled to push the rage aside...and he couldn't. It bore down on him. Crushing him. Suffocating. Not just because of what had happened today, but because of everything Aspen revealed that asshole had done to her.

Jesse had known the son of a bitch had hurt her. But hearing it out loud…it fueled his need to find the scumbag and tear him to fucking pieces.

CHAPTER 22

*A*spen strummed her fingers against the window frame. She was nervous. The kind of nervous that made her belly do funny little rolls and made sitting feel impossible.

She shouldn't be nervous. This was her mother, the woman she grew up with. Most people would be excited.

But most people didn't have Karen Davies as a mother.

She should have done this yesterday, but Jesse had encouraged her to spend the day resting. Well, not encouraged. *Enforced* in a very direct you're-not-moving way.

But he was right. And she'd been an emotional mess; waiting an extra day was probably for her mother's benefit even more than hers.

But if her mother confirmed that she'd given Dylan her address, she'd probably turn into that emotional mess all over again.

She dragged her gaze from the window to Jesse behind the wheel. "Thank you for coming with me."

"Until we find Dylan, you're not going anywhere by yourself."

Dylan...her fingers itched to touch the bruising on her neck, as if she needed the reminder of exactly what he'd done. She'd covered the bruising with makeup, but every time she looked in the mirror, it was all she saw. Every time she closed her eyes, *he* was all she saw…the anger as he choked her. The fury as he said she was his.

"Hey."

She jolted and swung to face Jesse.

His voice gentled. "Are you okay?"

No. For the millionth time in the last two days, she'd gotten lost in the darkness.

But she nodded because he was already angry and stressed enough. He didn't need her adding to any of that.

The muscles in his arms contracted…he knew she was lying.

"There've been no sightings of him?" she asked.

"Not yet. But there are a lot of eyes looking for him, and there are only so many places he can hide in a small town. We'll find him."

The rational part of her brain knew that. The part that kept remembering his fingers around her neck was wondering if that would happen before or after he got her alone again.

Jesse pulled onto a residential street. She frowned at the cabin when he pulled up. "You're sure this is where she's staying?" Her mother didn't have a lot of money, and this Airbnb had to be costing a fortune, especially considering how long she'd already been in town.

"George, the owner, confirmed she keeps extending her stay and is still there."

"Hm. Okay."

They both climbed out of the car, and she didn't miss the way he scanned the street before studying the cabin. He touched a hand to the small of her back and led her toward the door.

"Whatever happens in there…I'm sorry in advance," she said quietly, feeling obligated to warn him even though he probably didn't need it.

"You don't need to apologize for anyone else's behavior."

"Okay, but what if I attack her?" She half grinned at him, only kind of joking.

"I'll give you a five-second start before I jump in," he whispered before they stopped at the entrance.

Her half grin dropped when she looked at the door. She didn't knock right away. It always took a few seconds to work up the nerve to see her mother. What mood would she be in today? Happy? Angry? Would she start one way and switch to the other when Aspen started asking questions?

Jesse didn't push her. In fact, he didn't say or do anything. He just stood by her side, being his usual perfect self, the warmth of his hand seeping into her skin.

Twenty long seconds and a million unhealthy thoughts later, and she knocked.

Footsteps sounded from inside the house, then the door opened and Karen Davies stood in front of them.

Her mother's brows rose. "Aspen. What are you doing here?" Her gaze shifted to Jesse, and a small scowl crossed her face. "Are you—"

"I need to talk to you, Mom."

Her mother shifted her gaze back to Aspen. "I was going to pop out, but I suppose I can spare a few minutes. But only you, *not him*."

Jesse tensed. "I'm staying with her."

Her mother raised a brow. "Well then, I'm not talking to either of you. Have a nice day."

She went to close the door, but Aspen pressed her palm to the wood. "Mom. Really?"

"Really. Take it or leave it, Aspen."

Argh. Her mother couldn't be mature for two seconds.

Aspen turned to Jesse. "I'll be back in thirty seconds."

"*No.*"

Her mother smiled. The evil woman was enjoying this.

Aspen inched closer to him. "Jesse. Please. I need to do this. I'll be fine. I'll stay by the door."

His jaw clicked, and he looked inside the house behind Karen before returning to her. "Door stays unlocked, and you stay right at the entrance."

She touched his chest. "I will."

She sucked in a breath. She didn't like this any more than he did, but she needed to get some answers from her mother.

She stepped inside, and her mother closed and locked the door.

"Call out if you need him?" Her mother scoffed as she headed into the kitchen. "What does he think I'll do? Hit you over the head with a frying pan and rob you?"

Aspen unlocked the door and turned to her mother, not moving from where she stood. "What are you still doing here, Mom?"

Her mother stopped, back still toward her. "I'm here to see *you*."

"You haven't initiated any contact since you broke into Jesse's house and accused me of stealing your bracelet." To anyone else, those words would sound insane.

Her mother cleared her throat as she took two mugs from the cupboard. "Doesn't mean I wasn't *planning* on visiting again. And can you blame me about the bracelet? After the way you were staring at it, I'm surprised you didn't snatch it off my wrist."

It was so like her mother to not take responsibility. "Mom, I need to ask you something, and I need you to look at me when I do."

Her mother was good at lying, but her eyes usually gave her away.

Slowly, her mother turned. "What?"

"Did you give Dylan my address here in Amber Ridge?"

Her features didn't change at all. In fact, for a moment, she remained so perfectly still she was like a statue.

"Yes."

Aspen's stomach dropped. And the reaction was stupid. She'd *known* it was her mother—she was the only one Aspen had given her address to. But even after everything her mother had done to her, it still hurt. It always hurt.

"Why?"

"Because he asked for it."

That was it? He asked for it, so she gave it to him? God, she felt like throwing her head into a brick wall, she was so frustrated. "I told you that I left to get away from him. I told you our relationship wasn't healthy."

"What did you want me to do?"

"Say no! Protect your child!"

"Protect you from what? He's a nice guy. I was doing you a favor."

Anger darkened the room around her. "He *hit* me. Shocking, isn't it? He also used to grab me so tightly, I'd have bruises for days. And when I left him, he hit me so hard, I fell into the coffee table and it broke."

Her mother's brows flickered. "Come on, Aspen. Is that true? I know you have a tendency to make things up, and I don't want your overactive imagination to get that boy into trouble."

She flinched. She'd just told her mother the most painful things that had ever happened to her...and she didn't believe her. "You think I'd lie about something like that?"

"I think you like attention."

She blinked. Was this woman really her mother? The woman who was supposed to love her more than anyone else in the world? "What is wrong with you?"

"Excuse me?"

"I just told you that someone *assaulted* me, and you tell me that I like attention?"

"Aspen, I don't have the energy for your drama today. You asked me a question, and I answered it. Is there anything else?"

There was no point. Her mother would never change, and at some stage, Aspen needed to accept that. "No. That's all. I won't be visiting again. And I certainly won't be sharing information about my life with you ever again. Stay as long as you want, but leave me alone."

She turned and took a step toward the door when a sweater hanging over a chair caught her attention. She frowned, and her fingers shook as she lifted it. Immediately, she dropped it as she stumbled back.

It was his…the sweater was Dylan's. And it was also the same one she'd seen in the grocery store the other day.

She turned back to her mother, disbelief sending tingles through her limbs. "This is Dylan's."

Her mother pursed her lips but remained silent.

"This sweater is Dylan's! Is he here?"

The front door flew open and Jesse stormed inside, Glock in hand.

Her mother gasped and threw a hand over her chest. "What on earth—"

"Is Dylan here?" Jesse shouted, repeating Aspen's question.

"Get out!"

Jesse ignored her mother and moved through the cabin, opening doors, checking every inch of the space.

Her mother hurried behind him. "What the hell are you doing? You have no right to be in here!"

Her mother grabbed his arm and he spun, towering over her. "He's a wanted man, and keeping him hidden will see you arrested."

Her mother's face paled. "What are you—"

"*Is he here, Karen?*"

She jumped at Jesse's shouted words, and it took her a few seconds to respond. "He was. He's not anymore. The second your little deputy fixed the Wi-Fi router, he left. He didn't want to be caught on camera."

Aspen's jaw dropped. "You've been living with him?"

"Yes. So?"

Why did it keep hurting? "I can't be around you."

She spun and walked out of the house because she knew if she stayed a second longer, she would cry or scream or do something she couldn't take back.

* * *

JESSE WATCHED Aspen as she leaned against the counter at The Tea House and spoke to Mrs. Gerald. The second they'd left her mother's rental, this was where she'd wanted to come, and Jesse could see why.

She was smiling again. A big smile that lifted the corners of her lips and created little lines beside her eyes. She'd built a relationship with the older café owner. Which was good. She needed people in her life who treated her well. She certainly deserved a hell of a lot more than her mother gave her.

His biceps flexed at the memory of what she'd said to Aspen. At the way she hadn't even cared that she'd been living with the man who'd hurt her daughter.

What the hell was wrong with that woman?

He'd always known he was lucky to have the mother he had, but seeing Karen in action today just cemented that. And it made him want to share his family with Aspen. She deserved that kind of love.

Aspen returned to the table, setting a mug of hot liquid in front of him and a cup of tea in front of herself as she slid into the booth. "I had the best idea while talking to Mrs. Gerald."

The smile on her face was radiant. "Tell me."

"You know how she's close to closing this place because business has been so bad?"

"Yeah." Not that he was surprised. He'd been born in this

small town and didn't even know it existed. Plus, he didn't know one tea drinker.

"Well, I don't want that to happen. She loves this place. She said she wouldn't know what to do with herself without it, so I suggested a big reopening party."

He frowned. "A reopening party?"

"Yes! I'll do posters and get the word out around town, and she'll give free samples of her pies and scones. They probably think she only serves tea, but when people try her pie, they're going to die."

"I don't mean to state the obvious, but her coffee isn't the best."

"I know, which is why I suggested—in the nicest possible way —that her coffee machine is due for an upgrade. And when you buy a new coffee machine, they show you how to use it...hence, free coffee-making lesson. And I've told her all about my favorite coffee beans. Trust me, there is no bad coffee with these beans."

"That will be a big investment for her."

"I know. But it could also save her business." She cocked her head. "Perfect plan, isn't it?"

After the shitstorm that was the visit with her mother, anything that put that smile on her face was perfect. "It sounds great."

The smile slipped slightly from her face. "I hope so. I need something good to focus on."

He reached across the table and gave her hand a small squeeze. "I'm happy to help in any way." He lifted the coffee, only to cringe on the first sip.

Jesus, had it gotten worse since he'd last come here? The corners of Aspen's lips lifted again. It almost made the acid-tasting coffee worth it.

"Why did you order that?" she asked.

"Because after the twenty-four hours we've had, I needed

coffee." Really, he needed something stronger than coffee. A shot of whiskey wouldn't hurt.

"I told you, we could have gone to the diner. The instant coffee there's slightly better."

"Not really. And you like this place."

"Two pieces of pie."

Jesse looked up at Mrs. Gerald. "Thank you."

Aspen took one bite and closed her eyes. "It's heaven in a bite."

The older woman beamed at Aspen. "Thank you, dear. I would hope they're good after fifty years of perfecting the recipe. Call out if you need anything else."

As she left their table, he cut a piece of his own. While the coffee had been worse than he remembered, the pie was better. God, it was good.

"See," Aspen said, scooping more pie onto her fork. "The second locals taste this stuff, they won't be able to stay away."

She was right. The pie was addictive.

His voice softened. "I'm sorry about your mom."

Aspen frowned down at her pie. "I don't know why anything about her surprises me anymore. After a lifetime of her, I should be used to it, but for some reason, I just keep expecting more."

"It's not a bad thing to expect more from the people we love."

"No, but in my case, it kind of makes me a glutton for punishment." She shook her head. "I can't believe he was living with her."

"I'll put a deputy on the cabin to watch the place, in case he returns." After some pressure, Karen had said she'd let him know, but he didn't believe that for one second.

His phone rang, and he pulled the cell out of his pocket and cringed.

Aspen straightened. "Who is it?"

"My mother."

Aspen laughed. "You have a sane mother. We only cringe when mine calls."

"She's not going to be happy with me. I keep bailing on our family meals."

"You do?"

"Yeah. I've also been avoiding her calls, and I'm about to hear it." He answered the call. "Hi, Mom."

"Jesse Michael Hayes. Why haven't you been answering my calls?"

Jesus, she was middle naming him. "I'm sorry, I've been—"

"Don't you say busy. You should never be too busy for family."

"I know."

"You *are* coming to lunch this Sunday. That's not a request. It's happening. Already have plans? Cancel them. Your brother and sister are coming too."

"Okay."

"Good. And no last-minute canceling like last time."

"I won't. But I'm bringing Aspen with me."

Aspen's brows shot up, fork pausing halfway to her mouth.

"Of course. I expected her to come. Are you two—"

"Mom." He was not going to define what they were to his mother when he hadn't even talked to Aspen about that.

His mother sighed. "Butt out. I get it. It will be lovely to see you both. Is there anything she doesn't eat?"

"She doesn't like salmon, but that's it." He'd learned that the hard way in Misty Peak, when he'd cooked it, and she'd paled.

"No salmon. Done. I'll see you Sunday, darling. Remember, don't—"

"Cancel. I won't."

"Good. I love you."

"I love you too."

He hung up to see Aspen giving him a strange look.

He frowned. "Did I miss something? Is there anything else you don't like?"

"No. I just... I'm going to your family dinner?"

"If that's okay with you? If not, I could rain check." His mother would kill him, but for Aspen, he'd do it.

"Don't rain check. I'm looking forward to it."

"Good." It really was, because there was a huge part of him that was looking forward to her being a part of the family gathering, too.

CHAPTER 23

*A*spen groaned.

Tired. Way too freaking tired.

What was the time?

She cracked one eye open but quickly scrunched it shut again.

Why was it so bright in here when the curtains were closed? That meant it was late, right?

This was Jesse's fault. He'd kept her up late last night. Although, it had been worth it.

The heat in her belly did a little dance at the memory of everything they'd done in the shower...then out of the shower against the wall...then in bed.

She rolled over and reached for him, but her hand touched cold sheets.

Her eyes popped open. He wasn't here. This was the first time in days she'd woken without him. But then, it was late. Or at least, she was pretty sure it was late.

Something sounded in the other room. The subtle clatter of pans.

Jesse. He was clearly up. While her lazy butt had slept in.

She threw off the sheets and climbed out of bed before pulling one of Jesse's shirts over her head on the way to the door. The shirt smelled exactly like him and it enveloped her.

She stepped into the hall, then the living room, only to grind to a halt, fear shooting through her system.

A man stood by the coffee machine, back toward her. A tall man with broad shoulders. Similar to Jesse, but not Jesse. His hair was slightly lighter, and there was something different about the way he stood.

He turned and she gasped, lifting a lamp from a side table and yanking the cord from the socket. What she would *do* with the lamp, she wasn't sure. This guy was huge, in height and width. His biceps were freaking massive. But if he came toward her, she'd swing like her life depended on it.

"Who are you and what are you doing in this house?"

He glanced at the lamp, then back to her. He almost looked… amused? Did he find this *funny*?

He lifted his hands. "Aspen—"

"You know my name? How do you know my name? And where's Jesse?"

"I'm Holden. And I'm not here to hurt you. If I was, would I be making coffee?"

Well…no, but it was early, and she didn't know what the heck was going on.

"Holden…" Her frown deepened. "Holden, as in Jesse's best friend?"

"That's me. And Jesse's—"

The back door opened, and a shirtless Jesse stepped in. "Thanks. I needed that run." He stopped, eyes going to the lamp in her hand, moving down her body, then returning to her face. "Aspen."

Holy freaking shit. She was wearing his shirt. *Only* his shirt. No panties. No bra. In front of his best friend. Her nipples were probably poking through the material.

Her pulse picked up speed, but she plastered the fakest smile she could muster on her face as she looked at Holden. "Excuse me while I put on some actual clothes."

She spun and speed-walked back to the bedroom, almost running, before closing the door behind her with a loud thud.

She'd barely stepped inside when the door opened behind her. "Aspen—"

She spun. "I'm not wearing panties *or* a bra."

One side of Jesse's mouth lifted. "I know."

"*You* know, which means *he* knows!" She was shout-whispering, but she couldn't help it.

Jesse crossed the space between them and wrapped his fingers around the lamp. "I'm going to take this before you swing it again and hurt yourself."

She'd been swinging it? She hadn't even realized she was still holding it.

He set it on the dresser and turned back to her, his arms slipping around her waist. "With everything going on, I forgot to mention he was arriving today. He got here early, and you were still asleep, so I left you a note on your phone."

"You left me a note?"

"I did. But I should have woken you before I left. I'm sorry."

"I swung a lamp at him!" Her cheeks suddenly felt hot again.

He tugged her closer. "Hey. It doesn't matter. Although, in the future, if you see a stranger in the house, I'd prefer you run."

"Of course it matters! He's your best friend and he's moving to town and now he thinks your girlfriend's a psycho."

This time, both corners of Jesse's mouth lifted, his dimples on full display. "Girlfriend?"

Shit. They hadn't spoken about what they were.

"Aspen Davies...are you my girlfriend?"

She swallowed as she looked into his beautiful eyes. "Depends...are you my boyfriend?"

"Absolutely I am." Then he kissed her, and she almost forgot about every embarrassing thing she'd done that morning...almost.

* * *

"You sure the coffee hasn't gotten better?" Holden asked.

Jesse's lips twitched. "Nope. This diner has changed hands twice in the last twenty years, and it's still the same instant shit."

Aspen leaned forward. "Soon, you'll be able to get a good coffee at The Tea House."

"The Tea House?" Holden asked. "I've been to Amber Ridge a lot and never knew about a tea house."

"Hey, I grew up here, and I didn't know about it," Jesse added.

"Oh, it's here," Aspen said. "And it has amazing pie."

"I'm not sure—"

"Trust me," Jesse interrupted. "You want to go for the pie."

A waitress stopped at their table. "Hi, what can I get everyone?"

They each put in their breakfast order, and Holden was the only one to order coffee.

Jesse lifted a brow at him.

He shrugged. "I need to see for myself if it's any better."

"Don't say I didn't warn you. So, did the trip over go okay?" He still couldn't believe his best friend and former teammate was here in Amber Ridge. But it felt so damn good.

"Yeah, filled the truck and made the thirteen-hour drive in eleven and a half." He glanced around the diner. "It's crazy that this town never changes. Everything's always exactly the same."

"Not much changes here." Not even the bad coffee.

"You've been here often?" Aspen asked.

"I've crashed a few of the Davies family holidays."

"It's not crashing if you're invited," Jesse corrected.

Aspen frowned. "You don't celebrate with *your* family?"

There was a small tensing of Holden's muscles. It was so

subtle, most wouldn't have noticed. Jesse knew him too well to miss it.

"My mom died when I was a teenager, and I never knew my dad."

Jesse's stomach clenched. Holden's father had left his mother before he was born, and his mother had gotten sick with lung cancer and died when he was sixteen. Then he'd bounced around a couple of foster homes before enlisting in the military.

Aspen's eyes softened. "I'm sorry."

"Thanks. I heard you're having a rough time with *your* mother."

Aspen cringed. "Unfortunately, there's no such thing as a smooth time when Karen Davies is involved." She glanced at her phone.

She'd done that a couple times. "Are you expecting a message from her?"

"I asked her when she's leaving for Misty Peak, but she hasn't responded. She's also not answering my calls." Aspen lifted a shoulder like it was no big deal, but Jesse knew it was.

He squeezed her thigh beneath the table. "I'll touch base with George to see what the status is on the cabin."

She gave him a small smile. "Thanks. I'm just going to go to the bathroom."

He stood to let her out, but before she could step away, he grabbed her arm. "Don't venture too far, okay?"

Humor danced in her eyes. "The bathroom is right there. I think I'll be fine."

She kissed him and he watched as she crossed the diner.

When he lowered back into the booth, he caught Holden staring at him. "What?"

"You really like her."

"Yeah. Does that surprise you?"

"A bit. I've seen you date, but this seems different."

"Aspen's different."

Holden's mouth curved. "I'm happy for you."

"Thanks."

The smile dropped from Holden's face. "No progress on finding Dylan?"

"No. And it's driving me fucking crazy." He wanted eyes on the asshole, and he wanted eyes on him now. He felt blind and helpless, and he hated that.

"He won't be able to do much in this town without someone noticing."

"I'm counting on it."

Jesse was still in his head when Holden frowned. "Hey. I know we've spoken about Antwan on the phone, but this is the first I've seen you in person since all that went down. How are you doing after everything?"

His chest tightened. Sometimes he could almost forget about everything that took place in Misty Peak. Then he remembered, and *fuck*, it felt heavy. "As okay as I can be. You?"

"I wasn't there."

"Doesn't matter. He was like a brother to all of us."

Holden nodded. "Yeah. It hurts."

It more than hurt.

Okay, they needed a change of subject. "My mom's having a family dinner tomorrow night. Come with us."

"Is she making her famous pot roast?"

"I can put in the request."

"I'll be there."

Aspen returned to the table. "See? All safe."

He slid a hand back to her thigh as soon as she sat down. "Good."

The waitress returned with their food. The second she left, Holden lifted his mug of coffee to his lips. His expression didn't change as he sipped it. There was no cringe. No face pulled. But then, Holden could be a master at concealing his emotions.

Jesse lifted a brow. "And?"

"It's not so bad."

Aspen's jaw dropped. "What?"

Holden laughed. "I'm kidding, it's terrible. Like warm water mixed with dirt."

"That's my description too." Jesse laughed.

The diner door opened, and Luke and Bea stepped in. Jesse frowned. He didn't know they hung out.

Luke's gaze went straight to him, and he smiled before heading to their table. Bea followed closely behind.

"Hey. Looks like we got a day off at the same time," Luke said.

"Doesn't happen often." Jesse gestured across the table. "Luke, Bea, this is my friend Holden. Holden, Luke's a deputy at the station and Bea works our front desk."

Holden dipped his head. "Hey."

"What are you two doing today?" Aspen asked.

Bea smiled. "Getting a juice and going for a walk. It's such a nice day."

Luke stepped back. "We'll leave you guys to it. See you at work, Jesse."

They moved to the counter, and Aspen turned to Jesse. "Are they together?"

He shook his head, barely holding in the laugh. "No. Luke doesn't date."

Holden lifted a brow. "Ever?"

"I mean, he has women he sees on a more regular basis"—*like Margot*—"but I don't think Bea's one of them."

"I don't know," Aspen said as she glanced back toward the counter. "I think there's something there."

"That's probably the romance author in you wanting to couple them off."

Her smile softened. "I do like a good love story."

Just another thing he adored about her. He looked back at Holden. "So, are you spending the day settling in?"

Holden shot a look at his watch. "Actually, the agent to the place I bought is giving me the keys today."

Jesse's brows shot up. "You've got a place already?"

"Sight unseen. Guess I'm brave or stupid."

"Shit, you really *are* here for good."

"You sound surprised."

"I thought you'd stay for a few months, maybe a year, then be back on the move."

Holden shook his head. "Nah, it's about time I settled some roots. And Amber Ridge is as good a place as any."

CHAPTER 24

"Should I be nervous? Because I'm kind of nervous." Butterflies-in-the-stomach, clammy-hands kind of nervous.

Aspen was well aware that her level of nervousness was unwarranted. She'd met Jesse's mother before. She'd met his siblings too. But this was different. This was dinner in his mother's home. A meal with the entire family, where she needed to slot herself into their dynamic and not embarrass herself.

Jesse reached over and set a hand on her thigh as he drove. "Why are you nervous?"

"What if I say something wrong? Or try to use humor as a way to distract them from my complete awkwardness and I'm not funny? My humor never drops well when I'm nervous. Think strange-looks-and-cricket-silence kind of doesn't drop well."

"I think you're overthinking this."

"Am I? Or am I thinking about this the perfect amount because it's important that I make a good impression? If I make a joke, I want it to be funny."

He pulled up in front of a single-story ranch-style house. A truck was parked in front of them, and a small red convertible sat in the driveway.

Jesse turned to her. "You already made a good impression on my family when you met them. And your jokes are always funny."

"Not true. The other day I told you that I might kill off some characters in the book I'm writing and then added that it would spice up my autobiography, and you didn't even crack a smile."

And again now, not even a hint of a smile.

"If anyone's going to kill someone, it's me. You're to stay well away from dangerous situations."

She rolled her eyes as they climbed out, then grabbed the rhubarb pie from the back seat. She'd attempted to make a peach cobbler, but it was a disaster...think burnt crust and over-sweetened filling kind of disaster.

Luckily, Mrs. Gerald saved the day.

"What if they're disappointed that I didn't make the pie?"

Jesse slipped an arm around her waist. "They won't be. But you could always lie to them and tell them you did."

"Um, bad idea. My lying is as bad as my line dancing." Not that she'd done much line dancing in her life. "What if—"

"Aspen." They stopped at the door and Jesse cupped her cheeks. "You could knock the entire pot roast onto the floor, give everyone food poisoning with the pie, and they *still* won't hate you. They will love you."

She swallowed, her gaze shifting to the door, then back to Jesse. "I'm sorry, it's just...my mother's love always felt...conditional. Conditional to me being a certain way and her being in a certain mood. To me making her *feel* a certain way."

His eyes darkened, empathy and maybe a bit of anger skittering across his face. "We're not here to earn anyone's love. It's just a family dinner. And even if we were...you won't get that here. You are safe to be *you* in this family."

Safe...the word felt big and important. "Thank you."

He lowered his head and kissed her. The kiss was calming, when calm was the last thing she'd felt all day.

He lifted his head. "Ready?"

No. "Yes."

He took her hand, opened the door, and led them into an open living-and-kitchen area. His mother stood by the stove, while Clara and Becket seemed to be arguing about something by the fridge.

They all looked up, smiles spreading across their faces.

"Jesse, Aspen, you made it." His mother wiped her hands on a dish towel before moving around the island and tugging Jesse into a hug. When she pulled Aspen into an embrace, it was big and firm and warm, nothing like the hugs she'd received from her own mother over the years...not that they'd hugged that often.

"Thank you for inviting me, Mrs. Hayes."

The older woman stepped back. "Oh please, call me Pam. Anything else makes me feel old. And you are more than welcome."

"What is that divine-looking dessert in your hands?" Clara asked as her mother returned to the kitchen.

"Rhubarb pie from The Tea House." Aspen set the pie onto the island. "It's amazing."

"It looks delicious," Clara said, eyeing the dish. "I've been wanting to stop in there for a while. The desserts always look so good from the window."

"Well, she's actually having a big reopening celebration soon. I was just making fliers today. She'll have free samples of everything."

"This food-loving lady will be there," Becket said, bumping Clara's side with his hip.

Clara whacked his shoulder playfully. "Says the guy who once ate an entire plate of chocolate chip cookies when he was eight."

"And they were delicious."

Clara rolled her eyes, but there was a hint of a smile on her lips.

"It's true," Jesse confirmed. "There had to have been at least two dozen cookies on that plate and he wiped it clean."

"I took it as a compliment," Pam added, eyes warm as she looked at her kids.

"We have way too many stories similar to that one," Clara added.

Becket shook his head at Aspen. "Don't believe anything they say. They struggle with accurate accounts of the past."

Jesse scoffed. "One of us struggles and I'm looking at him."

"Do you see how they pick on me, Aspen?" Becket joked.

Aspen laughed. She'd always wanted a sibling. How lucky they were to have grown up with one another.

Pam watched her kids with affection. It looked like she knew exactly how lucky her family was.

"Can I help with anything?" Aspen asked.

Pam's brows rose. "Well, I would love someone to set the table."

"I can do that." She frowned at the pink roses centering the table.

Jesse gently bumped her hip. "Everything okay?"

"Yeah, I just…they're pretty…the pink roses."

"They're Mom's favorite," Clara said. "We alternate who sends her a bunch each month."

"Because I have wonderful children." Pam beamed.

Those flowers on that receipt…they *had* been for his mother.

"What are you thinking about?" Jesse asked.

She grinned at him. "Just how much I like you."

"Why don't I believe you?"

"All right, I've had enough of you guys, I'm going back to the grill," Becket said as he moved to the back door.

Jesse looked at Aspen. "Are you okay if I…"

"Go."

He leaned down and kissed her cheek. "Be back soon."

She was still watching Jesse as he stepped onto the deck when Clara sighed. "You make him happy. I like that."

She turned back to Jesse's sister. "No. He makes *me* happy."

Pam handed her some plates with cutlery on top. "Thank you, Aspen." But before she could turn, Pam touched her wrist. "Thank you for coming. Not just here tonight, but to Amber Ridge. I haven't seen Jesse smile like this in a long time."

Her heart gave a little kick. "He has the same effect on me."

Pam smiled softly.

When Aspen was done setting the table, she turned to see Clara frowning as she sipped a glass of wine. "I think Mom gave you one too many. There are only five of us."

Pam shook her head. "No, darling, Holden's coming."

Clara choked on the liquid before spinning toward her mother. "Holden's coming?"

At that exact moment, the front door opened and Holden stepped in, a wide smile on his face. "Hey, everyone. I was going to knock but—"

Pam shook her head as she rounded the island. "You don't need to knock. You're family." She pulled him into her arms. "It's so good to see you!"

Holden hugged her back. "You too, Pam."

When they separated, he moved over to Aspen and kissed her cheek. "It's good to see you again so soon."

"Same."

Holden turned to Clara.

Aspen frowned, noticing Jesse's sister was standing ramrod straight. And she almost looked...nervous?

"Hey, Clara," Holden said, his tone lower as he stepped toward her. He embraced her, and when he pulled back, Clara's mouth opened and closed a few times before she spoke.

"Hi. When...um, when did you get here?"

Aspen's lips twitched. She *was* nervous.

"A few days ago." He cocked his head. "I missed you."

"You missed me?"

He chuckled. "Yeah. It's been too long."

"I missed you too." She frowned. "As a friend," she quickly added. "A brother, even."

This time, Holden frowned. "A brother?"

"Well, kind of. I guess. But you aren't my brother. You're Holden. My brother's best friend. Very different. Not as different as a parent or a grandparent, but different."

Aspen grinned. She was rambling and making no sense—and it was definitely because she liked him.

Holden's smile widened. "Thanks for the clarification."

Pam cleared her throat. "The boys are outside."

Holden nodded but didn't take his gaze from Clara. "I'll join them."

The second he stepped outside, Clara dropped her face into her hands and groaned. "It's official...I'm an embarrassment to myself. One big, gigantic puffer fish of embarrassment." She lifted her head. "Not as different as a parent or a grandparent? What's *wrong* with me?"

"Nothing. You're perfect," Pam said as she walked past her daughter back to the kitchen.

Clara rolled her eyes. "You have to say that, you're my mother."

Aspen shook her head. "Not true. My mother has *never* said that to me. In fact, I could count the number of times she's complimented me on one hand."

Clara's eyes widened.

Shit, why had she gone and said that?

Pam almost looked sad. "I'm sorry to hear that, honey. But in this house, you get lots of compliments. It's the rules."

Aspen's heart squeezed. "I think I'm going to like this house."

"It's how we suck you in so you never leave," Clara said with a laugh.

* * *

"Shit, you guys are cute together."

Jesse leaned against the deck railing, beer in hand. "Thanks. Haven't been referred to as cute before, but I do know I'm a lucky bastard to have her."

A bit of the smile slipped from Becket's face. "The way you look at her...it reminds me of the way Dad looked at Mom."

That was a compliment if ever he'd heard one. His parents had loved each other. Like *really* loved each other, right up until the day their father had died. "It's the kind of relationship most dream of."

"I don't think you need to dream."

Even though Becket joked a lot, he had another side that he reserved for family and those closest to him. A side that took life more seriously than he often let on. "I think you're right. What about you? Any love in your future?"

Becket laughed as he turned back to the grill. A full belly laugh, like it was the funniest question he'd ever heard. "No love happening here. In fact, I am so far on the other side of love that I think the woman I see most often might murder me in my sleep."

"What have you done now?"

"Nothing. My neighbor's the one doing stuff. I was just getting home from work the other day and she exploded on me for the new cameras I installed on the side of my house. You should have heard the things she called me. I actually laughed when she used the word 'ogre,' and she looked like she wanted to stab me."

"Dammit, Beck, I'm going to get a call for a neighbor dispute, aren't I?"

"You absolutely will. And on that day, I want you to remember sibling loyalty." Becket flipped the chicken leg. "You can also be witness to how insane she gets. It's kind of cute. Her cheeks get red and her chest puffs up. It's like she forgets she's five foot nothing."

Oh, Jesus. "Beck—"

The back door opened, and Holden stepped out. "Hey. Room for one more?"

"Holden!" Becket pulled him into a hug. "It's good to see you, man."

"You too." When they parted, Holden eyed the grill. "Smells good."

"Pot roast wasn't enough," Becket said. "Mom decided we needed chicken as well. I heard you're living here now."

"I sure am. Just got a place."

"Damn, that's pretty official."

Holden lifted a shoulder. "Well, I tried moving back to Minnesota when the team was honorably discharged, but I can't be there. That's my past. So I thought, what the hell, this town has all my favorite people, I'll try here."

"Pretty good decision if you ask me," Jesse said.

Becket dipped his head. "Me too."

The small smile slipped from Holden's mouth. "Plus, an extra set of eyes around town can't hurt while this asshole ex of Aspen's is around."

Becket turned to Jesse, all humor gone from his face. "Still no word on his whereabouts?"

"No." His fingers tightened around his beer. "He was staying with her mother, but he's left now."

"What the fuck?" Holden cursed.

"Yeah, my thought too."

"We'll find him," Becket said, voice low. Every so often, the deadly former SEAL became obvious in his brother. This was one of those moments.

"I know we will. I just worry about what will come before that."

Over the last few days, a pit had formed in his gut, like his body knew something was coming. And that something felt dark and dangerous and made him want to chain Aspen to his side.

He turned to Holden. "I need a change of subject. Tell me about your new place."

They remained outside, chatting until the chicken was cooked. Over the meal, his family talked and laughed, and Aspen slotted right in as if she'd always been there. And it felt so damn good. And it felt right.

When he and Aspen finally climbed back into his truck, he'd just turned it on when she turned, touching his thigh. "Thank you."

"For what?"

"Sharing your family with me."

Another reason to love his family. They put that radiant fucking smile on her face.

He leaned over and touched a gentle kiss to her forehead before whispering, "Everything that's mine is yours."

When he lifted his head, it was to see tears in her eyes.

"Can I tell you a secret?" she asked quietly.

"Anything."

"I think you're healing all the damaged parts of me."

His heart gave a huge fucking thump. "No one should have hurt you, Aspen. You deserved better. And I will spend the rest of my life *giving* you better."

She tugged his head down and kissed him. A deep kiss. One where her tongue slipped between his lips and tangled with his. A kiss that weaved itself around his heart.

CHAPTER 25

*J*esse strummed his fingers on the wooden desk. He was supposed to be concentrating on writing this report, but he was distracted. Really fucking distracted.

Because Aspen was here.

He had a late shift tonight, and no part of him had wanted her home by herself, and she hadn't liked the idea of a babysitter—her words, not his—so here she was. Working in a room down the hall...within walking distance.

The station was quiet. It was just him, Luke, Claudia and Margot. Although, Luke was due to finish any minute now.

His chest rose and fell as he looked back at the screen.

Concentrate, Jesse. Jesus Christ.

The problem was, he knew exactly why he was itching to go to her. For days now, he'd wanted to tell Aspen that he loved her.

Love... He hadn't said that to a woman he'd dated...possibly ever. But he *did* love Aspen. And seeing her fit in so easily with his family last weekend had just confirmed exactly how right for him she was.

Would it scare her when he said the words? Would she run from him again? Shit, the thought terrified him. It had taken him a long time to convince her that she could trust him.

A knock on the door sounded, and he looked up as Luke walked in. "Hey, boss."

"Hey. You going home?"

"I am." Luke's phone buzzed with a text, and he looked down, only to cringe.

"Everything okay?"

"No. I fucked up."

"Fucked up how?"

Luke closed the door and dropped into the seat opposite Jesse. "There's this girl—"

"Of course there is."

"I've known she's had a thing for me for a while, and over the weekend, we went to the bar. I had a few drinks, so she offered to drive me home, and we…"

"You didn't."

Luke cringed. "I did…and I think I told her I loved her."

"You *think*?"

"We were in bed. It was getting hot and heavy. She said she loved me, and I just…I mumbled an agreement."

"*Luke.*"

"I know! I'm a terrible person! I was drunk and she was naked and…anyway. She's been blowing up my phone ever since."

"You have to be honest with her."

"Yeah. I know." Luke scrubbed his face. "I'm an asshole."

Yeah, in this instance, Jesse agreed.

Luke sighed and rose before moving to the door, only to stop and turn before he walked out. "Things are going well between you and Aspen?"

"They are." Really fucking well.

Luke nodded. "Good. You deserve to be happy. Even if it *does* distract you from your work." He grinned before stepping out.

How the hell did he know how distracted Jesse was? He looked back at his computer screen. Then his gaze quickly shifted to his cell.

Jeez, he had zero self-discipline. None.

He lifted his phone to text her.

Jesse: Are you okay?

Her response was instant.

Aspen: Depends what you mean by okay... I've spent the last hour on the phone with Callie and now I'm staring at a laptop screen.

Jesse: And here I was hoping the distraction had been thoughts of me.

Aspen: Even if it was you, I'd never tell.

Jesse: Why not?

Aspen: Your ego doesn't need the stroking.

Jesse: What if I told you that you're distracting me from my work?

Aspen: I wouldn't be surprised. I'm quite the distraction.

His lips twitched.

Jesse: I'm going to try and do some work now.

Aspen: Try all you want, you won't get me out of your head.

This time he laughed out loud. She was joking, but fuck, she was right.

He turned back to his computer for the fiftieth damn time. He had to get this report written before his shift finished.

Ten minutes passed, and he was finally getting into it when his work phone rang.

Goddammit.

He lifted the phone. "Jesse speaking."

"Jesse, it's Claudia." Wind blew over the line.

He frowned. "Where are you?"

"Outside by the power box. The power went out at our desks while Margot and I were working. I thought I'd check it out, but I can't get the power box door open. Can you come give it a go? I'm assuming it's just a fuse or a tripped switch or something."

He rose. "Margot's still inside?"

"Yeah. She's at her desk."

Good. As long as someone was still in here with Aspen. He sent a quick message to Margot, asking her to watch Aspen, then moved outside. On the side of the building, near the back, he spotted Claudia standing near the power box, flashlight in hand.

She glanced at him. "I don't know what's going on...it's like it's stuck or something."

He stopped beside her and tugged at the metal door. Jesus, it really was stuck.

He pulled harder, but again it didn't budge. He grabbed a pocketknife from his back pocket and slid it into the small gap between the door and the box. It took a few twists and some prying, but the door finally opened.

His gaze went to the switches and then the lining of the door. The *fuck?*

"Someone glued it shut," he muttered, almost to himself.

"Why would anyone do that?"

He opened his mouth to answer Claudia's question, but a distant scream sounded from inside the station—*Aspen's* scream.

* * *

ASPEN PUSHED HER PHONE ASIDE...WAY aside. She needed to stop distracting herself and do some work.

Although, Jesse *had* texted her first, so technically it was his fault. But calling Callie had been all her.

Focus, Aspen. You've almost finished the first draft.

She looked at the words on her laptop screen. Just a couple more chapters and she'd be there. But the ending was always the hardest part...for her, at least. She had to wrap the entire thing up, give her characters the happy ending they deserved, *and* give just a hint of the next story.

The next story... How long would that take her to release? If someone had asked her six months ago, she'd have laughed at their assumption that she'd even finish *this* book. But now? It might not take long at all.

Maybe music would help. When all else failed, music often got her fingers typing.

She was searching through a list of songs when a distant popping noise sounded, followed by a thump.

Her head shot up. What the heck was that?

She remained still as she listened for any more sounds. But there was nothing. In fact, the station sounded eerily quiet.

She nibbled her bottom lip. Should she go check it out?

Ha. What would be her next excuse to get out of writing? That she needed to assist the deputies in their next arrest?

She tapped her foot and looked back at the laptop screen, telling herself that she *needed to write*.

That lasted all of five seconds. She wasn't working anyway; she may as well check out what was going on.

She rose and stepped into the hall, turning left and passing the kitchen to step into the large workspace where all the deputies' desks were located. Only it was dark. Like, pitch-black kind of dark. The lights were off and the blinds down, although it was pretty much dark outside anyway, so open blinds probably wouldn't help much.

What was going on, and where was everyone? She flicked the light switch on the wall just inside the room.

Nothing.

A cool chill slipped over her skin. Something was wrong. There'd been at least three deputies here when she'd arrived with Jesse. Where was everyone?

She needed to find Jesse.

She was mid-turn when she saw it. A shoe sticking out from behind a desk, visible in the light from the hallway. Her heart sped up, and with shaking fingers, she lifted her phone and turned on the flashlight. She moved closer and aimed it at the shoe.

Not just a shoe…a person.

She rounded the desk and her heart stopped.

It was one of the deputies. What was her name? Margot? She lay still on the floor, blood seeping into her clothes from a wound in her chest.

Aspen stumbled back a step.

Shot! Someone had shot her right here in the sheriff's station.

Aspen ran forward and dropped beside her.

Pulse. She needed to find a pulse.

She touched the woman's neck, but there was nothing. She couldn't feel anything.

A choking sound tore from Aspen's throat. She bent down and listened for breathing. Watched for any rise and fall of the other woman's chest.

There was neither.

She was dead.

She fumbled with her phone, trying to find Jesse's name in her contacts. She could barely see anything. Her eyes wouldn't focus and she couldn't think. She finally found Jesse's name and was about to press Call when something sounded behind her—a light shuffle.

She turned her head and screamed at the blur of movement.

Something hit her hard on the head. She hit the floor and the phone fell from her fingers. Pain radiated throughout her skull. She blinked and spotted retreating red sneakers before her eyes closed.

A deep fog tried to pull her under. It was only the sudden sound of pounding footsteps growing closer that had her forcing herself to stay awake.

Was it the killer? Were they coming back to finish her off?

A deep, familiar voice sounded. The words were a blur, but that voice…she'd know it anywhere.

Jesse. He was here. Thank God.

Warm fingers touched her pulse. More indecipherable words, then his palm cupped her cheek, and she finally allowed herself to slip into the darkness, knowing she was safe with him.

CHAPTER 26

*R*age punched through Jesse's gut as he watched the doctor stitch up the wound on Aspen's head. Someone had knocked her out, Margot was *dead*, and it had all happened in his sheriff's office while he'd been outside.

Fuck, he was angry!

He wanted to hit something. Punch his fist through a damn wall and let the pain drown out the other emotions. The fury. The frustration. The fear that had been alive inside him since seeing Aspen still on the floor beside a bleeding Margot.

Was it Dylan? Of course it fucking was. It had been confirmed that he was here in Amber Ridge. He'd probably turned off the power to lure Jesse outside so he could target Aspen...only Margot had gotten in his way and paid the price.

Jesse's hands fisted. He wanted to kick his own ass for going outside. Aspen should have been safe in there. And Margot...shit, Margot was armed and well trained. No one should have gotten the jump on her.

"Okay, all done." The doctor stepped back. "Those are dissolvable stitches, so no need to get them removed. You were unconscious for about ten minutes and suffered a mild concussion. So take it slow for the next couple of weeks."

Aspen nodded. "I will."

Jesse slipped an arm around her waist. She wouldn't just be taking it slow. Jesse would be making sure she barely left the damn house. "Thank you, Doctor."

The young man dipped his head. "You're free to go when you're ready."

The second he stepped out, Jesse shifted in front of Aspen and gripped her hips. He was almost scared to touch her. "How are you feeling?"

There was a flash of something in her eyes...fear? Confusion? Then she blinked, and it was gone. "A bit groggy, but whatever he gave me for the headache is helping."

Jesse ground his teeth together. She shouldn't be in pain at all, dammit. She should have been safe in the station.

A knock on the door had them both turning.

Claudia stuck her head in. "Hey. You got a sec?"

The word "no" was on the tip of his tongue because he wanted to stay with Aspen. But Claudia had lost both a colleague and a friend tonight...they all had.

Aspen touched his arm. "Go. I'll be okay. I want to call Callie anyway."

He leaned down and pressed a gentle kiss to her forehead. "Call out if you need me."

"I will."

He crossed to the door but kept it open as he spoke to Claudia in the hall. "Did we get the asshole on camera?"

Please say yes. He needed solid evidence against Dylan so that every organization in the state was on the lookout for him.

She shook her head. "No."

"*What?* Why not? We have cameras at both the front and back exits of the building. We should have caught him entering *and* leaving."

"When the lights went off, so did the power to the cameras. It's like this person knew exactly which switches to flip."

Or he was the luckiest bastard around. Jesse scrubbed a hand over his face.

"Does she remember anything about the guy?" Claudia asked.

"Red shoes. She said everything was a blur, but she remembered the red shoes."

"It's something." She studied his face. "Want me to wait here?"

"No. You get back to the station. Unless you need to go home. Are you doing okay?"

A mixture of sadness and anger flashed over her face before she straightened. "I'm angry. And I need to keep busy right now. I'll head back to the station and call the rest of the deputies to let them know about Margot. I'll also see how the cleanup's going."

Cleanup...the cleanup from Margot's murder.

The band tightened around his chest. "Look after yourself, Claudia. And let me know if you need me to make some of the calls."

She nodded and had just turned to head down the hall when his phone rang, Luke's name on the screen. Jesse had left a message for him, asking him to call. As Luke's friend, he needed to take care of that himself. He wasn't sure exactly where the man's feelings sat with Margot, but regardless, the two had been close.

He shot a look at Aspen to see her still on the phone before answering the call. "Luke."

"Jesse...hey. Got your message. Everything okay down at the station? Or are you missing my witty humor already? I wouldn't blame you."

Jesse swallowed. "Something happened tonight."

"Cryptic. What kind of something?"

"The bad kind. Margot was shot."

An audible gasp sounded over the line. "Shot? What the fuck? Is she okay?"

"She's dead."

There was a pause. *"Dead?"*

"I'm sorry. I know you and her had a thing and—"

"Who did it?" There was a new edge to Luke's voice, one Jesse had never heard before. It was low and full of rage.

"I assume Dylan, as a way to get to Aspen, but we don't have any evidence. The killer turned the power off, which disconnected the cameras." At Luke's silence, Jesse ran his fingers through his hair. "I'm sorry. If you need some time off—"

"No. I'm heading into the station now."

"Luke—"

"I'm *going*, Jesse. I'm helping get to the bottom of this."

Jesse looked up to see two familiar people walking down the hall—Becket and Holden. Jesse had texted both when he'd gotten to the hospital.

"Okay," he finally responded. "Call if you need anything, Luke."

He hung up.

Jesus. What a fucking mess.

He turned to his brother and best friend. "Hey."

"How's Aspen?" Becket asked, an anger in his eyes that matched Jesse's.

His family was loyal, and the second Aspen had been introduced as his, she'd become part of that family. And today, their family had been threatened. "She's doing as well as can be expected."

"Are you thinking this was Dylan, and your deputy got in the way?" Holden asked.

Of course he was on the same page. They'd served on the same Ghost Ops team for so many years that they knew how each other's minds worked. "It's the most obvious conclusion."

Becket's gaze moved in either direction along the hall before landing back on Jesse. "We'll watch the hall and trail you both home."

Exactly why he'd called them. His deputies were good, but they weren't former special operations like Becket and Holden.

"I appreciate it." He nodded before heading back into the room just as Aspen was hanging up. "Get through to Callie okay?"

She nodded, but she looked pale.

Shit, he needed to get her home. He cupped her cheek. "Ready to go?"

"Past ready."

"Me too." He slipped an arm around her and led her out of the room, Holden and Becket sticking close.

It was late. She should be in bed. But Jesse was talking to deputies on the phone while he made hot drinks, and she knew if she got into bed alone, she wouldn't sleep. Because every time she closed her eyes, she felt Margot's warm but lifeless skin beneath her fingertips. Saw the crimson blood soaked into her uniform like it was still right in front of her.

She swallowed, watching Jesse as he balanced the phone between his shoulder and ear and poured hot milk into a mug while she sat on the couch.

He was certain this was Dylan. And yeah, there didn't seem to be anyone else it *could* be. But then that made Margot's death her fault, right? Or at least partially her fault. Dylan wouldn't be here in Amber Ridge if it wasn't for her. And he wouldn't have been at the station tonight if she hadn't been working there. That meant Margot would still be alive if it wasn't for her.

The thought sat in her belly like an immovable rock, weighing her down. Pressing on her.

Jesse hung up the phone and turned, two mugs in hand. He looked so big and strong and angry. He was trying to hide that anger, but she could see it in the darkening of his eyes. In the tensing of his jaw.

He handed her a mug. "Here, I made you a hot cocoa. My sister also gave me something to put in it. Don't ask me what, but she said something about a calming herb."

"Thank you." She took the mug from his fingers and the warmth slipped down her arms, moving beneath the surface of her skin.

Jesse sat beside her, but he felt too far away. She wanted to shift closer. Heck, every part of her craved the closeness of crawling onto his lap and pressing into him.

She didn't. Because she blamed herself for him losing one of his deputies tonight?

She lowered her gaze to her mug. "Does Margot's family live here in Amber Ridge?"

Jesse shook his head. "No. They live in Bozeman. Claudia called them."

She nodded.

"Hey. Don't do that."

Her head shot up. "Do what?"

"Blame yourself for what that piece of shit did."

She wanted to ask him how to *stop* blaming herself, but the words never made it out, because she had a feeling that no matter what he said, it wouldn't change her mind.

"What got you into writing romance books?"

Her brows flickered. He was asking her about work? She nibbled her bottom lip before lifting a shoulder. "I love to read. It led me to study creative writing. One of our assignments was to write a chapter of a story. The only guideline we had was that it had to be emotional. I finished the assignment, but then I couldn't stop. I kept writing until I had a complete book. I remember I couldn't believe how easy it felt, like I'd finally found what I was supposed to do with my life."

"And then you published it?"

"I did. I decided to self-publish because I thought, why not... and people read it. So I did it again. And people read that one too. That's when I figured out that I could actually be a writer. There's a bit more to it than that, with editing and cover design and marketing, but that's the simple, condensed version."

"Why romance?"

"So many reasons. The guaranteed happy ending. The ability to create flawed characters who fall in love. The escapism."

"Have you ever written a character based on you?"

Despite everything, she laughed. "Maybe a funnier, more put-together version of me."

"I can't see how that's possible."

She almost snorted.

His gaze was intense as it beamed into her. "So you must believe in love."

"I stopped believing for a while after Dylan." Her gaze returned to her cocoa. She watched the steam swirl into the air. "I think that's why I couldn't write for so long. It felt pointless, like I was writing about a type of man who didn't exist. A love that seemed *so* fictional, it felt forced when I read my work back."

His brows slashed together but he didn't say anything, just waited, like he knew she had more to say.

"It wasn't just my writing that he affected. What he did to me affected so many facets of my life. For a while, I lost faith in my own judgment." She looked up, that old familiar regret tightening her chest. "I *liked* him at the start. I didn't see what I should have seen. I thought..." She laughed, but there was no humor. "I thought he was a good guy. How stupid was I?"

Jesse slipped her mug from her fingers and set it onto the coffee table. She gasped in surprise when he reached over and easily lifted her onto his lap so her legs straddled him.

"You're not stupid. Men like Dylan make hiding their true colors an art form. They have to. Otherwise, they'd have no one to prey on." He cupped her cheek. "You'd have never seen that part of him until he wanted you to."

She swallowed the lump in her throat. It felt big and painful. "But if I hadn't fallen for his act, then none of this would be happening, and Margot—"

"It's *not* your fault."

The way he said it, with so much conviction, made her *want* to believe it. And it lifted a bit of that suffocating weight from her chest.

She pressed her palms to his chest. "I think it was you."

"What was?"

"You restored my faith in love."

His eyes darkened. Then his hand slipped behind her neck as he kissed her. There was nothing sexual about the kiss. It was comfort. Calm. And maybe something else. Something deeper... more healing.

The second their mouths parted, she pressed her head to his chest, right over his heart, while his arms wrapped tightly around her. Somewhere along the way, he'd become her safety. And right now, he felt like the only thing keeping her head above water.

CHAPTER 27

*J*esse shot a glance at Luke behind the wheel. They were driving to a callout and his friend was quiet. Had *been* quiet for the last week, since Margot was shot and killed.

"How are you doing, Luke? And tell me the truth. I don't care if it's messy."

Luke's jaw clenched. "I don't have a right to be upset. We weren't in a relationship. She wasn't my girlfriend. She wasn't my anything."

"Doesn't matter. You cared about her."

"I did." He turned right. "I'm angry. Really fucking angry."

"Me too, brother."

"Why haven't we found that asshole yet? Where is he?"

Jesse would pay good money to have the answer to that question. The entire station had been searching every goddamn day, but so far, nothing.

"I don't know," Jesse finally said, frustration leaching into his words. "But when we find him—and we *will* find him—he'll pay for what he did."

The asshole would never see freedom again. Jesse would make

sure of it. And people who killed law enforcement did *not* do well behind bars.

Luke didn't respond, but Jesse didn't miss the tightening of his fingers around the wheel.

The only good thing to come out of the last few days was George's call to confirm that Aspen's mother had finally checked out. Apparently, one of the two keys he'd left with Karen was missing, but if she or Dylan tried to enter the house again, they'd be caught on the surveillance cameras.

With any luck, she was already back in Misty Peak.

"So this is a neighbor dispute about a fence?" Jesse asked, trying to get his friend's mind onto something else.

"When's a neighbor dispute *not* about a fence?"

When Luke took another left, Jesse frowned. "Who made the complaint?"

"Uh...a Sky Williams, I believe."

Sky... As in his brother's *neighbor*, Sky?

Sure enough, they turned onto his brother's street, and he spotted Becket in front of his house, arms crossed, and a woman standing opposite him. They each stood on their own side of the yard, and there was a white truck on the street with what looked like fencing materials in the back.

Shit.

Luke frowned. "Hey, isn't that—"

"My brother."

Luke pulled over in front of Becket's house, and Jesse climbed out to hear his brother scoff. "You called the *sheriff* on me?"

"You're obstructing the fence from going up," Sky sneered. "Of course I called the sheriff."

Jesse walked over to the woman. "Miss Williams, I'm Sheriff Jesse Hayes, and this is Deputy Luke Pine. Can you tell me what's going on?"

"I got a Planning Division permit for a fence to be built

between our properties, and this *jackass* is stopping it from going up."

Well, Jesse agreed with one thing, his brother *could* be a jackass.

Becket lifted his hands. "Hey, I'm just standing here. They stopped working of their own accord."

The woman's eyes flared. "You threatened them! You said if they put one hole in the ground, you'd *hurt* them."

"I was a bit more specific than that. I said I'd kick their asses, then make sure they never worked a day again due to property damage."

Jeez.

"If she has a permit, she can put up the fence," Luke said.

"She didn't get the *right* permit," Becket corrected.

The woman's back straightened, and she waved a piece of paper. "I sure as hell did. I already said I got a Planning Division permit, which is what's required for—"

"A fence between four and seven feet tall," Becket cut in. "I asked them for the dimensions. The fence they've got is eight feet. You need a *building* permit."

Sky's jaw dropped, and Luke walked over to the men in the truck, no doubt to ask them about the height of the fence.

Jesse turned to the woman, his tone apologetic. "Technically, that information is correct."

Becket lifted a shoulder. "If my brother says it's true, it must be."

"Your *brother*?" Sky asked.

Luke returned. "The guys confirmed the fence is eight feet."

Becket smiled at the woman. "Sorry, peaches. No fence for you."

Was he *trying* to antagonize her?

Sky spun toward Jesse and Luke. "His camera films my front yard. Surely that's not legal?"

"Unfortunately, there's no law that says his camera can't cover a front yard where the public can see." Jesse almost wished there was, just because his brother was obviously getting a kick out of his neighbor's frustration.

Becket crossed his arms. "Told ya."

Sky's chest rose and fell with an exasperated breath before she threw her arms up in frustration. "Fine!" She stormed into her house.

Jesse looked at his brother. "Stop smiling."

"But she's so cute when she's mad."

"You're an asshole."

Becket's smile widened. "Never said I wasn't. Should I break the news to the fence guys?"

Luke sighed. "I'll do it."

After Becket threatened them, Luke was probably the safer bet.

As Luke walked away, Jesse cocked his head. "Why don't you want her to have a fence? She's already purchased it. At worst, you're just putting off the inevitable and inconveniencing these workers who have to haul the fencing materials back to their facility and store them until Sky gets the correct permit."

"I'm just following the law."

No. It was more than that and they both knew it. "Becket—"

"Want to come in for a coffee?"

Jesse shook his head. "We've got to get back. Just try to keep your neighbors happy so I'm not called back down here."

"Hey, every other neighbor loves me."

Jesse scoffed as he turned toward the car. "No more calls, Becket."

Once he and Luke were back in the car, they returned to the station. Luke followed him into his office.

"Lucky you didn't have to arrest your brother."

Jesse laughed as he lowered behind his desk. "If he actually did something wrong, I'd happily arrest him."

"Well, if I ever catch him breaking any laws, I'll call you and you can do the honors."

Jesse powered on his computer, and when he looked back at Luke, he frowned. There were dark circles under his friend's eyes. "Remember, if you need to take some time off—"

"No." Luke shook his head. "I want to be here. I *need* to be here. At least until we find the asshole who killed Margot."

Jesse nodded. He understood that. He'd feel the same way.

He opened his emails and frowned at the most recent one.

The Sheriff's Professional Standards Bureau.

What the hell did they want?

He clicked into it and skimmed the email before cursing.

Luke inched closer. "What?"

"Someone put in a complaint about me."

"A complaint? Who? And saying what?"

He skimmed the screen. "It was an anonymous complaint. But they're claiming I'm not doing my job properly. That I'm distracted. Working on personal matters. And a deputy died under my watch."

Who the hell had done this?

* * *

"So this is The Tea House I've heard so much about," Holden said, stepping inside.

Aspen nodded. "It is. Does it live up to the hype?"

"I kind of expected more curtains and carpet and high tea towers."

"Nope." Aspen slid into a booth. "This is more of a modern café tea house. It even has a mezzanine area, not that I ever sit there. I've become quite accustomed to my window booth. And the pie. I've become super-accustomed to that."

Holden cocked his head. "Why have you gotten so invested in this place?"

It was a fair question. They'd just spent the morning spreading fliers around town about the reopening.

She lifted a shoulder. "I like Mrs. Gerald. She kind of reminds me of the grandmother I never had. I also like this café. And when she told me that she was close to shutting down, I felt sad. I needed a project to throw myself into, to distract myself from all the other stuff. And did I mention the pie?"

He laughed. "You did. You may remember I tried the pie at Pam's place. It was good."

"It's not good. It's blow-your-mind amazing."

Holden laughed again.

She nibbled her bottom lip as she cast her gaze to Mrs. Gerald, who was behind the counter talking to a customer. "I hate that I have to tell her I can't attend the reopening."

She and Jesse had argued about it, and of course he was right. It was safest for her not to be in a roomful of people. Still, she felt like she was letting Mrs. Gerald down.

"She'll understand," Holden said quietly.

She would, but it would be disappointing for both of them, especially when Aspen had offered to help. "I told her I'd help hand out cake and coffee."

"I could always do it. People often tell me I have a certain charm. Add pie to the mix and I'll be fighting the customers off."

Aspen laughed as Mrs. Gerald stopped at their table. "Aspen. Hi. I'm glad you came in today."

"You are?"

"Yes, I got the new coffee beans, *and* the coffee machine was delivered earlier this week."

Aspen's brows rose. "Really?"

"Yep, and the lovely man who delivered it spent over an hour showing me how to use it. Thank you for encouraging me to do this. I wouldn't have had the courage without you. I've ordered you a shirt and had it personalized with your name!"

Aspen's heart dropped. "You did?"

"I did. Oh, and I've been baking up a storm. Apple pies. Strudel. Scones. All your favorites. I'll get you to hand them out—you're so good at talking up my pies. I've even been tinkering with some new recipes." The older woman reached down and took Aspen's hand. "This entire thing has just renewed my love of my shop, and it's all because of you. Thank you! I'll make a coffee for you both."

Then she was gone before Aspen could utter a word.

Aspen turned to Holden. "I can't do it."

"She made you a shirt."

"With my name on it! And she's making all my favorite pies for me to hand out." She nibbled her bottom lip as she glanced at Mrs. Gerald, then back to Holden. "I have to go to the reopening."

He lifted a brow. "Jesse won't be happy."

"I know, but you'll be there, and Becket will be there, and the three of you are super-badass former special forces soldiers. I can't think of anywhere I'd be safer."

"Your living room, where an entire town isn't squashed inside with you."

She frowned. "Whose side are you on?" Yes, he was Jesse's best friend, but after spending the entire morning together, she'd thought she'd earned some loyalty.

He leaned forward. "Keeping the woman my best friend loves safe. *That* side."

Her heart jolted. Love… It was a big word. One she and Jesse hadn't directly used yet.

Mrs. Gerald returned with two mugs of coffee. She set them onto the table. "Okay, tell me what you think. And be honest."

Aspen lifted the mug. She was kind of nervous. What if it was still bad? What if Mrs. Gerald had spent all that time and money improving her coffee and it wasn't any better?

She sipped her hot drink—and her eyes widened. "Holy crap. This is good. *Ridiculously* good." The first good cup of coffee she'd had outside of Jesse's home since arriving in Amber Ridge.

"You're not just saying that, are you?" the older woman asked.

"Absolutely not."

Holden tried his. "Jesus, this is like crack."

Mrs. Gerald frowned. "Crack?"

Aspen grinned as she touched her arm. "It's good. And once the town tries this and your pies, you'll be fighting off customers."

Mrs. Gerald sighed. "Oh, what a relief!" Then she touched Aspen's shoulder. "You've really saved me, dear. Thank you."

"No, this is all you."

A part of her didn't want to share her favorite café with more people, but better to share it than for the poor woman to go out of business.

Mrs. Gerald returned to the counter just as the door opened and Clara stepped in. Her gaze hit Aspen first, and she smiled... then it shifted to Holden. Her eyes flared and she stopped in her tracks. It almost looked like she was considering turning and walking out again.

Aspen bit back a laugh.

She didn't. She went to the counter.

Okay, Aspen needed to know what was going on between those two. Clara had acted so strange, almost nervous, around Holden at the family dinner, and now she was doing it again.

Aspen looked at Holden, who was watching Clara closely... almost possessively.

"Hey," Clara said when she finally stopped at the table. She shot a glance at Holden before shifting her gaze back to Aspen. "What are you guys doing here?"

Definitely not what she was supposed to be doing, which was pulling out of the reopening.

"We just tried the new coffee," Holden said. "It's good."

Clara swallowed as her gaze returned to him. "Good. That's good. We need a good coffee place here in town." She looked back to Aspen. "And are you okay? After everything that happened last week at the station?"

Her chest tightened. She hated remembering that night. "I'm okay."

Clara nodded. "Good. Remember, if you need any acupuncture to help your nervous system, don't hesitate to come by."

"Thank you." She'd never been into acupuncture, but maybe she should give it a try. She certainly needed to give *something* a try after all the stress.

Mrs. Gerald stopped beside Clara. "Here you go. One sweet tea."

Clara took the drink. "Thank you." Then she turned back to them...well, mostly to Aspen. She didn't look at Holden again. "I'll see you guys later."

The second she was out of the café, Aspen cocked her head at Holden. "So...I'm not sure if we're at the stage of this friendship where I can ask, but...do you and Clara have a history?"

"A history?"

"Have you ever dated?"

He turned his head to look outside, and she followed his gaze to where Clara was climbing into her convertible. "She's my best friend's little sister. That's it."

Nope. The romance writer in Aspen didn't believe it. Hell, a nun wouldn't believe it. Either something was going on between those two, or something was *going* to go on.

CHAPTER 28

"*H*e's never going to allow you to go to the reopening."

Aspen's back straightened, her fingers around the phone tightening. "Allow? Callie, I am a fully grown, independent woman. *I* decide what I do and don't do."

Her best friend scoffed. "Not when you're with an uber-protective, knows-fifty-ways-to-kill-a-man guy who is aware that your psycho ex is in town."

"Humph." She dropped back onto the couch. "When you put it that way, it doesn't sound great, but I'm going to that opening. I want to be there for Mrs. Gerald."

She glanced at the door. Holden was out there doing a perimeter check. If it wasn't for Callie on the phone, the house would feel entirely too quiet.

"She really means that much to you?"

Aspen fiddled with a loose thread on her jeans. "I see her every day. And she tells me about her grandson in Ohio. And her life in Manchester before The Tea House. And she always asks me about my life too. And when I speak, she listens. Not like those people who ask but their gaze is barely on you. She focuses on me and what I'm saying and, I don't know, I just really like her and her shop."

Callie was silent for a moment, and when she spoke again, her voice softened. "That town, and the people in it, have become your family."

Huh. She hadn't thought about it that way, but it was true. "Yeah."

"I'm happy for you."

"Really?"

"Yes. Do I miss you? Like crazy. Do I selfishly wish my best friend still lived in Misty Peak? Absolutely. But I love you so much that your happiness comes first. And if Amber Ridge has become your home, then I just have to accept you're not coming back."

"But we're still visiting each other, right?"

"Of course! If Mr. Overprotective would let me go there right now, we'd be having this conversation on Jesse's couch."

Nope. That was not happening, and not just because her best friend was pregnant.

"Jesse's not home yet?" Callie asked.

She shot a glance at the door. "Not yet. Holden's still outside checking that we're safe, but I'm not allowed to open the door for anyone, even if I know them."

"So, no takeout?"

"No takeout. Holden and I made some pasta bake, and we left some for Jesse in case he doesn't eat at work." She hated when Jesse did a night shift, and after Margot's death, he didn't want her working at the station anymore.

Her heart gave a little squeeze in her chest like it did anytime she thought about Margot.

Aspen sucked in a long breath. "I'm going to tell him I love him." Her heart gave a big, giant thump just saying the words to her friend.

Callie gasped. "Wow, Aspen, that's huge."

"It *is* huge. Do you think it's too soon?"

"No such thing. We don't decide when we love someone. Our heart does that for us, and we have absolutely no control over that organ."

She chuckled before quickly sobering. "What if he doesn't say it back?"

"Are you serious? I think that man fell in love with you the day he first laid eyes on you."

She scoffed. "You mean the night in the bar when Dylan dragged me outside—"

"And Jesse went after you and hit him? Yeah, that night."

She nibbled her bottom lip, that night still so fresh in her mind it was like it had happened yesterday. "I wish I'd pressed charges right then and there. Maybe then he'd know I was stronger and braver, and he wouldn't have thought he could follow me here."

"Aspen...everything he's done has everything to do with him, and *nothing* to do with you."

"Jesse's different." It had taken her time to trust that, but she was finally there.

"Jesse is Dylan's polar opposite, and he would *never* hurt you."

The click of the front door opening had her gaze shooting up. "Holden's back."

But it wasn't just Holden who stepped inside; Jesse was right behind him.

And man, he always looked so good in a uniform, with his broad shoulders and thick chest.

"I'll let you go," Callie said. "Good luck."

She watched as the two men spoke before Holden waved goodbye to her and stepped out.

"Thanks," Aspen said quietly to Callie. "I'm gonna need it."

She hung up as Jesse closed and locked the door. Then his gaze immediately went to her, moving up and down her body as if he needed the visual confirmation that she was okay.

"Hey. Have you been okay?"

"I've been great. Holden was a great babysitter."

"Not babysitter—protector." He dropped his bag, moved over to the couch and sat beside her. "I missed you." He leaned forward and kissed her.

Oh, God, his kisses...they softened every muscle in her body and made her want to melt into him.

No. She had things to talk to him about.

She pressed her hands to his chest and pushed.

He lifted his head and frowned, grazing a lock of hair from her cheek. "What's wrong?"

"Nothing, I just...I need to ask you something. *No,* not ask, tell. I need to tell you something."

His lips twitched. "Okay."

"I'm going to The Tea House's reopening."

The smile dropped. "No."

"Yes."

"*No.*"

"Jesse—"

"You've invited the entire damn town to that thing. The place will be crawling with people, and it will be too hard to maintain a visual on you."

"But it won't. You'll be there, and so will your brother and Holden. And you all know what Dylan looks like."

"No."

Goddammit.

"Fine." She pushed to her feet and got two steps away before strong fingers wrapped around her wrist and tugged her down on top of him.

She gasped, straddling his hips.

"Aspen." He cupped her cheek. "I *need* to keep you safe. That need is so strong, even the *thought* of having you near crowds makes me want to drag you back here and lock the door. Is that healthy? Probably not. Do I care? Hell no. Dylan almost *killed* the last woman he was obsessed with."

"I know that. I think about it every day. I think about *Margot's body* every time I close my eyes. But I also don't want to hide. We don't know how long this will go on. I need to live my life." And hiding meant he won, right?

Jesse's jaw clicked. He wasn't happy, and dammit, she didn't want to make him unhappy. But this was important.

She skimmed her hands down his shirt. "What about a compromise? We stay for an hour. I help Mrs. Gerald, make sure the event's going well, hand out some cakes. And you don't take your eyes off me."

His brows slashed together, something akin to pain in his eyes.

This time she cupped *his* cheek, his day-old stubble scratching her palm. "Please. One hour."

His forehead lowered to hers, his eyes closing. His chest rose and fell before he said, "Okay."

"Really?"

His head lifted. "I'd do anything for you. You know that, right?"

His brown eyes beamed into hers, the gold specks standing out like stars in a dark sky. God, he was beautiful. And this beautiful man cared about her. Wanted to *protect* her.

"I love you." The words fell from her lips. It was like the fear just vanished. She *loved* him. She loved him so much that she needed those words out in the world. She needed to give them to him.

His fingers tightened on her hips, his eyes darkening. "Say it again."

"I love you, Jesse Hayes. For a while, I stopped believing in love. I stopped believing in the goodness of men. But you...you are *all* good, and you reminded me that love exists." She shifted her gaze between his eyes. "You don't need to say it back, I just—"

"I love you too."

Her body seized and the air in her lungs got stuck. He loved her. This beautiful, selfless man, who'd entered her life when she'd needed him most, *loved* her. "Really?"

"I love everything about you, Aspen. Even the things you think are unlovable." Then his mouth crashed to hers.

* * *

JESSE LOST himself in the kiss. In Aspen's warmth…her softness.

She loved him. Hearing her say those words was the closest he'd ever come to *that* feeling. The one where everything felt so right and perfect, he knew if he even blinked everything would be different.

He slid his hand up her side, gently pushing her shirt up as he went. She lifted her arms, and he tugged the top over her head and dropped it to the floor.

His was next. Then her mouth returned to his, but this time her lips parted, and he slipped his tongue inside, touching hers. Tasting her.

He cupped her breast, his thumb finding her hard nipple through the material and swiping it back and forth.

She sighed, her head tilting back, and the sound weaved its way inside him.

God, he loved every sound she made.

He trailed kisses down her neck, then chest. Her skin was warm and soft, and it called to him. Made him want to touch and taste every inch of her. Learn her…memorize her body.

He wrapped his lips around her nipple, only the thin material of her bra separating them, and sucked. The sound that tore from her lips was something between a cry and a whimper, and he wanted to bottle it up.

He switched to her other breast, flicking the tight bud with his tongue, rolling it in a circle. But soon, it wasn't enough. He needed more of her. He needed skin against skin.

He reached behind her and unclasped her bra. It dropped to the floor with a delicate thud, and the second her breasts were free, he was cupping them. Holding their soft weight in the palms of his hands.

"You drive me crazy, Aspen." He lowered his head, wrapped his lips around her nipple and swirled that beautiful bud with his tongue.

She grabbed strands of his hair and pulled as she groaned. "God, Jesse."

He grazed her nipple with his teeth, blood roaring through his veins at those cries she made. He fucking burned for her.

He turned them and laid her on the couch. He held her gaze, getting lost in her blue eyes as he removed her jeans and panties. Then she was naked beneath him.

"Perfect," he whispered, unable to keep the word inside. "You're perfect."

He ran kisses down her neck, her chest, her stomach, before dipping his head between her legs. She went quiet under him. Then he ran his tongue over her clit. Her entire body jolted, and he gripped her hips, steadying her. He licked her again, but this time in a circular motion.

Every swipe made her body tremble beneath him, had her releasing sweet moans into the room.

He wrapped his mouth around her and sucked.

He wanted more tastes. To take everything she had to give. But she gripped his shoulders and tugged. "Jesse...please."

He kissed a path back up her stomach, then wrapped his lips around her nipple and sucked before returning to her mouth.

Almost desperately, she reached between them and unzipped his pants. He pushed them and his briefs down, then stood to shove them off completely. The second he was back with her, she reached between them and wrapped her fingers around his cock.

His entire body froze. He went so fucking still, he wasn't even sure he was breathing.

She slid her hand up and circled her thumb over his tip. He buried his head in the crook of her neck. He was so hard it hurt. *Jesus.*

She explored him, changing the pace of her strokes, her hold on him growing firmer. It was fucking torture. When he couldn't take it anymore, he gripped her wrist.

"Aspen...I need you."

"You have me."

He reached down to his pants on the floor and pulled his wallet from the pocket. He took out the condom he'd only recently started keeping there and tore it open with his teeth. The second it was on, he positioned himself at her entrance. But he didn't move right away.

Instead, he got lost in her eyes again. Eyes that would forever see into his soul. "Say it one more time."

She cupped both his cheeks. "I love you, Jesse."

His chest contracted and he lowered himself. Once he was seated deep inside her, every muscle in his body tightened again, and for a moment he couldn't move.

She lifted her head and nibbled his bottom lip. Her hips rotated in a little circle, and it fucking killed him.

He bit back a curse before lifting his hips and pushing back inside her.

Air whooshed from her chest, whispering over his face. He continued to move, lifting up and thrusting back down as he cupped her breast, once again pulsing her nipple between his thumb and forefinger.

She groaned and arched, her fingers sliding into his hair and tugging.

When he lifted his head, the world narrowed to only her. To her head flung back, eyes closed.

"Fucking gorgeous." The words had no sooner left his lips

than he was kissing her again. Tasting her sweetness as his tongue tangled with hers.

Quickly, he spun them so she was on top. She gasped but didn't miss a beat, lifting her hips and lowering back down.

He ran his thumb over her clit, and she groaned, her movement growing faster. Her breasts bounced as her thrusts became more desperate. He continued to swipe and stroke her clit, and he knew the exact moment she was on the edge. Her muscles tensed, her breaths shortening. Then she cried out as she broke.

Jesse kept rubbing his thumb over her clit, his eyes never leaving her. But when her walls clenched one last time around him, he couldn't stop himself. His entire body stiffened, then broke. He growled as he gripped her hips and thrust up inside her. Three thrusts...it was all he had left. Then he dropped to the couch, his chest pumping as the air barely made it into his lungs.

Aspen dropped onto his chest, and his arms wrapped around her. And suddenly he knew, this was his new favorite place, the only place he wanted to be—wherever this woman was.

CHAPTER 29

*J*esse's fingers tightened around the wheel. He'd had a bad feeling in his gut all morning.

He shot a glance in his rearview mirror. Nothing. No tail, anyway. But that didn't make him feel any better.

It was the evening of The Tea House's reopening. Holden and Becket were meeting them there, but so was the entire damn town. How many people would be there? Would they get in the way of protecting Aspen?

Aspen placed her palm on his thigh. "I'm so excited for Mrs. Gerald. I really hope the town comes, falls in love with her tea house, and her business flourishes."

At least one of them was excited. "As the only place in Amber Ridge that now sells a decent cup of coffee, I think Mrs. Gerald is going to be inundated with customers."

Aspen's smile widened, and *that* was exactly why he was doing this. He'd do anything to see that damn smile.

She leaned her head back against the headrest and glanced at him. "Do you ever imagine our lives if you hadn't offered me the spare bedroom in your home? I'd still be in Misty Peak, dealing with my overbearing mother and ex, but by myself. And you wouldn't have me."

He knew she meant it as a joke, but the very thought of not having her made him feel raw inside. "Don't say that too loud. We'll blink and none of this will be real." He lifted her hand off his thigh and kissed the inside of her wrist. "Thank you for saying yes."

"Best yes I've ever given."

He pulled into the parking lot behind The Tea House. Cars already filled the lot, and he hated that. He'd wanted to get here early, before the place filled up, but Aspen had distracted him with...other things, and leaving the house had taken far longer than it should have.

He climbed out and scanned the parking lot. People were climbing out of cars. Others were moving toward the building. None of them looked at him or Aspen, and none of them were Dylan.

When Aspen stepped beside him, he slipped an arm around her waist and headed toward the shop door. They were almost at the entrance when he paused, tugging her to a stop with him as he wrapped both arms around her waist.

She frowned and pressed her hands to his chest. "Jesse, what are—"

He kissed her, swiping his lips across hers and tugging her entire body flush against his.

He didn't want the kiss to end. He wanted to pause this moment and stay exactly as they were. It took far too much willpower to lift his head. And when he did, his eyes bore into her blue ones.

"Remember...stick close."

She tilted her head, a small hint of a smile spreading across her lips. "I'll never be more than a foot or two away."

"Have I told you I love you today?"

"About six times, but I was really hoping for that seventh."

"I love you."

Her eyes softened. "I love you too."

A throat cleared behind him. "Are we interrupting something?"

His lips twitched at the sound of his sister's voice, and he turned to see both Clara and his mother standing there.

He leaned down and kissed his mother's cheek. "Hi, Mom."

Clara hugged Aspen before grinning at him. "Is my badass big brother so in love that he can't go five minutes without kissing his woman?"

He grabbed her and lightly ruffled her hair, not caring about all the people passing.

Clara laughed and shoved him.

His mother wrapped an arm around Aspen's waist. "Let's go inside, honey. These two might be a while."

Jesse chuckled and followed. The second he was inside though, the smile fell. Too many people. Far too fucking many. He returned to Aspen's side. As they moved deeper into the room, he spotted Holden. Good. Now he just needed his brother and he'd feel semi-okay.

Holden dipped his head as he and Aspen stopped in front of him. "Hey."

Aspen smiled. "Hi, Holden."

"Sorry we're late." Technically, they weren't late, just later than they'd told Holden they'd arrive.

"You're fine. Is Becket still coming?"

Jesse frowned. "He's not here yet?"

"I haven't seen him."

Jesse searched the floor, then the mezzanine level upstairs. There were plenty of people but, as far as he could see, his brother wasn't one of them.

"He's probably just running late." Holden's gaze moved behind them. "I'm going to say hi to your mom and sister." Holden gripped his shoulder before stepping away.

Aspen inched closer. "Can I ask you something?"

"If it's whether we can leave, then the answer is yes."

She rolled her eyes, but there was a smile on her face as she did it. "Have Holden and Clara ever…"

When she didn't finish, Jesse frowned. "Dated?"

"Well, yeah."

"No. Why?"

She lifted a shoulder. "Just wondering."

Jesse looked behind him at Holden, Clara and his mother. They were standing in a circle talking, and as far as he could tell, everything seemed normal.

He'd never even considered them dating a possibility. Would he care if they did? He wasn't sure. Holden was one of the best guys he knew, and he trusted him with his life. But his best friend and his sister would be a strange concept to wrap his head around. And ever since Clara had been sick, he and Becket had been more protective of her.

"Aspen! Jesse!"

He turned back to see Mrs. Gerald joining them. The older woman gave Jesse a hug, then Aspen, before pulling back and looking at Aspen's shirt. "It looks great on you."

The T-shirt had "The Tea House" across the top, with a teapot graphic beneath, and on the back was Aspen's name.

Aspen beamed. "Thank you. I'm here to help, so put me to work."

"But just for an hour," Jesse added quickly.

They'd told The Tea House owner that they had a last-minute appointment they couldn't get out of. It was a shitty excuse for a Sunday night, but it was all they had.

"One hour," Aspen confirmed, reaching up and kissing him before following the older woman.

He was still watching them, following at a discreet distance, when his phone rang.

Becket.

He answered the call. "Hey. You close?"

A car engine sounded over the line. "I'm sorry, man. I was on my way, but I've been called into work. There's a huge fire in Bozeman, and they've called us in for backup."

Jesse's chest tightened, the sudden urge to whisk Aspen out of there almost overwhelming. He wanted his brother there, but he was the fire chief; if he was needed at work, there was nothing he could do. "Stay safe."

"Will do. Don't let Aspen out of your sight."

"Wasn't planning on it."

He hung up and was still watching Aspen when someone tapped him on the shoulder. He turned to see Luke.

"Hey." Jesse frowned. "I didn't know you were coming."

Luke lifted a shoulder. "You said there was good coffee. Thought I should get out of the house for something other than work."

Good. Luke definitely needed to get out. Since Margot, he hadn't been his normal self at all. But then, no one at the station had.

Luke lifted his chin, gesturing toward Aspen, who was now holding a tray of pie slices. "I'm surprised you let her come."

"Just for an hour."

"I'll help keep an eye on her."

"I appreciate it." There were so many people in this shop, he could use all the help he could get.

* * *

ASPEN COULD NOT WIPE the smile from her face. It was busy. People-everywhere, could-barely-move kind of busy. And locals were *loving* the coffee and pie. But she'd known they would. Both were amazing, and so were the scones and little finger sandwiches Mrs. Gerald had made.

She set another empty tray behind the counter and turned to

see Mrs. Gerald in front of her, mug of coffee in hand. The older woman was smiling from ear to ear. "Thank you."

Aspen shook her head. "All I did was make a coffee bean suggestion and hand out a few fliers."

"No, you did a lot more than that. You cared enough to help." She pulled Aspen into a one-armed hug. "Thank you."

"Thank you for letting me occupy one of your booths for hours on end." No, *days* on end.

"You may occupy a booth whenever you want, for as long as you need." She pulled back and handed Aspen the mug of coffee. "Now, this is for you. I added the creamer you like. You have ten minutes before you have to go, so inhale that coffee and have fun."

"But—"

"No buts. You've volunteered enough of your time." Then Mrs. Gerald gave her a little push around the counter.

Aspen chuckled as she slipped into the crowd. Someone brushed her shoulder, knocking her drink and almost spilling it. "Whoops, sorry."

The woman didn't look back or stop, just kept walking.

That was a bit rude.

She took a small sip of her coffee, only to flinch. Hot. Good, but hot. If there was one teeny-tiny criticism she had of Mrs. Gerald, it was that she tended to make the coffee on the boiling side.

Her gaze lifted, and she spotted Jesse. He was on the other side of the room talking to Burt, the pizzeria owner she'd been introduced to earlier. But Jesse's gaze was on *her*, exactly as it had been every other time she'd looked for him that evening.

Her heart did one of those funny little squeezes. The kind that reminded her of just how lucky she was to have the people she had in her life.

She took another step toward him, only to crash to a stop

when a woman cut in front of her. Not just any woman—her mother.

What the *hell*?

"Mom…what are you doing here? I thought you left." Well, she'd assumed she'd left after the Airbnb owner had confirmed she'd checked out. Plus, Aspen hadn't heard from her mother in weeks.

"No, I stayed. I need to talk to you." The words came out fast. Almost breathless.

"Are you okay?"

Her mother stepped closer. "Aspen—"

"Do you have a black eye?" Oh, God. She did. And it looked fresh.

Her mother's mouth opened and closed. "I…no, it's just bags under my eyes from not sleeping well."

She was lying. And she wasn't even lying well. Suddenly, a sickening thought hit her. "Mom, was it Dylan? Have you been in communication with him again?"

"Yes."

Aspen's jaw dropped. The confirmation came so quickly, it felt like a kick to the stomach. "Yes?"

"I know you're angry, but—"

"I'm not angry. I'm *furious*. I shouldn't be. I should be used to you disappointing me by now, but for some reason, I'm still not."

"I *am* sorry, but I need to tell—"

"I don't want you to be sorry. I want you to do better! I need —" She stopped speaking when a wave of dizziness passed over her.

What was that?

Her mother kept talking, but for some reason her words didn't make sense. They were a blur of sounds that morphed into the noise of the room.

Something was wrong with her. Something was very wrong.

She needed Jesse.

She mumbled something she hoped sounded like, "I need to go," but everything was so fuzzy she had no idea what came out. Her mother reached for her, but she shrugged off her touch and pushed into the crowd.

Jesse…where was Jesse? Was she moving toward him? She didn't even know.

Two more steps and an arm slipped around her. Who was that? Her mother? It wasn't Jesse. The body was softer. Shorter.

She tried to pull away, but her muscles wouldn't cooperate.

Panic tightened her chest. What was wrong with her?

Her knees started to tremble, like her legs could barely carry her weight, and her eyes shuttered, too heavy to keep open. The arm around her tightened, almost dragging her.

A door opening sounded, then there was wind on her skin.

She was outside. Someone had taken her outside.

Fear gripped her chest.

Her legs suddenly crumpled, and strong arms wrapped around her…but not Jesse's arms.

Her heart took off at a gallop as she was thrown onto what felt like the floor of a car. Pain seared her side, but she was too tired to do anything about it.

A door slammed closed, and a few seconds later, a car engine sounded. She was just losing consciousness when a voice pricked her ears. A voice that was both familiar and terrifying. A voice that made the darkness around her turn into a nightmare she couldn't wake up from.

Dylan's voice.

CHAPTER 30

*J*esse watched Aspen as she hugged Mrs. Gerald. Burt probably thought he was rude. He was barely looking at him...barely listening. What was he saying? Something about the wrong type of pepperoni being delivered and it was too spicy for customers?

When was the hour up? He was ready to leave, and he was ready now.

Jesse nodded at something Burt said, not entirely sure what he was agreeing to, before looking back at Aspen. She sipped her coffee and cringed. When she lowered the mug, her gaze collided with his, and for a moment, he couldn't breathe.

Would that feeling of breathlessness when he looked at her last forever?

"Hey, is your sister okay?"

Burt's words finally had Jesse looking at him. "What?"

"Your sister." Burt nodded behind Jesse. "I think she passed out, and looks like your friend caught her."

Jesse turned his head to see Holden with his arms around his sister. She was grabbing her head and she looked pale. Shit. Was it her chronic fatigue?

He moved toward his sister, putting a hand on her back. "Hey...are you okay?"

"I'm not sure." Clara grabbed her head. "I just feel...really lightheaded all of a sudden."

"Is it the fatigue?" Holden asked, his arms still around her.

"I don't know. It kind of feels different." Clara frowned at him. "You need to be watching Aspen."

Shit.

"Go," she pushed, shoving Holden's hands off her. "I'll go outside with Mom."

Her mom's arm replaced Holden's, and they both stepped out of the shop.

Jesse turned to look for Aspen, only to walk almost straight into Karen Davies. Her hair was disheveled and...was that a bruise on her left eye? "Karen—"

"Get her out of here."

Cold slipped over his skin. "What?"

"Aspen's not safe. Dylan asked me to drug her at this very event and deliver her to him. I said no. He wasn't happy. Then tonight, I saw him outside with someone...some woman."

Dylan was here?

His gaze shot back to where she was standing—but she wasn't there anymore.

The fuck. Where was she?

He looked around the room. There were too many people, and none of them Aspen. Panic crawled up his throat, choking him, but he pushed it down. She *had* to be here.

"I'll check outside, you check inside," Holden said from beside him.

He pushed through the crowd to the place where she'd been standing, his gaze searching.

Nothing.

He scoured the crowd, checking every face.

Less than a minute later—less than sixty fucking seconds—

and he knew, she wasn't here. The realization hit him so hard, his knees almost caved.

He ran outside, pulling his phone from his pocket and calling her number as he moved. It rang out.

Holden rounded the building and shook his head at Jesse.

Gone. He'd taken his eyes off her for one fucking minute and she was gone.

* * *

THE DULL HUM of a car engine swelled in Aspen's foggy mind. Where was she? And why did everything hurt? Her stomach, her head…it was like one big ache.

She scrunched her eyes before opening them, the brightness immediately making her snap them shut again.

Someone cursed, and her entire body froze.

Dylan.

For a moment, she had to remind herself to breathe. To suck one breath in after the next.

Little things started to come back to her. The Tea House. Her mother. The room as it blurred around her. Then nothing.

Now she was in a car with Dylan. Maybe on the floor of the back seat. It didn't matter that she didn't remember how she got here. Or that everything hurt and she had no idea why. What mattered was that she was here now, and she needed to *get out*.

Dylan cursed a second time, and the car made a sharp turn, sending her body into what she could only assume was the bottom of the seat behind her.

Slowly, she forced her eyes open. They wanted to snap shut again, but she refused to let them. Definitely the floor of the back of a car, and she was facing the front.

She tested her wrists, moving them just a fraction. She wasn't bound. If he didn't want to bind her, why wouldn't he have put her in the trunk? Did he assume she wouldn't wake up?

Her belly rolled, and she just kept herself from grabbing her stomach.

You can't be sick now, Aspen. Hold it together.

He must have drugged her. How? The last thing she remembered drinking was her coffee. Could someone have slipped something into it? Who? Mrs. Gerald wouldn't have. Her mother?

The thought made her belly roll a second time.

No. She'd sipped her coffee *before* speaking to her mother.

Something pricked at her thigh.

Silently, she reached down. Her fingers brushed over cold metal. She wrapped her fingers around it.

A key. A key for what, she wasn't sure, but it didn't matter. It was all she had; the end was surely sharp enough to use as a weapon.

She gripped the key with her fist, the end pointing out.

Bile crawled up her throat at the thought of what she was about to do. But what was the alternative? Let this psychopath take her God knew where and kill her? She'd end up like his ex, but she probably wouldn't make it out alive.

She took a couple of deep breaths, trying to calm her racing heart.

You can do this, Aspen. You have to. You don't have any other options.

One last deep breath and she shot straight up.

Dylan's gaze swung to her in the rearview mirror. "What the fuck?"

A wave of dizziness almost had her dropping back down again, but she locked her knees and swung her fist, nailing Dylan in the temple.

He cried out and the car swung. Aspen screamed and grabbed onto the back of Dylan's seat. The car hit a telephone pole hard, bashing her head into the seat padding before she flew back.

Then there was stillness. For a second, she didn't move, shock rendering her completely motionless.

Silence filled the air, making the ringing in Aspen's ears loud.

She lifted her hand, biting back a whimper at the sight of the blood.

Oh, God. Had she killed him? Was it possible to kill someone like that?

With trembling arms, she pushed herself up to her knees on the back seat. Dylan was hunched over the wheel, seat belt still on and completely still.

She focused on his back. It was moving. He was breathing...he was alive.

She had to get out.

Her fingers wrapped around the door handle and she pulled, but it didn't budge. She tried again, then the window. Still nothing.

Crap, crap, crap.

She crawled to the other side. Same thing.

Her gaze shifted to the front. It was her only way out.

Slowly, she climbed onto the center console. Her knee slipped, landing in Dylan's side, and she froze, holding her breath, expecting him to wake—he didn't.

She crept onto the passenger seat and tried the door. It opened. Thank God! Quietly, she pushed it farther open, wincing when the hinges creaked. She was about to step out when strong fingers wrapped around her ankle and tugged, dropping her to her belly.

"Aspen—"

She screamed and kicked, nailing Dylan in the face. He growled and she fell out of the car and slammed into the concrete.

Pushing up to her feet took every scrap of energy she had, but she did it. Then she ran, her feet pounding against the ground with each step.

Familiar shops bordered the street. She was still in Amber Ridge. But none of them looked open. It was Sunday evening in a small town—of *course* everything was closed.

"Get the fuck back here, bitch!"

Her heart crashed against her ribs at Dylan's shouted words, and she almost stumbled to the asphalt. She shot a look behind her. He was already out of the car and following.

Shit.

She turned a corner and tried the first business door—a bookstore...locked. She tried the second store. Also locked. As she moved, she reached into her back pocket for her phone but it was gone. Dammit!

A big business sign across the road caught her attention.

Sky's Doggy Daycare. The lights were on. That meant someone was there, right?

She took off, sprinting across the street. When she pushed on the handle, it opened, and relief shot through her system.

She all but fell inside and slammed the door closed behind her. She looked for the lock, but there was only a key lock with no key.

Dylan appeared across the street. Their eyes locked.

She spun and ran around the front counter and into a dark hall. She passed a bathroom, a few medium-sized rooms with dog beds, and a couple more with toys. But none of the rooms had anywhere to hide.

A door leading outside to what looked like a backyard caught her attention. Hope lit her chest. She tried the handle...locked. *Jesus.*

A door opening near the entrance sounded, then his voice. "Aspen. Get the fuck out here."

Panic tried to seize her lungs, but she breathed through it. She needed to hide. Someone had left the front door unlocked and the light on...so someone would come back. And that someone might be able to help her.

To the left was a big open wet area with individual dog bathing stalls. And at the end of the hall was a kitchen.

She was out of rooms. She had to choose between the kitchen or the shower stalls.

She ran into the wet area and chose a bathing stall that was second to the end. Even though there were no doors or curtains, there were side walls that shielded her from the hall.

She grabbed a bottle of soap...then she waited.

CHAPTER 31

*S*tupid adorable dog collar charms. She'd thought they were cute. So cute that she'd rifled through the box while driving to have another look. And what had happened? She'd dropped the entire stupid box everywhere. Yep, that was right.

Sky reached under the seat and yelped when she scratched her arm against something sharp.

Ow. Why was everything a mess today?

A huge...colossal...mess.

Okay, maybe things weren't that bad. Maybe a certain six-foot-five tower of *annoying* was affecting her on a deeper level than she cared to admit. She shouldn't *let* him affect her. So he'd temporarily blocked her fence from going up, and now she had to watch him walk outside his house every morning, gloriously shirtless, for a while longer. And so he had a camera pointed right at her driveway and was basically filming her comings and goings. She shouldn't care so much. She still owned the fence, and as soon as she got the *right* permit, it would go up.

Maybe she cared so much because he was annoying. Had she mentioned annoying? It was like he got his kicks out of seeing her angry. This morning, he'd whistled at her as she'd climbed into her car and followed it up with a, "Hey, peaches," a nickname he knew she hated. She'd been so startled, she'd hit her head against the doorframe. Then she could have sworn she heard a chuckle.

She hated him. Big move-next-door-to-someone-else kind of hate.

She grabbed the last charms she could find and dropped them back into the box. More would probably pop up. Heck, she'd probably find one a day until Christmas.

Really, she shouldn't be complaining about this *or* her neighbor.

She needed to focus on the good. Her doggy daycare business was going well...really well. Why she was here on a Sunday evening though, she had no idea. Because she didn't have a life? Because work *was* her life?

That should be okay though because she loved her work.

She climbed out of the car, dog charms in hand. There was a parking lot around the back, but she hated entering through there when the place was empty. It kind of creeped her out, probably because it was so dark and quiet.

She stopped at the entrance and frowned. The door was open. Wide open. Only...she hadn't left it like that. Unlocked? Sure. No reason to lock it in the small town of Amber Ridge when she was coming right back...but not open. She'd once left a door open when she'd worked in a café and a stray bird had flown in. It had taken an entire afternoon to get the creature out. Never again.

She took slow steps forward and quietly set the charms down on the counter.

Was someone here? The thought made a chill sweep over her skin.

Slowly, she moved toward the hall. A voice whispered in her head that this was a bad idea. That she should go back outside where it was safe. But she'd never listened to that voice in the past, so why start now?

She turned into the hall and inched forward, sticking close to the wall, glancing inside empty rooms as she moved.

Silence and stillness surrounded her.

She was just passing one of the dog playrooms when a noise stopped her. A man stepped out of the second playroom—and in his hand, he held a gun. Her heart stopped. But he didn't so much as glance her way. He turned straight toward the kitchen.

Silently, Sky slipped into the room. The air in her lungs whooshed so quickly she almost felt lightheaded, and when she pulled her cell from her pocket, her fingers shook.

She didn't want to make the call. She didn't want to make any noise at all, but she needed help. She didn't know who the guy was, but the gun told her he wasn't friendly.

She dialed 911, praying someone could get there, and they could get there fast.

* * *

"Faster," Jesse growled from the passenger seat.

"I'm going as fast as I can, Jesse," Holden said, far too fucking calmly.

It wasn't fast enough. *He'd* wanted to drive, but Holden refused to let him. And yeah, maybe he wasn't in the best state to be behind the wheel, but sitting here in the passenger seat, *knowing* Aspen was with Dylan...he felt so fucking helpless he could barely breathe.

Deputies were scouring the streets looking for her. Pulling over cars. Running license plates and looking for rentals or stolen vehicles. But the asshole could be anywhere, including already in hiding.

There were too many options and not enough answers.

His fingers tightened around his Glock as he scanned the streets around him.

"Remember when Lock went missing?"

Jesse frowned. "The mission in Frankfurt."

"Yeah, we thought we'd never find him, but not only did we find him within the hour, he was kicking ass. He'd basically done all the work before we got there."

"That was different. Lock's trained in a hundred ways to kill someone. He knows how to protect himself."

"He still shouldn't have made it out. He was outnumbered and the assholes had machine guns."

"Lock's smart."

"So's Aspen. Don't lose hope."

Aspen *was* smart. But this asshole had almost killed a woman before, and hell, there might be women he *had* killed that they didn't know about.

"She's going to be okay." Jesse said the words quietly, and more to himself than to Holden, almost like he was willing them to be true.

"She's going to be okay," Holden repeated.

They turned a corner—and Jesse straightened. A crashed BMW. It had hit a telephone pole and sat partly off the road.

He lifted his phone and called the station.

"Amber Ridge Sheriff's Office, Deputy Finch speaking."

"Claudia, I need you to run some plates."

"Give them to me."

They pulled over behind the car, and both climbed out as Jesse relayed the plates.

The typing of keys sounded over the line before Claudia spoke again. "Rental car, under a Karen Davies."

Aspen's mother. "It's him."

Jesse studied the inside of the car. Blood. It was on the driver's side, mostly on the headrest. But where was the driver?

Holden popped the trunk. "Empty."

Where the hell were they?

He was about to tell Claudia to send all the deputies to his location when she spoke again.

"Hang on, Luke has a call on another line from a woman by the name of Sky Williams. She's in the doggy daycare on Fifth and says there's a man with a gun in the building." There was a short pause. "He matches Dylan's description."

"Get everyone there *now*." Jesse hung up and turned to Holden. "They found Dylan. This way."

Jesse took off, pushing his body to move faster than he'd ever moved before. It was just around the corner, but it felt too far. He had to make it to Aspen before it was too late.

CHAPTER 32

*A*spen pressed a hand to her chest as if that could somehow slow the thumping of her heart.

Breathe, Aspen. Just breathe.

She had a plan for when he found her—squirt soap into his eyes, then run. It was a good plan. If he had a weapon, which she was sure he would, he might even drop it, and she could make a grab for it.

So why was the fear making her heart want to jump out of her chest?

The crunch of his footsteps as he stepped into the bathroom made her fingers tighten around the soap. When her teeth began to chatter, she clenched her jaw. She could *not* give her position away too early. Her advantage was that she could hear him, but he couldn't hear her.

He continued to grow closer. A couple more steps and he'd be right there. She lifted the bottle and aimed.

Suddenly, a subtle noise sounded from somewhere else in the building—the squeak of a floorboard.

Dylan's footsteps stopped…and when they started again, they moved away from her in quick succession.

Oh no, had whoever left the front door unlocked come back?

She inched her head up to see Dylan turning into the hall.

She couldn't let someone else get shot because of her.

She crept to the hall and stuck her head out to see Dylan still moving away from her, but slower now, gun raised.

Suddenly, someone popped their head out of a room—a woman. Her eyes widened and she quickly ducked back inside as Dylan fired.

Aspen flinched.

She had to do something. She couldn't let him kill her.

Without caring for her own safety, she ran out of the wet room and sprinted down the hall. Dylan turned his head just as she got close, and she squeezed the soap bottle, nailing him in the face. He growled and swiped at his eyes but didn't drop the gun.

Quickly, she kneed him between the legs. When he hunched over, she kicked the wrist holding the gun. The weapon fell to the floor and Aspen lunged for it and wrapped her fingers around the wooden stock before rolling to her back.

Before she could take aim, Dylan dropped on top of her. His eyes were bloodshot and full of rage, and blood dripped down the right side of his face.

"I'm going to fucking kill you!" he growled as he grabbed her wrists and threw an elbow into her cheek.

Pain radiated through her skull, and her head fell back onto the cold floor. Her vision blurred as the gun was ripped from her grasp.

"It's time you learned a fucking lesson." He was lifting the gun even as a shadow appeared behind him.

Something hard came down on Dylan's back, followed by a loud *crack*. He grunted, his weight dropping onto her. The air was knocked from her lungs, but Dylan was only down for a second. He twisted at the waist and pointed the gun at the woman behind him as she lifted the chair a second time.

Aspen punched him in the gut at the same time a gunshot sounded.

Aspen flinched, expecting the woman to drop. But it was Dylan who collapsed, his body once again suffocating her. She tried to push him off but it was impossible. He was deadweight.

Fast, pounding footsteps sounded, and a second later, Dylan was shoved off her. Air rushed into her lungs and she rolled to her side. Someone dropped to their knees beside her.

"Aspen!"

Her entire body relaxed at the sound of his voice.

Jesse.

A warm hand touched her back, fighting off the chill that had overtaken her. She tried to sit up, and Jesse's fingers circled her upper arms, helping her.

His gaze narrowed on the left side of her face. She could already feel it swelling from the elbow to her cheek.

He growled before inspecting the rest of her. "Are you okay?"

She nodded, his brows slashing when he obviously caught the flicker of pain in her expression. "I'm okay." But only because Dylan was gone and Jesse was here.

She looked down at Dylan's lifeless body. To the bullet wound in the side of his head, almost in the exact same place she'd nailed him with the key.

"He's dead." She wasn't sure if it was a question or just her saying the words out loud to make herself believe they were true.

"He's dead," he confirmed.

She looked back to Jesse. "How did you know I was here?"

"I called."

Aspen looked up at the woman standing beside Holden. Her chest was moving fast, and Holden was gently easing the chair from her grasp.

"I'm Sky," she added.

"Aspen. I'm so sorry I brought him in here."

She shook her head. "Don't be. I don't know the whole story, but I *do* know that guy wasn't one of the good ones."

That was an understatement.

She swallowed as distant footsteps sounded. Then the store was filled with people. Deputies with guns. Paramedics.

She was about to push to her feet when Jesse cupped her cheek. "Are you sure you're okay?"

"No. But I will be."

* * *

JESSE'S FINGERS were firm around the wheel as he drove home.

Today had been what nightmares were made of. For a short while, Aspen had been out of his reach, and that time had almost killed him.

He shot a glance at her in the passenger seat. She was already asleep, her cheek resting against the sweater she'd pushed between her face and the window. She'd fallen asleep almost the second he'd started the engine. Paramedics had looked over her, but that wasn't enough. Jesse had wanted her to go to the hospital and be properly checked out by a doctor. They needed to know what she'd been drugged with.

Luckily, the hospital had been fairly empty, so they'd be seen quickly and would get the results of the blood test soon. His sister had also taken a blood test, and Jesse was betting that whatever had been slipped into Aspen's drink had been slipped into Clara's too as a way to pull his attention from Aspen. Thank God, they'd both only drunk a small sip of their coffees, so neither had been out for long.

He pulled into his carport but didn't get out right away. Instead, he just watched her, thoughts plaguing him. Dark thoughts. Of how differently today could have gone. If they'd stepped into that building a second later, Sky would have been dead, and, likely, Aspen next.

The thought made his heart lurch and darkness fill every crevice of his mind. He didn't fear much in life, but losing her? The thought fucking terrified him.

He climbed out of the car. When he reached her side, he lifted her into his arms. She fit so damn perfectly against him. If there was anything he believed in this world, it was that they were always meant to find each other. It was always supposed to be them.

He walked through the house and into his bedroom, where he laid her on the bed. But again, he didn't leave immediately. Instead, he removed her shoes, then her jeans. Once the covers were tucked around her, he perched on the side of the bed and grazed a lock of hair from her cheek.

"You scared me today, Aspen." He'd never been more scared in his life. The fear had been like a parasite, sucking the life from him. "Never again."

He swallowed and was about to rise when her hand grabbed his, and she whispered, "Hey."

Her eyes fluttered open, her blues colliding with his brown, so damn captivating they paralyzed him.

"Thank you for saving me," she whispered.

He shook his head. "I didn't save you. *You* saved you. By forcing that asshole to crash the car and running. By being smart."

She'd told the entire story to him and his deputies, and every word she'd spoken had both terrified him and made him proud as hell. She'd fought, and she'd fought hard.

He cupped her cheek, letting her warmth slip into his skin. "I just need to lock up the house."

"Don't be gone long."

"Never." He leaned down and kissed her, his lips lingering, needing to feel her against him.

He eventually forced himself to rise even though the motion

went against every one of his instincts, which told him to stay as close to her as possible.

Her eyes shut the second he stood.

After locking the front door, he moved around the house, checking every window and door. He was just returning to the bedroom when his phone rang, Becket's name on the screen. He'd already updated his brother on everything through text but hadn't actually spoken to him yet.

"Becket."

"I'm so fucking sorry, Jesse. I should have been there."

"It's not your fault. You had work, and Dylan would have found a way around us regardless, I'm sure of it."

"So he's really dead?"

"He's really dead. The bullet to the skull made sure of that." He stood by the bedroom doorway, watching Aspen as he spoke with a lowered voice. "But this isn't over. Someone in that building drugged her. And that same someone took her to Dylan. I don't know who, but we *will* find them."

"Of course we will. Keep her close, brother, and let me know what I can do. Until then, rest."

He wasn't going to rest. Not after the day they'd had. He'd be lucky to get an hour of sleep. "Thanks."

He hung up and entered the room. After stripping off his clothes and turning off the lights, he slid between the sheets. Before he even had a chance to reach for her, she rolled and snuggled her head over his heart, like she knew exactly where he was even while asleep.

He wrapped his arm around her but didn't close his eyes. Who had helped Dylan tonight? It had been someone in that tea house. Someone who'd probably walked past him and he hadn't even given them a second look.

It would torment him until he had an answer.

CHAPTER 33

*J*esse watched the rise and fall of Aspen's chest. Felt the warmth of her breath against his skin.

It was early. He should still be sleeping, particularly after how long it had taken him to finally drift off last night.

But he wasn't. Because every time he closed his eyes, he saw the same thing. Aspen beneath Dylan on the floor. The gun in Dylan's fingers. And even when he managed to shove that memory aside, just for a second, the same thought hit him in the chest—it wasn't over.

His arm tightened around her waist.

It *should* be over. It was *supposed* to be over. Kill Dylan and the danger dies with him, then they could finally start their lives together.

But that's not how it had played out.

He traced the bruise on her cheek with his gaze, feeling the rage rise in his chest all over again.

The ringing of his phone pulled him out of his thoughts. He reached for it, noticing it was his mother. The ringing didn't even stir Aspen. God, she must have been exhausted.

Even though he didn't want to, he slipped out from under her.

After pulling on some pants, he waited until he was in the living room before answering.

"Hi, Mom."

"Honey, I'm sorry to call so early, but I was just speaking to Clara. Becket told her that Aspen was *kidnapped* last night?"

Nothing stayed quiet in his family for long. "It's true. But she's here and she's safe."

The exaggerated sigh sounded from over the phone. "I'm so relieved! Is she okay?"

"She has a black eye and will probably wake up with a headache." So physically, yeah, she was mostly okay. Mentally and emotionally? He'd have to wait and see.

"Oh my gosh. What can I do?"

"Nothing, Mom. She just needs rest."

"What about you? Are you okay?"

No. The answer screamed in his head. "I'm glad I have Aspen back." It wasn't really an answer to her question. "Is Clara okay after she passed out yesterday?" With everything going on, it had completely slipped his mind. He should have checked in on his sister as soon as he'd woken.

"She's been pushing herself too hard," his mother said, concern in her voice. "Her daily runs, her acupuncture business, her new house. It's too much with her chronic fatigue."

Shit. He needed to check in on her more. When this was all over, he would. "I'll call her today."

"I'm sure she'd like that. And I'm going to drop a meal off to you."

"No." The word came out faster than he meant for it to. But he didn't want her or Clara close until they found Dylan's accomplice. They'd get a description of this person from Karen, then he wouldn't feel so blind. "Sorry, I just...would it be okay to give Aspen some time?"

"Oh, of course, honey."

"Thanks, Mom."

"I love you, darling."

"I love you too." He hung up and turned—only to freeze at the sight of Aspen in the bedroom doorway. The blond locks of her hair tumbled over her shoulders, and she wore his shirt. Sexy didn't even begin to describe her.

But then he focused on that black eye again, and the murderous rage returned.

"You should be in bed," he said quietly.

"*You're* not."

He crossed the space between them and cupped her unbruised cheek. "How do you feel?"

"Like I was kidnapped by my crazy ex last night."

The growl ripped from his chest.

She cringed. "Sorry. I'm okay."

"I hate what happened."

"Me too." She reached up and touched her fingertip to the line between his brows. "You're still worried. About the person who drugged me?"

She read him too well. "Are you sure you don't think it was your mother?"

"That would make it easier. But I don't think so. I sipped the coffee, then spoke to my mother, which is when I started feeling disorientated."

"I'll bring her in for questioning. Get a description of this woman she says she saw with Dylan. I'll also talk to Mrs. Gerald and ask her if anyone had contact with the coffee before you." A muscle clenched in his jaw. "Someone else in this town helped him." It was like he had to say it out loud because he still couldn't believe it.

Fear flashed over her face. Then she blinked and visibly tried to conceal her emotions.

"Hey." He lowered his head. "I'm not leaving you unprotected, okay?"

"I know. It's just a really unnerving feeling knowing that

someone helped him. Someone we probably know, because everyone there last night was local. And someone who wants to harm me for reasons I can't begin to guess."

It wasn't just unnerving...it was sickening. "When we catch them, they're going to wish they'd never involved themselves."

She nodded quickly.

He hated that she'd already gone through so much yesterday, yet danger still lurked in this town.

He lowered his mouth to hers, trying to give her in one kiss the calm and safety and love he knew she needed.

* * *

ASPEN SAT on the back porch, legs tucked under her, hot cocoa in hand. It was raining. Figured. Couldn't have a gloomy day without rain.

Becket was inside while Jesse had run down to the station. He'd tried to be discreet about why he needed to go in the day after she'd been kidnapped, but she'd seen right through him...he was questioning her mother.

Her fingers tightened around the mug.

She already knew her mother had been living with Dylan. Jesse had told her that the car he'd used to kidnap her had been rented in *her* name. Was there more?

Her black eye flashed in Aspen's head. There probably was.

It hurt. Even when she was certain she expected nothing from her mother, the deceit still felt like a kick in the stomach.

She sighed.

So far, Becket hadn't come out to check on her, but she knew he'd been watching from the window. In a lot of ways, he reminded her of Jesse. He was protective. And kind. And when things got serious, so did he. But he was also different. He used humor to lighten the mood a lot more.

She startled at the ringing of her phone.

Jesus, she was jumpy.

She lifted the cell, immediately sucking in a sharp breath.

Her mother.

Was she done at the station? A part of her didn't want to answer the call. She wanted to let it ring out, then block the number. Cut all ties so the woman didn't have the opportunity to hurt her ever again.

But the other part of her needed to know the extent of her relationship with Dylan.

"Mom."

"Aspen, I just got out of the sheriff's office. They told me what happened. Are you okay?"

She frowned. Did her mother really care? "I'm fine. What did you tell them?"

"What?"

"They were asking about your involvement with Dylan, right? What did you tell them?"

There was a small pause before she spoke. "That he paid for me to come here. He paid for the Airbnb. He paid for my food, the rental car. Everything."

Aspen closed her eyes, breathing through the hurt, almost not wanting to ask the next question. "And what did he get in return?"

"He got to put everything in my name. I also promised I'd help him get close to you. Encourage you to return to him."

Everything in her name to conceal his movements, and using her mother to give Aspen a little nudge. She massaged her brow, not sure whether to laugh, cry or scream. Maybe all three.

"He kidnapped me, Mom."

"I know, but—"

"He would have *killed* me." She didn't have confirmation, but deep down she knew it was true.

Another pause. "He wouldn't—"

"He *would*. Did you know he almost killed his ex a few years ago? She ended up in a coma. Almost died before she *disappeared*. No one's known where she's been ever since. She could be hiding, or she could be dead."

Her mother gasped.

"I was next," Aspen added. "And *you* made it easy for him."

There was another small pause. Was her mother finally understanding? "I didn't...I wouldn't have thought—"

"But that's the thing—you never think about anyone but yourself."

"He seemed like an okay guy. Kind, even."

"It doesn't matter how he seemed! I *told you* he wasn't a good guy. I even told you what he did to me. But you didn't believe me!"

"I'm sorry. I...I gave Jesse all the information I had. I even described the girl I saw Dylan with."

It wasn't enough. "Are you going to get help?"

"Help?"

"For your mental health, Mom. Are you going to get help?"

"No, I—"

"Then I can't have a relationship with you. Because you'll keep hurting me without even realizing that's what you're doing."

"Aspen—"

"Goodbye, Mom."

She hung up and leaned her head back against the seat. When a tear fell, she scrubbed it away, almost angry at herself for being upset. Her mother didn't deserve her tears.

"Hey."

She jumped at the sound of Becket's voice, and her eyes flashed open. He lowered to the seat beside her, concern in his normally humorous eyes.

She straightened. "Hey."

"Want to talk about it?"

"I don't know why I still let her actions bother me. My mother has been the same for my entire life. She's never been what I needed, and yet, I always expect her to be more."

"Because she's your mom and you love her."

"I love the *idea* of her."

Becket shook his head. "You love the good in her. And there *is* good. It just doesn't come out very often."

"How do you know? You've never met her."

"You wouldn't hang on to hope so hard if there was never any reason to."

She swallowed. He was right. Her mother had her good moments, and in those moments, she gave Aspen a glimpse into who she *could* be. And Aspen hung on to those moments even when she shouldn't.

"She's sick, even if she won't acknowledge it. I wish she would get help."

"When family's sick, it creates a helplessness that can be debilitating. I felt that with Clara."

She swallowed and nodded. She'd never have expected to have such a deep conversation with Becket, since he'd never shown her this side before.

"Thank you. I needed someone to validate that I'm not crazy. And give me some wisdom."

He chuckled. "I can be pretty wise when I want to be. But don't tell anyone. I've become quite accustomed to people thinking I'm just a pretty face."

She laughed, and God it felt good.

CHAPTER 34

*J*esse leaned back in his seat, his fingertips tapping on the wooden desk.

Where was she? She was supposed to be here already. Was she stuck in traffic? Picking up something on the way to the station?

He lifted his phone.

Jesse: Hey. Are you almost at my office?

Aspen: Fifteen minutes.

Jesse: You left home ten minutes ago. You should be here now.

Aspen: Are you spying on me?

Jesse: Yes.

Aspen: You're lucky I like you.

Jesse: Like?

Aspen: Okay, maybe a bit more than like. I'm still fifteen minutes away because I convinced Holden to stop to pick up coffee at The Tea House. If he hadn't said yes, I wasn't above army rolling out of a moving car. My need for coffee is equal to my need for oxygen after you kept me up so late last night.

Jesse: Fine. But no more stops. I want eyes on you. And I have a very clear memory of who kept who up last night, and it wasn't me keeping you up.

Aspen: Totally worth it. See you soon, Mr. Grouch.

Jesse dropped the phone onto his desk. A week had passed since Aspen had been kidnapped. An entire week, and they weren't any closer to figuring out who had drugged her at The Tea House and taken her to Dylan. Aspen had no recollection of who'd led her out the back door and the description from Karen, who'd only seen the back of the woman, had been too common— mid-twenties, brown hair tied into a ponytail, slim and average height.

He'd wanted it to be Aspen's mother, because that would have been easy. They'd have had their person and the threat would have been taken care of. He wasn't taking Karen off the table as a suspect though until they found the person responsible.

He blew out an exasperated breath. It had been a long week.

His desk phone rang, and he lifted it. "Yeah?"

"It's Claudia. I found something you're gonna find interesting, but not in a good way."

Just what he needed. "Tell me."

"I was going through the cameras from the Airbnb that Karen Davies booked, like you asked, and I found footage of Dylan entering the cabin through a back window. I'm guessing he didn't realize there was surveillance footage there."

"Not surprising. We know he was staying there. He was paying for the entire stay."

"Yes...but this footage of him is on the night Margot was killed."

He straightened, a bad feeling churning in his gut. "What time?"

"The same time Margot was shot...almost to the minute."

A chill slipped over Jesse's skin. "No. That can't be possible. He killed Margot. He *had* to have killed Margot." Because if he didn't, it wasn't just an accomplice of Dylan's on the loose—it was a killer.

And it left a lot more questions than answers.

Claudia's voice softened. "I'm sorry."

"Send it to me."

He hung up, but he didn't actually need to see the footage. If Claudia said it was him, it was him. The air in his lungs moved too quickly, and his chest felt too fucking tight.

Someone else had killed Margot. Who? And why? He'd just assumed it had been Dylan making a play for Aspen, and Margot had gotten in his way. But if that wasn't true...had Margot been the target all along? And all this time, her killer had been out there...

And he hadn't even been looking.

Was this person the same one connected to Dylan? They couldn't be, because Margot and Aspen weren't connected. Were they?

There were too many unanswered questions.

The night Margot had been shot, the killer had known exactly which switch turned off the cameras and the lights. They'd also known how to enter the building and find Margot.

Shit. He'd been so focused on it being Dylan, he hadn't put it all together...

It was someone on the inside.

The same person who'd made the formal complaint about him? That had to have been an inside job too. Who else would have known about what Jesse was prioritizing in his work life?

Was this about him rather than Aspen?

A knock at the door pulled him out of his thoughts. "Come in."

Bea stepped inside. "Hi. I have the files you requested." She crossed the room and set them on his desk.

"Thanks." He barely looked up. His head was a damn mess. He was the sheriff, a former fucking Ghost Ops soldier. He should be among the best of the best. But he'd missed something, and that something was huge.

"You're welcome. How's Aspen doing after everything?"

He looked at the receptionist, trying to give her his attention when his mind was firmly everywhere else. "Better now that Dylan's gone."

"Good. He deserved to die after he killed Margot. Now we don't have to worry about some psychopath shooting unarmed deputies."

Jesse nodded...only to stop and frown. "How do you know she wasn't armed?"

"Oh, um. Luke told me." She cringed. "Sorry. He probably shouldn't have."

No, he shouldn't have. Bea wasn't a deputy, so she wasn't privy to all the details of crime reports.

Something started to tick in his brain. Bea was close to Luke. He'd seen them together more than once. But Margot had been close to Luke too. They were connected.

Bea cocked her head. "Aspen still can't recall who led her to Dylan?"

"No, unfortunately not."

"Hopefully soon." She turned.

The door opened wider and Aspen entered the office, but Jesse was focused on something else. He stared at Bea's shoes as she stepped past Aspen. Shoes she didn't usually wear.

Red sneakers.

* * *

ASPEN SIPPED HER COFFEE, only to cringe.

Hot. *Really* hot.

But at least it was good coffee.

She stared out the window, the frown she'd been wearing all day deepening. Something had been niggling at her mind. A dream she'd had last night. Or maybe it wasn't a dream. Maybe it was a memory. She couldn't get it out of her head, it was on permanent repeat.

"That's a deep frown. I thought you liked Mrs. Gerald's coffee."

She turned to look at Holden behind the wheel. She still didn't have a car, and Jesse didn't want her walking around town by herself until Dylan's accomplice was found.

"Oh, this coffee is the best thing to touch my tongue today. Hot, but good." And sure, it was also the *only* thing to touch her tongue, due to her lack of appetite these last few days, but she was pretty sure any competing foods or drinks would lose.

Holden shot her another glance. "What's on your mind then?"

"I had a dream last night, about the day I was kidnapped."

Holden's brows flickered. "Tell me about it."

"There's not much to tell. Everything was a blur. I could feel this person's hands on me as they led me through the crowd. And even though I can't understand what they said to Dylan, I remember the voice. It was female, and I woke up with this feeling like I'd heard it before, but I don't know where."

Holden's fingers visibly tightened on the wheel. "It wasn't your mother?"

She almost flinched at the mention of her mom. She hadn't spoken to her since that phone call the day after her kidnapping. "No. It wasn't familiar enough to be her."

"It's a small town. I wouldn't be surprised if you've run into the person once or twice."

And somehow, the person hated her enough to drug and help kidnap her? "I just don't understand why anyone would help Dylan. I thought he was the only person who hated me enough to hurt me like that. Then I thought maybe he was paying someone, but the deputies looked into his accounts and there were no big withdrawals or transfers."

It didn't make sense. Any of it.

"Unfortunately," Holden said quietly, voice hard, "I've learned that some people need little to no incentive to do really shitty things. But when Jesse finds them, you'll get your motive."

She nodded almost absently as Holden pulled up in front of the sheriff's station. He started unbuckling his seat belt, but she shook her head. "You don't need to come in."

"Aspen—"

"You've been driving me around all week. You've done enough, and I know you're on a deadline with a cabinet you're making."

He'd already gotten so much work here in Amber Ridge. Not that she was surprised—she'd seen his woodwork. He was good at what he did.

She slipped off her seat belt and opened her door. "You can watch me go all the way inside though."

His gaze moved around the station before returning to her. "I will."

"Thanks again for picking me up." She lifted both her and Jesse's coffees. "Hopefully I won't need you to take me places much longer."

He lifted a shoulder. "I don't mind."

Yeah, but he shouldn't have to.

She smiled before climbing out of the car and heading into the station. The front desk was empty as she passed, and Jesse's door was half closed. She knocked before stepping inside.

Aspen smiled at Bea as the other woman walked toward the door. "Bea! Hi."

"Hi, Aspen. Jesse was just saying you're doing a bit better."

She stopped, her belly doing a strange roll. Bea's voice...why did it make every hair on her body stand on end?

She glanced at Jesse, but he wasn't looking at her. She followed his gaze to Bea's shoes.

Red sneakers. *Familiar* sneakers.

Aspen gasped, stumbling back a step.

Bea frowned. "Are you—"

"*You.*" Aspen's gaze flashed back up to Bea. "*You* hit me the night Margot was killed, and you took me to Dylan the day he kidnapped me!"

Anger, shock, and maybe a bit of fear flashed over Bea's features—then everyone moved so quickly that Aspen didn't have time to comprehend what was happening.

One second she was standing there, facing Bea; the next, Jesse was reaching into his holster while Bea kicked the door closed, grabbed Aspen around the neck and swung behind her, causing one of the coffees to drop to the floor. A gun was pressed to her temple the same time as Jesse aimed his Glock.

Air stalled in Aspen's chest.

"I knew it was a good idea to start carrying," Bea said.

Jesse's eyes were black with rage. "What's the plan, Bea? You're in the sheriff's office. You kill either of us, a shitload of armed deputies come in here and arrest you."

Bea's arm tightened around her neck. "I've got a go-bag in my car. I just need to get to my vehicle before they stop me."

"Not gonna happen." Jesse rounded his desk, gun still trained on Bea.

"Why?" Aspen whispered, so confused she wanted to scream. "I barely know you. Why would you help Dylan? Why would you *kill* another deputy?"

"Because I love him."

Aspen frowned. "Who?"

It was Jesse who answered. "Luke."

Bea inched back a step. "Yes. And he said he loved *me*. But then he went back to that whore, Margot! I was so angry and hurt, I could barely function."

"So you killed her?" Aspen gasped.

"With everyone so fixated on Dylan, and with you working here in the station, it was easy. I knew everyone would suspect it was him." She paused before sneering, "And our new *sheriff*

271

would look incompetent by allowing one of his deputies to be murdered in his own station, right under his nose. I lodged a complaint against you the next day, thinking Luke would get the job that should have been his all along, and with Margot out of the picture, he'd come back to me. It was so fucking perfect!"

Jesus. Her plan was so detailed.

"So you wanted me out so Luke would be in," Jesse said.

"Yes! How dare you walk back into this town after being away for years and just take a job that was rightfully his! He's *been here*, serving the community all along."

"He didn't want—"

"It wasn't fair!" Bea cried, cutting off Jesse's words. "*He* should have been sheriff. His office would have been right next to *my* desk instead of next to Margot's."

The cold metal pressed harder against Aspen's temple. She swallowed before asking, "Why drug *me* though? Why help Dylan?"

"I asked Luke to meet me at a motel. He didn't show, and when I was leaving, I saw your mom and Dylan fighting. I saw how angry he was. Well, I was angry too. Angry that my complaint had accomplished nothing. Angry that Jesse was still sheriff and Luke still didn't want me. I knew losing you would tip Jesse over the edge. And with Luke as sheriff, he'd work more closely with me. He'd come back to me eventually."

She did all of this for unrequited love.

"It's over, Bea," Jesse said quietly. "Put down the gun."

Bea laughed, but the sound was almost hysterical. "You really think I'd just put down my gun and give up? It would mean everything I've done was for *nothing*!"

Jesse inched another step forward. "You know there's no way out of this."

"There is...but not for either of you."

Jesse's eyes narrowed. "Bea—"

The door behind them opened, and Luke's voice sounded. "Jesse, I— What the fuck?"

Aspen yanked the lid off the coffee in her hand and threw it over her shoulder into Bea's face.

Drops of scalding liquid splattered onto Aspen's neck and cheek, but she ignored the burn as Bea screamed. The second she moved the gun to grab at her face, Luke tackled her to the floor.

Jesse was across the room in a second, cupping her face and looking intensely into her eyes. "Are you okay?"

She wrapped her arms around him and breathed him in, air whooshing from her chest. "I'm okay." Her gaze moved to Bea, struggling beneath Luke on the floor.

This entire time, it had been her...and no one knew.

"It's over." There was a thread of disbelief in her words.

"It's over," Jesse breathed.

CHAPTER 35

*P*eople moved around him. Deputies. Paramedics. But Jesse's entire focus remained on Aspen perched on the edge of the ambulance.

Twice he'd almost lost her, in just over a week. Twice he'd had to relearn how to breathe after seeing her gripped in the hands of evil. It was two times too many.

This entire time, Margot's killer had been sitting right outside his office. He couldn't wrap his head around it because it didn't feel real.

He should have known it was Bea. He should have worked it out. Why didn't he see it?

"Stop it."

He looked down at Aspen, her soft words breaking into his internal battle. His gaze zoned in on the small burn marks on her neck. She said she was fine. *He* was the one who wasn't fine. *He* was the one who needed every inch of the woman he loved checked by the paramedic.

"Stop what?" he finally asked.

"You know what. You're spinning everything around in your

head to make it your fault. You're blaming yourself when her actions were her own."

"Her desk was right outside my office."

"It was."

"She *killed* one of my deputies and aided in your kidnapping."

"She did."

"And I didn't know."

"No one knew."

He shook his head. "*I* should have known. I'm the sheriff of this town. It's my job to keep everyone safe, especially you."

She stood and cupped her cheeks. "Stop holding yourself to impossible standards. We had no reason to think Margot's murderer wasn't Dylan. Bea knew that. She set it up that way because she was smart. But she didn't win."

"You never should have had a weapon put to your head."

"But I'm okay."

He frowned and looked behind her. "Where'd the paramedic go?"

"He took one look at my burns and told me I was fine, just like I knew he would."

He had? Jesse had been so deep in his own head, he'd missed it. He looked up to see Luke moving toward them, a deep frown between his brows.

Aspen gave him a little push. "Go. I'll be fine."

"I'm not leaving you."

"I'll stay with her," Claudia said, stopping in front of them.

"See?" Aspen said softly. "I'm looked after."

His jaw clenched before he leaned down and kissed her temple. "I'll be right back."

"Take all the time you need."

He blew out a breath before straightening and crossing the parking lot toward Luke.

"Paperwork's done, and she's in a holding cell," Luke said quietly before Jesse had even stopped walking.

"Good. Are you okay?"

Luke shook his head, his gaze moving around the parking lot. "It's my fault. I should have been more honest with her about my intentions."

"Luke—"

"I slept with her, and I told her I loved her when I didn't. I knew she had feelings for me. She'd had feelings for me for years."

Yeah, that had been stupid, but... "You couldn't have predicted she'd do this."

He frowned. "She killed Margot."

"She did."

"It will take me a while to process."

He gripped his friend's shoulder. "If you need time off, it's yours."

Luke nodded almost absently. When he looked back at Jesse, there was resolve in his eyes. "I don't know if this needs to be said, but I *was* happy when you became sheriff. I never wanted the position, and I knew you'd be great."

"I know."

"Good." Luke's gaze shifted over Jesse's shoulder. "Is Aspen okay?"

"She's strong." So much stronger than him. "I'm going to get her home."

"I'm gonna stay, pull a double shift."

Jesse frowned. "Are you sure?"

"Yeah. I need to stay busy."

Jesse watched his friend head back into the station. Just like him, Luke was blaming himself.

Fuck, today had been a lot for everyone.

He ran his fingers through his hair before turning back to Aspen. She was looking straight at him, and for the millionth time, he felt the relief in his gut that she was alive and safe even after everything that had been thrown her way.

* * *

ASPEN WATCHED the thick cords of muscles in Jesse's arms bunch as he spoke to Luke. She hated what had happened today. She hated that Margot's murderer had been someone Jesse had trusted.

"I wish he wouldn't shoulder the blame," Aspen said, more to herself than to Claudia.

"You almost died today. He's going to shoulder the blame no matter who held the gun on you."

It was true. She still didn't like it.

Claudia bumped her side. "I heard you were pretty badass in there."

Aspen scoffed. "I threw coffee in her face—it was hardly a great act of bravery."

"You gave Luke a chance to grab her, and no one got shot. You were smart."

"Really, it was Mrs. Gerald's coffee that saved the day."

Claudia chuckled. "Yeah, well, she's been saving my mornings most days lately too, so that doesn't surprise me." The smile slipped. "You're okay?"

"I'm safe, and so is Jesse. So yeah, I'm okay. Are you?"

"We lost a deputy and now Bea. It will take a while for everyone here at the station to recover. But we will."

"I'm sorry."

Claudia dipped her head. "Thanks."

Aspen looked over at Jesse and, as if he could feel her gaze on him, his dark eyes collided with hers.

All it took was one look, and any anxiety or fear just...vanished.

When he started back toward her, her skin began to tingle. He was so big and fierce, she couldn't *not* feel safe around him.

He slipped an arm around her waist before looking at Claudia. "Thanks."

"Need anything else?"

"Not right now. I just want to get Aspen home to rest."

"Call if you need anything."

The second Claudia was gone, Aspen stepped in front of Jesse and splayed her hands over his chest. "How's Luke?"

"Not good. He thinks this is his fault because of his history with Bea and Margot."

"It's not."

"That's what I told him." His brown gaze bore into her as his strong arms wove around her waist. "Are you ready to go home?"

"I'm dreaming about being in bed with you."

His eyes darkened. "Let's go."

He went to step toward the car, but she grabbed his arm, stopping him. "Wait."

"What's wrong?"

"I'm sorry."

He frowned. "For what?"

"You trusted Bea, and that trust was broken. I'm sorry she did that to you."

Pain flashed through his eyes. "You're safe. That's what I'm focusing on. Thank you for fighting in there, just like you fought Dylan."

"I'll always fight to return to you."

Emotion flickered in his eyes. "I love you."

"I love you too." She lifted to her toes and kissed him, a long, deep kiss that almost made her forget everything that had come before it. "Take me home."

CHAPTER 36

The Tea House was actually busy. People-everywhere, almost-every-booth-taken kind of busy...and it was just a normal Tuesday. She couldn't take her eyes off the windows as they pulled into the parking lot.

They'd done it. They'd actually kept Mrs. Gerald in business.

It was official—the smile could *not* be wiped off her face.

Jesse parked and turned to her. "I love it when you do that."

"Do what?"

"Smile."

Somehow, her smile widened. "Do you see how many people are in there? Heck, do you see how many cars are in this parking lot?"

"I do."

"*We* helped Mrs. Gerald do that."

"*You* helped Mrs. Gerald do that."

Her grin softened. "She kind of feels like family, and this town really feels like home."

"Because it *is* your home."

"It is, isn't it?"

He squeezed her thigh before they both climbed out and

walked toward the shop. Just as they were about to step in, her phone rang, her mother's name flashing on the screen.

She stopped. She hadn't spoken to her mother since their conversation the day after the Dylan mess. Her mother hadn't tried to call her at all.

A couple weeks had passed since Bea was arrested. She assumed her mother had returned to Misty Peak, but she had no confirmation.

"You don't need to answer that if you don't want to," Jesse said from over her shoulder.

She nibbled her lip. She knew she didn't...so why was she considering it? "I think I want to hear what she has to say."

Jesse inched closer. "Want me to stay with you?"

"Is it okay if I meet you inside?"

Concern flashed in his eyes, but he nodded. Then he bent and pressed a lingering kiss to her forehead before heading inside The Tea House.

She sucked in a breath before putting the phone to her ear. "Hi, Mom."

"Aspen. You answered."

"You thought I wouldn't?"

"I thought you wouldn't." There was a short pause before her mother added, "I'm home in Misty Peak."

"Good."

Another pause. "How have you been?"

"Okay. We found Dylan's accomplice. It was someone from the station. She's been arrested."

"Oh, I'm so glad. I'm happy you're safe."

"Are you? Or are you just glad that you weren't implicated in anything that happened?" It was a low blow, but Aspen was past niceties.

"Aspen, I know a lot has happened between us, and I'm sorry that I trusted Dylan over you. But I *do* love you, and I want you to be okay."

Aspen bit her tongue. There was so much she could say in response to that, but nothing that she hadn't said before.

"I'm seeing a therapist and taking medication," her mother added.

Aspen's brows shot up. "You are?"

"Yes. You've been telling me for years that I need help, and for a long time, I've been in denial. But this was my wake-up call. I *do* need help. My therapist has already helped me recognize that I suffer from dissociative identity disorder...or what used to be called split personality disorder. It makes it hard for me to maintain healthy relationships."

Aspen couldn't believe what her mother was saying. For so long, she'd dreamed about hearing similar words come out of her mouth, and now they were. "I'm glad you're seeking help."

"I know a lot has gone on between us, but would you ever consider...forgiving me? Maybe even having a relationship with me? A new one. Like a fresh start?"

Aspen swallowed and looked down at her black boots. A part of her, the part that had never had a mother she could rely on, wanted to say yes. But the other part, the part that had been burned so many times, was scared to feel hope in case she got hurt again.

"I promise you," her mother hurried to add, "that nothing like what happened with Dylan will ever happen again."

"It's not just about that, Mom. It's about everything that's *ever* happened between us. Our past is...heavy and complicated."

"I know. I'm sorry. It was selfish of me to ask. Um...I should go. I just needed you to know how sorry I am and that I'm trying to do better."

"Mom..."

"Yes?"

Aspen swallowed. "Give me time. Then, maybe, we can see about a relationship." How much time, exactly, she wasn't sure. But it was the most she could offer.

"Okay. Yeah, that…that sounds good. Thank you."

"I hope you stay well, Mom." In more ways than one.

"Thank you. And I hope you enjoy the life you've created in Amber Ridge. Despite all the adversity I threw your way, you've built a great life."

On that, they could agree. "Thanks, Mom."

When the call ended, Aspen's chest rose and fell on a deep breath. She felt lighter. A kind of lightness she'd never really felt before. Her mother had finally acknowledged she needed help, which meant for the first time ever…sometime in the future… they might actually have a shot at a healthy relationship.

She stepped into The Tea House and caught Jesse's gaze across the room. He was watching her so intensely.

She *had* built a great life here, and one man had a lot to do with that.

She crossed the space between them, reminded with every step how lucky she was that Jesse had come into her life, and that she finally had the love she'd always written about and dreamed of.

* * *

JESSE LEANED back in his seat and watched as Aspen stood behind the counter and spoke to Mrs. Gerald. While she'd been speaking to her mother, every protective part of him had wanted to march outside, take that phone from her fingers and hang up on Karen so she couldn't hurt her daughter anymore. He hadn't, and surprisingly, the conversation had gone well.

Something he was slowly learning was that Aspen didn't need him to shield her from hard things. She was strong and fierce, and those were just two of the reasons why he loved her.

He was about to get up and drag her back to him when his phone rang, Lock's number appearing on the screen. He'd been updating his former Ghost Ops team member about everything going on. Just as Aspen had been updating Lock's partner, Callie.

He pressed the phone to his ear. "Hey."

"Jess, hey, I just wanted to check in and see how everything's going. I hate that I haven't been there."

"Callie's pregnant and she needs you there, so that's where you *should* be. I had my brother and Holden, and we're doing good now."

"So, since Bea was arrested…"

"Everything's been quiet."

"I'm glad. You had not only me worried but Callie as well. And I'm doing everything I can to try to keep her calm during this pregnancy."

Jesse nodded. He was in full agreement. Callie needed a calm pregnancy, considering her medical history. "I'm sorry. This definitely couldn't have helped her."

"Don't be sorry, just keep telling us you're all right."

"I'm better than all right. I'm drinking great coffee, watching the woman I love smile, and waiting for Becket, Clara and Holden. Life's great."

Lock blew out a breath. "I'm happy for you, brother. You deserve every bit of good that comes your way."

"Thank you. I'm just trying not to pinch myself in case I wake up and realize this isn't my life."

"Pinch yourself. Give yourself that confirmation that it's real. Trust me, I've felt the disbelief myself, and then the overwhelming relief that it's all true."

When Aspen hugged Mrs. Gerald, Jesse straightened. "I've got to go. But we'll talk soon."

"Check in often, okay?"

"Definitely."

He hung up, unbelievably grateful that his friend could live across the country and they could still have the relationship they had. When you served with a person, that person became family, and distance didn't change that.

He rose from the booth before Aspen reached him and wrapped his arms around her waist. "You took too long."

She laughed, and the sound was fucking beautiful. "I was gone for five minutes."

"It felt longer."

She leaned into him. "I missed you too."

He studied the navy in her eyes. "This is it, you know."

"What?"

"The magic you were chasing."

Her smile softened. "It kind of feels like magic, doesn't it?"

"No 'kind of' about it."

Her fingers skimmed his chest. "I pushed you away for a long time."

"I wasn't going anywhere."

"Thank God."

He cocked his head. "Have you sent your manuscript to your editor yet?"

Her face lit up. "I did. And I put it up for preorder and announced a release date to my readers. It's like this weight has been lifted from my chest."

"Good."

"Thank you for helping me believe in love again."

"I didn't do anything."

"You did *everything*." She rose to her toes and hovered her lips an inch from his. "I love you, Jesse Hayes."

"And I love you, Aspen Davies." Then he kissed her and thanked every fucking star that he got to call this woman his.

CHAPTER 37

$\mathcal{B}$ecket pulled into the parking lot of The Tea House.

Shit, he was tired. He'd worked well into the morning after a fire at an e-bike store a few towns over. His station had been called because they'd needed all hands on deck. The damn store should have known better than to charge multiple batteries in one area. Lithium-ion batteries could cause fatal fucking fires. Everyone knew that.

He leaned back and closed his eyes. He was used to surviving off a few hours' sleep. He'd done it plenty as a SEAL. But right now, he needed a strong fucking cup of coffee.

He slipped off his seat belt and was about to climb out of his car when a familiar face across the lot caught his attention.

Sky. His beautiful, feisty neighbor.

A smile twitched at his lips. She'd hated him since the day she'd moved in next door. He had no idea why. He was great fucking company.

She stood opposite an older woman. A woman he recognized as a frequent visitor to Sky's house. Her mother? Probably. They had the same hazel eyes.

Whoever she was, they argued a lot, and by the deep-set frown on Sky's face, they were arguing now. But they also hugged and smiled a lot. A complicated relationship?

He shook his head and climbed out of the truck. It wasn't his damn business.

He still couldn't believe she'd become entangled in the Dylan mess. Every muscle in Becket's body had tightened at the story Jesse had told him. Jesse had thanked Sky, and Becket had tried to, also. But the conversation had quickly turned into an argument about his cameras again. The woman wouldn't let it go.

He entered The Tea House, the scents of coffee and pie already teasing him. Damn, it was good to finally have a place in Amber Ridge with a decent cup of coffee. But it wasn't just the coffee that was good. The food was un-fucking-believable too. The scones. The bagels. Even the turkey sandwiches.

He spotted his brother, sister and Aspen in a booth by the window.

His brother looked happy. A hell of a lot happier than he'd looked when Aspen had been living with him and they weren't dating.

Good. He deserved it.

Becket slid into the booth beside his sister, snagged her fork, and stole a mouthful of her pie.

She slapped him on the shoulder. "Hey! Get your own."

"But yours is right here."

"Yeah, key word, *mine*." She slid the plate away from him.

"You've always been terrible at sharing."

"Because sharing with you means giving up ninety percent of my food. Plus, this pie's too delicious to share."

She wasn't wrong. He looked across the table at his brother and Aspen, the smile on his face a bit gentler. "Hey. How are you both doing?"

Aspen nodded and smiled back. "We're good."

"Great, actually," Jesse added, his arm visibly tightening around Aspen's waist. "Aspen's got a new book releasing soon."

Clara straightened. "Oh my God, really? Don't mess with me, Aspen. Is it the next in your West Valley series?"

"It sure is. It's written and currently with the editor," she said.

Clara squealed.

Jesus Christ.

While the women talked about the book, Becket rolled his eyes at his brother. "I'm going to get coffee."

"It's usually table service."

Becket lifted a shoulder. "I'll save Mrs. Gerald the trip."

A couple of tables over, he noticed Sky was now sitting at a table with the woman she'd been talking to outside.

His neighbor leaned over, and he couldn't help but hear her say, "Mom, I love you, but you need to stop. This is *my* life, and I'll live it the way I choose."

Ah, it *was* her mother. And by the sound of it, he'd been spot on with the complicated relationship.

"Skylar, honey, I just want you to be happy!"

"I—" She stopped, and even though Becket wasn't looking at her, he could feel her eyes on him as he passed their table.

Don't stop on my behalf, Peaches.

He grinned to himself as he stopped at the counter.

Mrs. Gerald glanced over from the coffee machine. "Becket, honey, sorry I'm taking a while to get to you. I've hired more staff, but I think I still need more."

"Don't apologize. I just came for a closer look at your pies."

"Oh, you want to try the caramelized apple and rhubarb. It's my flavor of the week, and it's been popular."

"You sold me at caramelized."

"Great. And a double shot long black?"

He grinned. He'd been here daily for the last few weeks, so he shouldn't be surprised they were on a first-name basis and she remembered his coffee order. "That would be great. Thanks."

"I'll bring it over."

He turned, and his gaze immediately went to the back of Sky's head. Her mother was still leaning forward, and the conversation looked tense. He was just passing her table again when her seat suddenly pushed back and she rose, stepping straight into him.

She almost rebounded off his chest, and he grabbed her arms to steady her.

Her eyes widened as they swung up to his face, her palms pressing to his chest. "Becket."

"Hey, Peaches." He wasn't sure why he called her that. He'd used the endearment once and it had annoyed her, so the name just stuck. "I know you miss me when we're not arguing about fence permits, but throwing yourself into my arms is a bit much."

Her eyes narrowed, and she shoved off him. He didn't move, just reluctantly lowered his arms.

"Peaches?" her mother asked, sitting straighter now.

"It's nothing, Mom. He's just my annoying neighbor."

"Annoying? From you, that's almost a compliment." Yesterday, he was "the biggest ass on the planet," and the other week, she'd told him she was jealous of people who'd never met him. He'd say "annoying" was an upgrade.

"It's about as close to a compliment as you're going to get," she retorted.

"Ouch."

"You'll be fine. I'm sure you have enough people stroking your ego."

"Ah, but the only ego stroking I want is from you."

"It will be a cold day in hell before that happens."

The smile on his face stretched. "Still mad about that fence?"

"Mad that you seem so obsessed with filming my front yard." She cocked her head. "Now, as fun as this has been, I need to go to the bathroom. Excuse me."

He watched her go...and she was right, it *was* fun arguing

with her. For some damn reason, it had become a highlight of most of his days. She was cute when she was angry. And maybe there was a bit more to it.

More than either of them wanted to admit.

Order book two, Becket and Sky's story, UNRAVELED, now!

ALSO BY NYSSA KATHRYN

PROJECT ARMA SERIES

Uncovering Project Arma

Luca

Eden

Asher

Mason

Wyatt

Bodie

Oliver

Kye

BLUE HALO SERIES

Logan

Jason

Blake

Flynn

Aidan

Tyler

Callum

Liam

MERCY RING

Jackson

Declan

Cole

Ryker

BEAUTIFUL PIECES

Erik's Salvation

Erik's Redemption

Erik's Refuge

SHORT CHRISTMAS STORY

Hidden Shadows

RECKLESS SERIES

Reckless Hope

Reckless Trust

Reckless Fall

Reckless Faith

Reckless Love

AMBER RIDGE SERIES

(Series ongoing)

Unafraid

Unraveled

JOIN my newsletter and be the first to find out about sales and new releases! CLICK HERE

ABOUT THE AUTHOR

Nyssa Kathryn is a romantic suspense author. She lives in South Australia with her daughter and hubby and takes every chance she can to be plotting and writing. Always an avid reader of romance novels, she considers alpha males and happily-ever-afters to be her jam.

Don't forget to follow Nyssa and never miss another release.

Facebook | Instagram | Amazon | Goodreads

www.ingramcontent.com/pod-product-compliance
Lightning Source LLC
Chambersburg PA
CBHW050553190726
48283CB00007B/2122